One Last Wish

Samantha Baca

Cover Design: Oh So Novel

Contents

One	3
Two	11
Three	13
Four	17
Five	33
Six	49
Seven	55
Eight	65
Nine	79
Ten	87
Eleven	97
Twelve	111
Thirteen	117
Fourteen	123
Fifteen	135
Sixteen	143
Seventeen	155
Eighteen	167
Nineteen	183
Twenty	191
Twenty One	199

Contents

Twenty Two	211
Twenty Three	225
Twenty Four	229
Twenty Five	235
Twenty Six	239
Twenty Seven	247
Twenty Eight	259
Twenty Nine	267
Thirty	279
Thirty One	293
Thirty Two	303
Thirty Three	311
Thirty Four	321
Thirty Five	327
Thirty Six	329
Thirty Seven	333
Thirty Eight	337
Epilogue	351
Other Books By Samantha Baca	355
Acknowledgments	357
About the Author	359

They say that time heals all wounds. But that's a lie. Sometimes the damage is too immense. Too raw. It penetrates your soul so deeply that nothing can unhook its claws once it's grabbed hold. If you're lucky, time might take pity on you and let you take one last breath before the pain sucks the life out of you and pulls you into the depths of darkness.

But I wouldn't count on it.

One

"Hey," I grunted into the phone as I hopped across the tile floor of my studio apartment, trying to force the Spandex-clad trousers up my legs. Note to self—don't buy the hype of finding work pants that promise to slim you unless you plan to do a workout every time you need to put them on.

"What's going on?" Charlotte asked, the sound of traffic coming through as I turned on the speakerphone and tossed it on the bed.

"I'm trying to find an outfit to wear for the interview tomorrow," I huffed, shimmying my way into the death trap, aka slim-fitting pants.

"What are the options?"

"I have the yellow silk shirt with the black blazer and dress slacks, but I feel like I look like a—"

"Bumblebee," she finished for me with a laugh.

"Or I have the same outfit that I wear to every interview and feel like it's now a bad omen to wear it to this one." I gave up trying to pull the pants the rest of the way up my thighs and plopped down on the bed. "I want this job so bad, Char. The interview has to go perfect."

"Well then, I guess we're just going to have to go shopping and find you something to wear. Now get your butt down here so we can get going. I have to get to Lily's school in an hour, and lucky for you, there's that strip mall with those cute shops right down the street."

"You don't have to take me shopping. I'll find something," I protested, looking at myself in the mirror across from me and grimacing. I was already grabbing at straws with these stupid pants.

"I'm already downstairs, so hurry your butt up, Emma."

I heard the phone click as she hung up. I grumbled one last time then got up to get dressed. Thankfully, the pants were a lot easier to get off than to put on. I grabbed my favorite pair of sunglasses and pushed them up my nose, taking a moment to check my hair before I left. The one good thing working in my favor so far was the gorgeous cut and color I had gotten yesterday as my reward to myself for getting the interview. Another candidate had pulled out at the last minute, which led me straight to the salon to cut off 3 inches of dead weight. My confidence was boosted when I looked in the mirror at the chin-length bob that framed my face perfectly, hiding the scar by my ear. I stuck with a honey brown color that made my charcoal eyes pop and added some highlights, knowing that the California sun would soon lighten it on its own anyway. Finally, I grabbed my purse and slung it over my shoulder as I rushed downstairs to meet her.

"Hey," I said as I climbed into her car and pulled the seatbelt across me. She waited impatiently, tapping her fingers on the steering wheel until she heard it click into place. I playfully rolled my eyes and made sure to stick my tongue out at her when it locked. For as long as I had known her, she'd always been the overprotective mom.

It was a beautiful spring day in San Francisco as we drove with the top down, letting the breeze whip through our hair. I was convinced that it was a sin to live in California and not own a convertible. There was something about the freedom that you felt as you breathed in the salty air while sticking your head out the window like a dog that made it feel exhilarating.

Fifteen minutes later, we were parked and making our way into one of the stores that had looked promising from what the models in the window were wearing. I made my way over to the long-sleeved, business-appropriate shirts in the back while Charlotte casually perused the tank tops that I would never be caught dead wearing.

I was flipping through the hangers, unimpressed with the options, when I heard Charlotte call me from across the store. I gave up and tried to remind myself that there was still plenty of time to find something to wear before I allowed myself to feel the wallow and despair that were creeping up on me. Finally, I rounded the corner and saw her squatting down, looking through the boxes of shoes piled under a shelf.

"What did you find?" I asked, trying to keep my disappointment and frustration out of my voice.

She moved a few more boxes around before she popped up, her blonde hair bouncing behind her.

"Yes!" she squealed, handing the box to me.

I eyed it suspiciously before taking off the lid and looking inside. There were a pair of black heels that were my size. I looked up and furrowed my brow.

"You know I don't wear heels," I said, handing the box back to her.

"I know, but I thought maybe you could try them," she replied softly, reaching behind her to pick up the clothes that she had set on the bench against the wall. "With these!"

She forced them into my hands and clapped excitedly.

"Now go try them on," she urged, gently pushing me to the back of the store where the dressing rooms were.

I groaned and tilted my head back, making sure she saw the fit I was throwing as I walked to the dressing room and waited for an employee to unlock the door for me. I went inside and set my purse down on the small seat in the back, along with the outfit she had picked.

"Hurry and let me see it. I've gotta get to Lily's school soon," she hollered from the waiting area.

"What does she have going on today?" I asked as I pulled my shirt up and over my head, making note that I eventually needed to buy new bras at some point. The black cotton one I was wearing had seen better days and had a hole in the bottom that was starting to get bigger.

"It's show and tell day, and Lily took the blanket that she and I have been knitting together. It's *soooo* beautiful and soft," she gushed. "Lily loves it already, and we haven't even finished it."

There was pure excitement in her voice that made me wish I could be there to see Lily talk about it. I loved seeing them talk about things they were working on together, even though it tugged at the emptiness I felt when I thought about all of the unfinished stuff my mom and I never got around to doing.

"I don't want to make you late. Why don't you get going, and I'll find a ride back when I'm done?"

"No need for that," she laughed. "Trust me, *that* is the outfit. I'm sure of it."

I slid the black satin tank top over my head and brushed my hands along my sides when I saw that it fit perfectly. It wasn't too tight and hugged my curves perfectly without drawing attention to the areas that made me self-conscious. I quickly pulled on the pair of boot-cut black dress slacks and then slipped on the heels, turning in the mirror to check each angle. Thankfully, the pants looked tight-fitting, but they were so unbelievably comfortable that I didn't notice.

She was right. *This* was *the outfit.*

"Well?" she called impatiently.

I opened the door and stepped out, making sure to keep my foot on the door, so I didn't accidentally lock myself out. She lowered her phone and stood up, coming closer to look at her work. Her cheeks split into a huge grin as her baby blue eyes lit up.

"It's perfect," she said, taking a deep breath. "You look amazing. I'd hire you in a heartbeat."

"Thanks," I laughed, running my hand down the miracle shirt again. "I actually feel amazing in this."

"Good." She raised her eyebrows, and her voice cracked a little. We had been friends since we were nine, and she knew how big of a moment this was for me. Needless to say, we were both feeling a little emotional given our success with finding me an outfit, knowing how picky I was about what type of clothes made me feel comfortable. I still had a hard time swallowing the pill that I was starting over with my career this late in life. I had never imagined that I would spend twenty years working for the same company, climbing the ladder to get to the top, only to start over with a new company before I turned forty.

"Okay, go get changed and toss everything over the door so that I can go pay," she said, breaking out of the moment.

"You're not buying my stuff," I countered and went back inside the dressing room to get changed.

"Yes, I am. It's good luck if I give it to you as a gift. Now hurry, or we're gonna be late."

I stripped down quickly and tossed everything to her, sliding the shoes under the door. By the time I had changed, she had already paid for everything and waited by the door for me. She handed me the bag as we got in the car and headed for the school.

"Do you and John have plans for the weekend?" I asked, knowing that their fifteen-year wedding anniversary was coming up in a few weeks, and he wanted to take her out of town to celebrate. Unfortunately, his work schedule was busy, and this was the only weekend that he wouldn't be out of town for work.

"We haven't made any yet," she said, glancing at me out of the corner of her eye.

"You don't have to worry about me this weekend. I'll be fine," I reassured her, looking out the window to avoid having a breakdown.

"I'm not leaving you." She turned her head to the side, checking oncoming traffic before she pulled out into the intersection to turn left. Traffic was somewhat heavy today, and I knew that we'd be sitting here for a solid hour if she didn't push herself out there.

"It's been thirty years since my parents died, and yes, it still hurts, but I'm not a kid anymore. I appreciate you wanting to be there for me, but I think you should let John take you out of town."

She let out a heavy sigh as she turned to look at me for a second before turning her attention back to the road and inching forward to make the turn. She turned the steering wheel and went for it.

"You deserve to get—"

The sound of metal crunching and glass shattering filled the air around us as my head whipped forward before everything went black.

Two

"Ma'am, can you hear me?"

"I need you to wake up… stay with me."

"Help is on the way!"

"Did you see the driver of the other car?"

"I think he was drunk, the way he came flying through that intersection with no intention of stopping."

"Someone call 911!"

"Is she alive?"

"I've got a pulse on this one, but it's shallow. We need to get her to the hospital!"

Three

I've heard that when it's your time to go, you know. I've always expected it to be like the movies where you see the bright white lights and soft music floats down from heaven as you find your way to the loved ones that have passed before you. Everything is so calm and peaceful. That would have been nice.

My head throbbed as I woke up to the sound of someone saying my name over and over. *Emma, can you hear me? Please wake up, Emma. You can't do this to us. Please don't leave us, Emma. We need you.* Man, heaven sure was annoying. Or at least that's where I wished I was when my eyes scanned the room and landed on John sitting across the room from me.

He hung his head, his wedding ring glistening in the dingy light above him. He was rocking back and forth, chanting something that sounded like, *let her be okay, please let her be okay.*

"What are you doing?" I tried to ask, my voice weak and rough. His head whipped up as he looked at me, relief washing across his face. And that's when it hit me.

The accident. The truck that came flying into the side of the car when Charlotte turned to clear the intersection as the light changed to yellow. Panic flooded through me as I tried to remember any details, but there wasn't anything more than that. *Was she okay? What happened? Was anyone else injured? Where was the driver? Was she in the hospital too? Please let her be okay.*

He got up and rushed over to the side of my hospital bed, gently reaching down to squeeze my hand that didn't have an IV sticking out of it.

"Where is she? Is she okay?" I asked, feeling the way his

hand fell limp on mine when I asked about her. A tear slid down his face, his eyes red and swollen. He lowered them and looked away, refusing to answer me. My stomach sank when I knew what he was trying to say but couldn't.

"Is she okay?" I repeated desperately, trying to sit up in the bed. "John… is she…"

He shook his head before covering his face with his hand, his body shaking as he cried.

I pulled my hand away and covered my mouth as I screamed, the tears rushing down my face. I gasped for air as my body crumbled with the grief. John's hand gently held onto my shoulder as he tried to comfort me.

"That's not possible," I stammered between sobs, unable to catch my breath. "She… she… she… has to be… alive."

I looked up at him, begging for him to tell me that it was a mistake, a misunderstanding of some sort. Instead, he shook his head but didn't say anything.

"No!" I cried harder, letting my head fall forward. "It's… all my… fault!"

"What's all your fault?" a little voice asked.

I looked up, the tears clouding my vision as I saw Lily standing in the doorway, holding a blanket. She looked so little standing there, it didn't feel like she was ten years old. Her innocent face reminded me of the little girl that still needed her mom. I wiped my face with my hands and tried to pull myself together as I sucked in rapid breaths to replace the oxygen I lacked. My body heaved uncontrollably; my mind unable to process anything other than the fact that my best friend was dead.

"Nothing, sweetie," John assured her, pulling her close to him as he thanked whoever had brought her up to my room. I couldn't see much past the tears that were still blurring my eyes.

"Do you want to come say hi?" he asked her, gently rubbing her back as she looked unsure of whether to come any closer. She nodded and took a few steps closer. I had no idea what I looked like and prayed that I didn't scare her or further traumatize this poor child.

"Hi, Aunt Emma," she whispered as she stood next to my bed and clutched the blanket to her chest.

"Hey, sweet Lily," I whispered back, a loud sob escaping my throat while doing my best to give her my bravest smile.

"My mom died," she said sadly, lowering her chin to her chest.

I nodded, biting the inside of my cheek to keep from crumbling in front of her. I covered my mouth with my hand and wiped away the fresh tears that were falling.

"Are you going to die too?" She tilted her head, a look of concern etched on her beautiful little face. Her voice cracked, and I saw her struggling not to cry. I scooted over as much as I could and pulled the blanket up, waving my hand for her to sit with me. She gently climbed up onto the bed, making sure not to touch any of the tubing hooked up to me. I was in a decent amount of pain and hadn't spoken with the doctor yet, so I had no clue what the extent of my injuries were, but that didn't stop me from pulling her into me and hugging her with everything I had. As far as I was concerned, it was nothing too extreme, or I imagine I would have nurses and doctors flocking to my bed the moment they knew I was awake.

I felt her small body tremble as she cried, her heart breaking along with mine. I cried with her, knowing the pain she was feeling after losing my parents around her age. I would never wish this pain on anyone, let alone a child. I looked up to find John whispering to the nurse at the door, asking her to give us a moment before they came in to talk to me.

I held Lily and rubbed her back, hoping to bring her even an ounce of comfort. I had lived through this pain and knew that there was nothing that could even begin to dull it. It was like a tattoo, permanently embedded inside of you, forever dictating who you were from that point on. Charlotte had gone out of her way to be there for me when I lost my parents, and now it was my turn to do the same for Lily.

Four

I stood at the podium, my fingers trembling as I looked into the crowd of people with red, swollen faces, wearing all black. I turned to the picture on the table beside me and looked to Charlotte for help. It was one of my favorite pictures of her, taken shortly after she had Lily. She was glowing in this picture, pure happiness radiating from her. Her smile stretched across her face, and big blue eyes lit up like a child on Christmas morning.

Seeing the picture was supposed to be helpful, to draw the words out of me that I needed to say. Instead, I felt my throat closing up as I struggled to keep the tears from running down my face. There were so many things that I wanted to say, that I needed to say. But the only words that I could find were the ones that I couldn't say because no one wanted to hear about how she would still be alive if it weren't for me.

If I hadn't been freaking out about what to wear for the interview, she wouldn't have come by to take me shopping. She would have never been at the strip mall, which meant that she wouldn't have been at that intersection. Instead, she would have taken a different path to get to Lily's school, and she would still be here today, smiling as she told us how proud Lily was to show her class the blanket they were making together. Instead, she died on the side of the road after a drunk driver ran a red light and plowed into her car, forcing it around the light pole. She died on impact while I was spared my life and walked away with a few broken ribs, a couple of burns from the airbag, and some minor scratches and bruises.

I felt the anger building inside of me, the same rage that I felt every time I remembered that I lived, and she died. It wasn't fair. It was beyond unfair. I didn't have anyone to leave behind—not even a job that I loved. Yet death chose her, the one with the family who adored and needed her. And it pissed me off.

I heard someone clear their throat beside me and looked up to find John standing next to me, his hand resting on my lower back.

"Are you okay?" he whispered, covering the microphone in front of us with his other hand.

"I can't do this." I shook my head, gritting my teeth.

"It's okay. You don't have to. She knew. Whatever it is you were going to say—she knew."

My eyes filled with tears as I looked away, frustrated with myself. I owed Charlotte better than this. I needed to get it together and honor her in whatever way I could.

"I'm okay," I said forcefully, pulling my shoulders back. I had to convince myself first, then maybe he would believe it too.

He nodded and took a step back, staying behind me in case I needed him.

I cleared my throat and slowly pulled in a deep breath.

"Charlotte was the first person to show me what it meant to be there for someone through thick and thin. She saw me at my absolute worst and held me while I cried on the bathroom floor as I grieved the loss of my parents, the only family that I've ever had. That was the hardest thing I had ever gone through, and she stepped up and went through it with me. When I was overwhelmed with anger, she took me to the mountains and screamed with me at the top of our lungs until we lost our voices. She spent every holiday with me and silently sat next to me every year on the anniversary of their death when I was too broken to find the words I wanted to say.

"She was there when I opened acceptance letters, nervous that I wouldn't get into the college that I wanted. I remember her showing up with tequila in one hand and champagne in the other. Luckily, we were only a few shots in before I got the letter I was looking for, and then we switched to champagne. That might have been a disaster if not," I laughed.

"I was there when she first met John, and she tried to convince me later that she didn't like him," I laughed as I glanced over my shoulder to see him laughing with me, shaking his head while looking down at the carpet. "Even when she wouldn't stop smiling and checking her phone every thirty seconds, she was *still* trying to pretend that she wasn't interested. Then, six months later, I was asked to be her maid of honor at their wedding. Five sweet years after that, I was blessed to be one of the first people that they told when they found out she was pregnant. I was so excited to be in the room when Lily was born." I smiled, remembering that moment and how breathtaking it was to see her bring that sweet baby girl into the world.

I stopped for a moment, getting choked up by the memories. I found Lily sitting in the front row, next to her grandmother, looking up at me with tears in her eyes.

"She prayed every day for you, Lily. There wasn't anything in life that she wanted more than to be your momma. She was so proud of you, and I hope you always know that."

She nodded before tucking her head into her grandmother's shoulder to hide her tears. I switched to a few lighter memories about the fun times we had and how much I loved Charlotte's adventurous spirit before I wrapped up and joined John in the front row as a few other people got up to share their stories.

The wake was at their house and was put together by his mother when he argued that they didn't need to have one. He was worried that Lily would already be overwhelmed and exhausted from everything else, and he was right. It was a lot to put on a child, and I understood why he was concerned. But she had insisted, so there he was, wandering around the house, trying to make an effort to thank everyone for coming today.

I spent as much time as I could with Charlotte's parents before they left since they were the only people I really knew. I had met a handful of women at different events here and there, but no one that I knew well enough to sit and talk to for more than a few minutes. I tried to keep my distance and stayed only to support John and Lily. I didn't know the majority of his family as they had never been around much in the time that I'd known him. Charlotte had mentioned several times that he wasn't close to his parents and was even more distant from his extended family. As I moved about the house, I could see why when I heard the hushed whispers when they thought no one was listening.

"Poor John, how's he going to raise that little girl on his own? Doesn't he know that she needs a mother?"

"I heard that he's going to have to step down from his position at work and take a *huge* pay cut so he can be home to take care of her."

"Well, if he would just take Sandra up on her offer to move in and help… I don't see why he's refusing his mother's help. She deserves to get to know her granddaughter. It's only right after her mother kept her away from everyone all these years."

"I heard that the other girl in the accident wasn't even injured. Such a freak accident that it killed Charlotte on impact, but her friend escaped with a few broken ribs and some bruises. Something about it seems off if you ask me…."

I pulled my bottom lip in between my teeth and clenched my fists at my sides as I tried to force myself to walk away and not say anything. If they knew the guilt that I carried with me daily, they might understand that I asked God every day why he didn't take me instead. If I could have traded places with her, I would have in a heartbeat.

The voices faded behind me as I walked upstairs and made my way to the guest room where I used to stay on occasion. It felt weird to be in there now, knowing that I would never spend the night here again. Those days were over, and I had no idea what would happen with my relationship with John and Lily. I prayed that I wouldn't lose them too, but I wouldn't blame them if I did.

I pulled open the French doors to the closet and stopped when I heard sniffling under the coats hanging on the bar. I pushed them to the side and looked down to find Lily curled up with her arms around her knees as she cried. She looked up at me, her face red and splotchy.

"Is there room for me too?" I asked softly.

She nodded and scooted over. I knelt down and climbed in beside her, pushing the suitcases out of the way to make room. I wrapped an arm around her shoulders and pulled her into me as she cried. We sat there in silence for who knows how long before John wandered into the room and stood by the door, smiling when he found us.

"I was looking for you," he said, coming closer and sitting on the edge of the bed.

"Am I in trouble?" Lily asked, wiping her face with her arm.

"Not at all. I just wanted to make sure you were doing okay." He smiled at her before looking up to smile at me and mouthing thank you. I smiled and squeezed her a little bit tighter.

"Yeah, I'm okay," she said, resting her chin on her knee. "I just didn't want to be around all of those people anymore. They wouldn't stop crying and telling me how I look just like mommy."

I felt my heart squeeze inside of my chest, remembering that feeling when so-called distant relatives forced themselves into my life after my parents died. When they realized that there wasn't any life insurance money, they quickly ran for the hills to avoid having to take care of a minor child and deal with a house about to go into foreclosure. My parents were good people—wonderful people, but they sucked at knowing how to manage their money. My mom's only sister, Willow, adopted me and cared for me before she passed shortly after my eighteenth birthday. Fate was funny like that, keeping someone around long enough to care for me until I was legally responsible for myself before throwing me into the world with no freaking idea of what to do.

"I'm sorry, baby," John said softly to her. "Everyone is gone now, so why don't we put on our pajamas and have a pizza and movie night?"

Her face lit up with happiness for the first time that I'd seen since her mom died almost two weeks ago.

"Really?" she asked in disbelief. "But it's a school night… are you sure we're allowed to do that?"

He raised an eyebrow at her and folded his arms across his chest.

"Who's the boss around here?" he teased, his attempt at being serious making her giggle even more. "Besides, I've already talked with Ms. Summers and let her know that you'll be out the rest of this week."

Her eyes widened at this news before her smile pulled even tighter across her face.

"Now go get your pajamas on, and I'll order the pizza. Just cheese?"

"Just cheese," she squealed and got up, giving him a quick high five before she ran out of the room.

He leaned forward and rested his elbows on his knees, his sandy brown hair falling in his eyes. There was no doubt about it—he needed a haircut. But I imagined that had been the last thing on his mind when planning his wife's funeral. It was hard enough to find the perfect arrangement to place next to her picture and the urn at the service, but adding additional, unnecessary things was just a waste of time. And time had proven to be incredibly precious.

"How are you holding up?" he asked, looking up at me with exhaustion etched onto his face. He was a handsome man, but I could tell that he hadn't been sleeping. It was apparent with the dark circles under his usually vibrant green eyes. The light that used to be in them seemed to disappear when Charlotte died, and I didn't know if I would ever see it again.

"I'm okay," I said, shrugging one shoulder and pulling my mouth into a crooked smile. "You?"

"Same."

We sat in silence for a few minutes, too tired to do much else. Finally, he pulled his phone out of his pocket and dialed the number to Lily's favorite pizza place.

"Do you want the meat lover?" he asked, waiting for them to answer.

"Oh no, I'm going to get out of here in a few minutes. Let you guys enjoy your time together."

I pushed myself up off the floor, feeling the exhaustion from the past few weeks settling in my bones. Or maybe that was just old age. I was almost forty, but I really thought I had a good stretch ahead of me before I started complaining about the pain in my hips and knees.

Then I had to remind myself that it likely had nothing to do with being forty but instead being the anomaly that happened to survive *two* horrific car accidents that had taken the lives of everyone I loved, my parents and Charlotte. The doctors had warned me that it might take a few weeks to a few months before I was completely healed and no longer in pain.

"Yeah, can I get a small cheese pizza and a medium meat lover?" John said, holding up his hand to stop me before I could walk off. He answered their questions and gave them his address before hanging up.

"Stay and have dinner with us?" he asked, desperation deep in his eyes. "Please?"

"John," I sighed sadly. "It's not that I don't want to stay—because I do, but I think that you guys need to get back to normal sooner than later and having me here every day isn't going to help you do that."

"Do you really think we have a normal at this point?" he asked shyly. My stomach sank, knowing that he was right. Neither of us were trying to be rude or hurt the other, but it sucked, and there was no way around having to deal with the one thing we had been trying to avoid: moving forward.

"No," I shook my head. "The normal we all knew is gone, and now we have to make our own. But I don't know if it's going to be confusing to Lily if I'm constantly here."

"You're her Godmother. I don't think she would mind the company for a little while longer."

I rubbed my lips together, trying to figure out what the best thing was to do. I loved Lily more than anything, and I knew how vulnerable she was right now. I was the same way when I lost my parents. I couldn't imagine being alone, and thankfully, I had Charlotte and my aunt to make sure that I was never alone again from that day forward. But Lily didn't have anyone to do that for her, except for me.

"Okay, I'll stay for a little while," I agreed.

I saw the relief flash across John's face, a shimmer of happiness that faded as quickly as it had appeared. We went downstairs and found Lily sitting on the couch, wearing her Christmas pajamas that matched John and Charlottes from their family photos. She sat there and stared at the tv, tears rolling down her face.

"Honey, what's wrong?" I asked softly, walking over to sit next to her. I placed my hand on her knee, bringing her attention to me. It was a loaded question given everything that had happened and turned her world upside down.

"I miss mommy," she cried, the tears falling harder down her face. "I just wish I could see her one last time."

I looked up to find John standing in the wide doorway that separated the kitchen from the living room, looking at us. He looked completely lost, unsure of what to do. His face scrunched up in anger, his fists balled at his sides—the frustration of not being able to give his daughter what she needed unbearable.

"You know what," I said, forcing as much excitement as I could in my voice. "I have an idea."

I jumped up and walked over to the bookshelf in the corner of the room, standing on my tiptoes to see the DVD cases on the top shelf. Finding the one I wanted, I pulled it down and waved it happily in the air.

"How about, instead of watching a regular movie, we watch one of your mom?"

My palms started sweating, wondering if I had overstepped. I felt as desperate as John to make Lily feel better and didn't think about asking him first. What if this further upset her, and I did more damage than good?

She looked from me to John before asking, "Can we, dad?"

"Of course," he said quietly, his voice cracking at the end. "That is a great idea, Emma. Thank you."

I felt the tension leave my body as I got the confirmation from him that I needed. Over the past few weeks, we had developed a new language between the two of us that we used whenever Lily was around. I knew the smile that pulled the corners of his lips up was when he was saying thank you. Just like the one that seemed to require every muscle in his body was the one he forced when he was trying to keep it together and not break down in front of her. Our goal was to be there for her however she needed us, but the problem was that we didn't actually have a clue what that meant.

Twenty minutes later, the doorbell rang, and John passed a wad of cash to the young, freckled face kid who delivered the pizza. Lily and I were cuddled up next to each other under a blanket on the couch, watching the video John had put together for Charlotte as her first Mother's Day gift. It was a collection of random videos he had taken the first year they had Lily, and watching it broke my heart when I saw how much love she had for that little girl.

A couple of hours later, we had finished the second video, this one of Lily's first year and the massive birthday party John insisted on throwing her, before she got tired and went upstairs to bed.

"Just leave the mess, and I'll get to it in the morning," John said as I helped carry our empty plates and cups into the kitchen. I set them in the sink, stacking them neatly.

"I don't mind helping now," I offered, feeling the same anxiety that I felt every night when I left to go to my empty apartment. I had lived on my own for years but not having a daily phone call or random text strings from Charlotte made it abundantly clear just how lonely I was there by myself.

"Na, really, it's okay."

He stacked the empty pizza boxes and piled them next to

the trash can that still needed to be emptied from the wake. I had offered to do that earlier as well, but he had declined.

"Do you think that it's a good idea to keep Lily home from school the rest of the week?" I blurted out, surprised that I had decided to bring it up. It had been weighing on my mind all night, but I didn't want to overstep by questioning his decision.

"Honestly, I don't know." He shrugged. "I feel like nothing I do these days is the right decision, and I really miss having Charlotte here to help me figure all of it out," he laughed.

I raised an eyebrow at him and smirked.

"Okay, okay," he said, raising his hands in front of him. "I miss having her do it all for me. There—I said it."

We laughed together, knowing that it was true. John's work kept him busy and allowed them to have Charlotte stay home with Lily after she was born. It ended up working out better, having her home with Lily since the only family they stayed in touch with were Charlotte's parents, who lived in New Jersey.

"She did so much, and I never thanked her enough for it," he admitted sadly.

I lowered my head, trying to force the tears away before he could see them.

"Charlotte knew how much you appreciated her, John. She adored you more than you could ever know."

"Well, hopefully, she can start giving me some tips from heaven before I screw everything up."

I pulled the barstool out from under the island and sat down.

"I don't ever want to overstep, so please tell me if I do. But I think that Lily would do better if she were to go back to school and not miss so much. I know that you've already excused her for the rest of this week, and I get why you did it, but she's already having a hard time there. So, I wouldn't make it worse for her."

He ran a hand down his face and paused.

"What do you mean she's having a hard time?"

"Didn't Charlotte talk to you about it?" I suddenly felt guilty for talking to him about something that I knew she had planned on telling him. It didn't feel like it was my place to let him know what was going on, but there weren't any other options given the circumstances. He shook his head no, his arms folded across his chest as he waited for me to tell him.

"Lily has been having trouble with a few of the girls in her class. It's the typical pre-teen drama, but Charlotte was working with the teacher to try to figure out how to make it stop."

"Stop what?"

"They were bullying her. Making fun of her for being a momma's girl. Things like that."

My heart broke saying the words, knowing how cold and callous girls that age could be. What if she went back to school, and they were worse now? If they said even one word about Charlotte, I would be the one down there beating their ass, and that wasn't something that I wanted to happen.

"She didn't tell me," he said, the frustration filling the room.

"I know she was going to. She might not have had a chance…."

I looked away, unable to finish the sentence.

"Thanks for letting me know. I'll talk to her teacher tomorrow."

I forced a smile and started to stand up when he walked around and pulled the stool beside me out and sat at the end of the island.

"Did you ever hear anything about that job you were supposed to interview for?" he asked, changing the subject.

Not that it was a better subject, it just shifted the pain from his side to mine.

"After I explained why I didn't make it to the first interview, they were kind enough to give me a second one, but I don't think I'm going to get the job."

The interview was yesterday, and I struggled the entire day trying to get my head right before I got there.

"Why not," he pressed.

"Well," I laughed. "Because I burst into tears the moment I sat down, and they asked me why I wanted to be their creative marketing manager. I didn't mean to break down, but I couldn't get Charlotte and the accident out of my head, and so I just sat there and cried the first fifteen minutes while they looked at me like I was crazy."

"I'm sorry, I know how much you wanted it."

"It's okay. I blame the outfit," I joked, trying to make light of it.

"What did you wear?"

"The same outfit that I've worn to every interview this month. It's like the annihilation of my career. I wear that outfit, and everything I touch crumbles."

"Again—what in the hell did you wear?" he laughed, finding humor in my misery. I laughed with him, covering my mouth when the giggling started to get louder.

"My black dress slacks and a black button shirt. It's not a terrible outfit," I justified. "It's professional without being flashy."

"Well, at least it wasn't the bumblebee outfit…." He smirked.

"You know about that?" I groaned, covering my face with my hands while making a note to get rid of that damn yellow shirt.

"I know everything." He winked.

"At least one of us does," I laughed, not finding as much humor in it when the truth slapped me in the face that I had no idea what I was doing with my life anymore. Before, I used to have Charlotte to talk things out with and get advice from, and now I had no one. That was a hard pill to swallow.

32

Five

The rest of the week passed by painfully slow as I tried my best to stay out of John and Lily's hair for a few days. I knew that it was comfortable when we all spent time together and that it almost dulled the pain of Charlotte being gone, but I wasn't doing anyone any favors by keeping up our little routine. It had been nearly three weeks since she passed, and we needed to make the transition of John and Lily being on their own before it was too late. Rip the Band-Aid off while the pain was still fresh, and so you wouldn't have to feel it again later.

My apartment was still eerily quiet, and even with the constant stream of rom-com movies blaring through it, I still felt the void of not talking to Charlotte every day. I couldn't remember a single day that we hadn't spoken since we were little girls, other than in seventh grade when she found out that I liked the new boy at school, and I hadn't told her before she found out from Sandy Pickler. Sandy was always such a bitch, trying to start drama wherever she could.

By Monday, I was crying in my coffee, feeling myself on the verge of another breakdown when I opened my mail to another rejection letter. I had yet to hear anything from Marshall Advertising, which was the job I *really* wanted, but I knew that crying through my interview probably wasn't the best way to win them over. I glanced over at the outfit that Charlotte had bought me to wear for that interview, still in the bag with the tags on it because I couldn't bring myself to do anything with it.

I flipped through the rest of the mail, ignoring the junk mail. I was about to toss everything to the side when a letter slipped out between the sale ads and fell into my lap. My stomach knotted as I opened it, knowing what it was before I even read it. There was no address or return address on it, just my name scribbled in black ink with three lines marked underneath it.

The knot in my stomach turned sour as I read the eviction notice, demanding that I be out of my apartment in two weeks. As if I had somewhere else magically lined up to move to or some fancy job that would pay me the two months' worth of rent that I owed. After receiving the first warning, I reached out to the landlord and explained my situation, but it fell on deaf ears. Since then, I had been living off the severance pay from my last job—which was a very generous package, but I knew that it would run out soon.

My goal was to be aggressive and nail the interview with BayView Advertising and become their next Creative Marking Director. They had been the direct competition of the company that I had worked for before they had to eliminate a few positions—mine included, so I knew their salaries were comparable, given how many of our employees they had attracted.

I tossed the letter to the side and rubbed my temples with my fingers, praying that the tension headache that had been haunting me for days would give me one day of relief. There were plenty of things to worry about—eviction included, but I couldn't think about any of them right now. Everything felt overwhelmingly out of control, and I had no idea where to start trying to pick up the pieces as my life crumbled around me.

My cell phone rang, startling me, as I wiped the tears away

with the back of my hand. I looked down to find John's name on the caller ID. Suddenly, I panicked, worried that something had happened to Lily on her first day back at school.

"Hey," I answered, chewing my fingernail anxiously.

"Hi," he said heavily. "I'm sorry to bother you, but I need to ask for a favor."

"Sure, what's up?"

"I'm a total bonehead and spaced that Lily had volleyball practice after school today, and unfortunately, she gets done right when I have a meeting that I have to attend. Is there any way that you could pick her up for me?"

I drew in a long breath, allowing my nerves a moment to calm down.

"Of course," I agreed. "Did you already call the school to let them know?"

"Not yet, but I'll call them right now and let them know. Thank you, I owe you big time."

He sounded relieved when he hung up, which made me feel somewhat better that I had been able to help him. I was still feeling frustrated and overwhelmed with everything falling apart around me, but I pushed all of that aside and got ready to go pick Lily up.

I waited in the parking lot, standing next to the light pole with my sunglasses blocking out the harsh sun that was beating down on me. It was unseasonably warm for the end of April, and the local meteorologist confirmed that it was only going to get warmer this week. I groaned when

I thought about the flocks of people who would soon start making their way down and crowding the nearby beaches.

I closed my eyes for a second, daydreaming about what it would be like to take a vacation. To have the money to say *screw it all!* and live vicariously for a few weeks without a care in the world. Images of walking down the beach with a cold drink in my hand were interrupted by a tap on my shoulder. I opened my eyes and turned to look at the young woman, probably in her late twenties, smiling the fakest smile I had ever seen.

"Hi, we don't allow visitors on campus without checking in first," she said with a whiney tone, pressing her hands together as her face scrunched in a phony apology.

"Sorry, I didn't know that I had to check in since school was out for the day. I'm here to pick up Lily Wright. Her dad, John, called earlier to let them know I was coming."

She narrowed her eyes slightly as she stepped back and looked at me as if I wasn't what she was expecting.

"Yes, well, John needs to call earlier next time so they can make sure we all get the message."

"And you are?" I asked, pushing my sunglasses back up my nose.

"I'm Ms. Summers, Lily's teacher."

I bit down on my lower lip, trying to hold my tongue so I didn't say something I would regret. Instead, I turned my head to the crowd of girls who were finishing up and running inside to put their gear away.

"Are you going to be picking Lily up from now on?" Ms.

Summers probed, her tone still getting under my skin.

"When they need me to," I replied stiffly.

"Well, then, I feel it's best to let you know that Lily is falling behind on her schoolwork, and perhaps it's not in her best interest for her to miss any more school this year." She folded her arms over her fake boobs and shifted herself to stand directly in front of me. "We wouldn't want to have a negative impact on her schooling, now, would we?"

I watched as the group of girls walked out of the gym and found Lily, walking by herself with her head down and her backpack pulled tightly across her back as she held onto the straps. Behind her was a group of girls, whispering and laughing as they looked in her direction.

"Yeah, we wouldn't want to interfere with the bullying that she goes through daily, now, would we?" I snapped, pulling my glasses off my face so she could see my eyes. "Now, if you'll excuse me, I better get her home so I can teach her all of the things that she sure as hell didn't learn in your class today."

I slid my glasses back on my face and pushed around her, not waiting to hear if she had a comeback. The school year was almost over, and Lily didn't have anyone to stand up for her. While I hated the idea that I might have made things harder for her with her teacher, I hoped that for once, I would catch a break and Ms. Summers would mind her business and do her job. There were only four weeks left until school was out, which gave me some comfort that Lily wouldn't have to put up with too much for too long. June 1st couldn't come soon enough. Then she would be free of all this drama and have the summer to be a kid again.

I glanced over my shoulder to see the girls rush over to her, smiles on their faces as she walked with them out to the other parking lot. And now it all made sense as to why she hadn't stopped the bullying. She was the damn ringleader.

"Hey!" I said excitedly as Lily got closer. My heart thumped in my chest when I saw the smile on her face when she saw me standing there, waiting for her.

"What are you doing here?" She ran the rest of the way over and wrapped her arms around my waist.

"Your dad had a work meeting that he couldn't get out of, so he asked if I could come pick you up."

Her features changed as the disappointment etched on her face.

"He always has meetings," she mumbled and pulled the straps, adjusting the position of her backpack.

"I know," I said softly. "But that means that you and I get to spend some time together this afternoon until he gets home," I offered, gently nudging her with my arm as we walked side by side to my car. I wondered how long it would be until I had to get rid of it with everything else.

"Are you going to stay for dinner?" she asked, looking up at me as the sun slightly blinded her.

I hated answering this question because it didn't feel like there was a correct answer. If I said yes, then I felt like I was forcing my way into their lives and not letting them find their own groove. If I said no, I risked hurting their feelings and making them think that I didn't want to spend time with them.

"I don't know," I answered honestly as we got to the car.

"But, if you want, I can help you make dinner tonight. It would be a nice surprise for your dad when he gets home."

She climbed into the car and set her backpack on the floor in front of her. I was waiting for her to answer, and she knew it as she dramatically did everything in slow motion, from buckling her seatbelt to turning to look at me.

"On one condition," she said, tapping her finger to her chin.

"What's that?" I asked, one eyebrow raised suspiciously.

"We make pizza."

I let out a laugh, enjoying the brief happiness.

"Fine, we'll make pizza." I pretended to groan and make a big deal out of it as I turned the key and started the car. Then, suddenly, I had a flashback of the accident with Charlotte, and I froze. My hand hovered over the shifter, unable to do anything, when I thought about what would happen if I were in an accident with Lily. What if I were the catalyst in every single equation and had somehow been the cause of the accidents and yet survived each one?

"What's wrong?" she asked, fear echoing in the air around us.

I whipped my head to look at her, unable to pretend like something wasn't wrong. Her eyes found mine, searching for any clues as to what had frightened me.

"Nothing," I lied, my voice hoarse as it burned from the strain of trying to keep it together.

"Are you afraid that we'll get in a car accident?"

Any resolve I had at that point vanished. I nodded as the

tears slid down my face, burning the already raw skin from crying.

"I'm sorry, sweetie, I didn't mean to scare you. I just had a quick moment where I—"

"Had a panic attack," she finished for me calmly. "My therapist says that they're normal, but they don't ever happen to me. She told me what to look out for, in case I have one. But I haven't yet."

I leaned back against the seat and studied her. She was so brave for her age, and I tried to remember what I was like as a ten-year-old who had just lost my parents. Here she was, looking like she had all the answers to the world. For all I knew, I was probably a hot mess who didn't know what day it was as I tried to figure out life without them. But then again, that could be said about me these days too. Losing Charlotte sent me back into the same tailspin that I was in when I was Lily's age, and I still didn't know how to handle the loss of someone I loved any better than I did back then.

"You have a therapist?" I asked, wondering when she had started seeing one. John had mentioned that he wanted to set up an appointment for her, but I hadn't heard anything more about it when we talked last week.

"Yeah, I just started seeing her last week. Daddy took me on Friday, and then we went to dinner after. I think he wants to do it every Friday because that's the only day that he doesn't work late. He promised that he won't be working late anymore now that mommy's gone, but I don't think that's true."

"You never know, your dad has a habit of surprising

people," I laughed, remembering how wild and adventurous he and Charlotte had been when they first met.

"I'll believe that when I see it!" she chuckled.

The change in conversation helped calm my nerves as I drove us to Lily's house and helped her with the small amount of homework she had. She was an intelligent kid, and I had been telling Charlotte and John for years that she needed to be in a gifted class, but the school didn't want to test her. Even after missing almost a week worth of school, she had already caught up on everything she missed and was ahead of most of the other students in her class, despite what her teacher had just tried to tell me. I went over Lily's work with her and confirmed that she didn't have any other assignments that she was missing. It was at that moment that I hated her teacher even more.

Around five o'clock, we started getting the stuff together to make pizza. I was worried that John would lose track of time and not get home until eight or nine like he usually did. So, I sent him a quick text, letting him know that Lily was making him dinner tonight and to please be on time so he didn't ruin her surprise. He texted back, confirming he would be home by six, and asked if I wanted to join them for dinner. I gave him the same answer that I had given Lily: I don't know.

Why was that such a hard thing to decide? It was dinner with my friend and his daughter. MY goddaughter… Yet, I still felt like I didn't belong in the picture anymore. Now that Charlotte was gone, I wasn't sure that there was a place for me anymore.

I was relieved when I heard the front door open, right at

six o'clock. Lily's mouth curved into a smile as she danced excitedly around the kitchen. The dining room table was set, and per Lily's request, a glass of red wine was waiting for John at his seat. She had asked if I wanted a glass as well, but I still couldn't force myself to make a decision.

"Something smells *amazing*!" he exclaimed as he walked into the kitchen and pulled Lily into him for a hug. I looked away, feeling out of place watching them. It felt too personal, too much like being part of their family if I sat here and felt the love between them.

"We made pizza!" Lily said, pulling him by his hand over to the oven. He bent down and looked inside, a smile tugging at the side of his lips as she walked him through all of the toppings she had put on his pizza before explaining that the little pizza was just for her.

"Looks like you did a great job," he replied, patting her on the back. "And you did too, Emma," he added as he turned to look at me. "Thank you again for picking Lily up for me. I owe you one."

"Don't worry about it. We've had a wonderful time together this afternoon, and she even let me help her decorate your pizza," I laughed.

"My pizza? You're not staying for dinner?"

They both looked at me, the disappointment on their faces crashing into my heart and pulling on every single string.

"I don't want to impose," I said quietly, looking away.

"It's not imposing when you were invited."

"Yeah, we invited you, duh," Lily chimed in.

I looked over to find her sticking her tongue out at me.

"Well then, it would be my honor," I joked, standing up and curtsying.

"I'll get you some wine," John offered after scanning the table and spotting the glass Lily had asked me to pour for him.

"Thank you."

We sat and ate in silence for the most part, with Lily telling us about her first day back at school and how she didn't want to play volleyball anymore. I felt that it had nothing to do with the sport itself but with the girls on the team.

"It seems rather sudden," John said carefully. "Are you sure you want to quit?"

"Yeah, I don't think volleyball is fun anymore." She shrugged and studied her pizza, taking a bite to avoid having to discuss it any further.

"Well, if you're sure," he sighed, gripping the side of his plate. "I'll figure out a way to change my schedule around at work so I can be there to pick you up."

Lily's eyes jumped up with excitement, and I knew that she thought this meant that he would be home with her in the afternoons after school.

"I can always take a late lunch to come pick you up, then head back to the office," he added quietly as if talking to himself.

Just as quick as the excitement came, it vanished with his words.

"I'm done. May I be excused?" she said with a slight quiver.

"Sure… I guess if you're done…"

Lily pushed away from the table, stormed out of the kitchen, running up the stairs before slamming her door shut. John lowered his head and closed his eyes.

"What did I miss?" he asked without looking at me.

"She thought you were going to change your schedule so you could pick her up from school, then be home with her in the afternoons."

"It's not that easy," he huffed, scrubbing a hand down his face. He opened his eyes and looked at me. The same tiredness that I had seen right after Charlotte died somehow took up a permanent residence with the dark circles that sat right above his cheekbones.

"I would love to be able to cut my hours at work so I could come home and take care of her every day, but I can't. Not yet anyway."

"I know," I assured him.

"I've worked for years to get to where I am within the company, and unfortunately, the title of vice president comes with far more responsibilities and late hours. If I'm going to change either of those, that means that I have to step down, and we can't afford that. So, I'm in a bind, and I have no freaking clue what to do."

"At least you have a job to worry about," I snorted. "I'm soon to be homeless and won't have a penny to my name."

I said the words before I thought them through. My cheeks immediately burned with embarrassment as his face changed from frustration to pity.

"Why will you be homeless?" he asked, leaning forward.

"It's nothing," I fibbed.

"Emma…"

I shifted in my seat uncomfortably, trying to find a way to move the attention away from me. Finally, after a few minutes of awkward silence and John still staring at me, I gave in.

"Fine, I got an eviction notice today. I have to be out in two weeks. And given that I've yet to find a job, I can't pay the two months' worth of rent that I owe, let alone my car payment that I'm also behind on."

I waited for him to start his lecture about how I was an adult who should have known better or to go on about how much things have changed in the job world since I first got hired on at my last job fifteen years ago.

"Shit," he muttered, lifting his wine glass to take a drink. "I'm sorry, I had no idea."

"It's fine," I said, even though it wasn't. "I didn't mean to blurt it out. It's just been weighing heavily on my mind all day, and I have no idea what I'm going to do. The good thing is that my car is big enough to hold most of my stuff, and I'm hoping that I can sell whatever doesn't fit."

"Don't be ridiculous," he scoffed, setting his glass back down on the table.

"I'm not," I laughed. "I'm one hundred percent serious."

I lifted my glass of wine and tossed back what was left. We sat there for a few minutes, drinking our wine and worrying about our problems.

"I have an idea," he exclaimed excitedly, leaning across the table to take my hand. "Move in with us!"

I pulled my head back in surprise and narrowed my eyes. He had to be out of his mind.

"John, I don't need the pity but thank you—"

"It's not pity," he interrupted. "It's a win/win situation. You get a place to live—rent-free, and I have someone here with Lily in the afternoons after school until I can figure out my work schedule."

"But what am I supposed to do when I find a job? Lily still needs someone to pick her up and be here with her. I can't guarantee that a new employer would have that kind of flexibility with me—or that I would even be on this side of town and could make everything in time."

His eyes lit up as another idea ran through his mind.

"What if I hired you? Like as a nanny? You can live here with us and help me take care of Lily. I'll pay you for helping out so then you don't have to worry about finding a job right away, and you'll be helping Lily and me."

I tapped my fingers nervously on the table.

"I don't know, John. Do you really think this is a good idea? We've already been blurring the line so much with how often I've been hanging out since Charlotte passed. What if Lily starts to get the wrong impression about why I'm here all of the time?"

"It's a great idea, and I think Lily would be fully on board with it. If I don't hire you to be her nanny, then I'm going to have to hire someone else, and that's even more disruption in her life. Plus, you already have your own room here anyway, and I know how much you love that room."

He was right. I did love that room. Hell, I loved everything about this house. It was the only place that I felt calm and relaxed, even without having Charlotte around. It was warm and inviting, and I desperately needed something to ease the loneliness I felt.

"Okay," I said shakily—half excited, and half scared that this was a terrible idea. "I'll do it."

ONE LAST WISH

Six

I left John's house feeling relieved for the first time since Charlotte died. While I was excited about the possibility of starting over and helping him out with Lily, I was reluctant to jump on packing my stuff up, just in case this didn't pan out after all. When I left, I made sure that he was going to go upstairs and talk to Lily. I didn't want to stick around for their conversation about me moving in and helping out because I needed her to have the chance to say no if she wanted to. And if I was there, I couldn't imagine that she would.

I loved Lily with every fiber of my being, and her happiness was more important to me than a roof over my damn head. I wanted only the best for her and knew how vulnerable she was right now. So, if there was a way to make *anything* easier for her, I was going to do it. Even if it made my life harder.

It was a little after nine when I got home. I had no desire to come back to an empty apartment, but I also couldn't justify driving around town and wasting gas that I might not be able to afford next week. I got comfy, made a cup of chamomile tea, and sat down on the couch with the book I had started reading before the accident. Reading had always been my escape, but lately, I couldn't read more than five words without getting lost in my thoughts.

I sipped my tea and opened the book, letting my fingers trail over the worn-out bookmark that Charlotte had bought me for my eleventh birthday. It was the first one that I had to spend without my parents, and she saved her allowance to buy me a copy of James and The Giant Peach and a bookmark with two tree frogs having a tea party.

She knew that the book was my absolute favorite and that I had checked it out so many times from the library that my name was practically the only name on their check-out list. The bookmark was supposed to be her and me when we got older, enjoying our books, and drinking tea.

I closed the book and wiped the tears away from my cheeks with the back of my hand. I set my tea down on the coffee table and tried to take a deep breath. Just as the grief was starting to build up again, I got a text message from John. I opened my phone and read it.

John: Lily is 100% on board with you moving in and being her nanny.

John: She wants to know if you start tomorrow, or if you want to start tonight and stay over?

I felt my cheeks splitting as my grin spread from ear to ear. His last text was a picture of the two of them sitting on her bed, and hands pressed together as she begged with her eyes squinted closed.

Me: It's late, and she has an early day at school tomorrow. How about I pick her up after school and officially start then?

I waited for a few minutes, chewing my nail nervously when the dots started bouncing then disappeared. I didn't want to disappoint her, but I also didn't want to just rush over there. Suddenly, my phone started ringing. I rolled my eyes and swiped my finger across the screen to answer John's call.

"I can't do all this texting crap," John said with a chuckle.

I could hear Lily in the background, scolding him for his language. "Sorry," he added, more to her than to me.

"That's alright. I always prefer phone calls over texts anyway," I said sarcastically, thankful that it was just a phone call and not a FaceTime request. I had already washed off my makeup and tossed my hair up onto my head.

"Really? That's so—"

"No, I'm messing with you," I laughed, hearing his disappointment when I cut him off.

"Maybe I should reconsider this arrangement after all… I don't know if I want someone who prefers electronic communication over verbal."

"This—coming from the guy who is the *Vice President* of a global tech company?" I had to bite the inside of my cheek to keep from laughing.

"Hey, I'm just saying that I grew up in a world where people talked about things. Not the constant text messages and IM and emails."

"Who do you know that still uses IM? Do they have a landline?" I teased, enjoying razzing him.

"Very funny," he quipped. "Anyway, Lily wants to know if you want to come stay the night *tonight*."

"I wish I could, but I'm already in bed."

I felt terrible for lying, but it was for the better.

"Bull. Shit."

I felt my face flush at least seven shades of red when he called me out.

"What?! It's true. I'm in bed," I paused to force a yawn. "And I'm so sleepy already."

"I'll make a deal with you," he said, pressing the phone closer to his mouth. "If I can guess at least three out of five things that I think you're doing right now, you have to get your ass over here and stay the night. Deal?"

I pulled in a deep breath and slowly let it out. He wasn't going to win. There was no way he could possibly know that much about me.

"Fine. Deal. But you're going to lose."

I heard him laugh in the background, moving the phone from his face, so the loud sound didn't hurt my ears. "Lily, please go get Emma's bedroom ready for her."

I rolled my eyes again at how cocky he was being.

"Okay, are you ready?" he asked.

"Are *you*? Because you're still going to lose."

"Oh, Emma. You have no faith in me."

"Nope."

"Alright, I'm going to go with… you're sitting on your couch, wearing no makeup, with a cup of tea getting cold on the coffee table, and a book sitting next to you that you don't plan to read."

How in the world did he know all of that? I leaned forward and looked around to make sure he wasn't somehow hiding in my apartment, and I hadn't seen him. That would be the only possible explanation of what had just happened.

"Those were only four things," I said dismissively,

brushing off the fact that he was right.

"Alright, I'll add in that you left the kettle on the stove, and now you're wondering if you turned it off."

I hadn't thought about it until he said something, but I found myself jumping up and rushing over to make sure that I had turned it off.

"So, what was I? Five for five?"

I could hear the satisfaction in his voice and pictured the smirk he likely had on his face.

"Those were all easy guesses," I countered, walking back over to the couch and sitting down.

"Oh really?"

"Yes," I laughed nervously, feeling the pressure from the other end of the phone. It felt weird, but there was something different about how John and I acted with each other. It was almost as if… we were… *flirting*. My heart immediately sunk in my chest, and I closed my eyes. Shame flooded over me as I realized that I *had* been flirting with my *dead* best friend's *husband*. I was a terrible person and deserved all the misery that was washing over me.

"I don't think it had anything to do with being easy. I think it had to do with me knowing you better than you think. Now go pack your bag and get your ass over here. I'll be waiting for you at the door in twenty minutes."

I didn't have to worry about what to say because he hung up after that. Instead, I was left to deal with the guilt and mix of emotions still racing through me from what I had done. Maybe moving in with them was a terrible idea after all.

<u>Seven</u>

I couldn't tell if I hated myself more for absentmindedly flirting with John or for giving in to my guilt and showing up at their house at nine o'clock on a Monday night. I should have said no and given myself time to stop and process what was happening before I just jumped in, but something about how Lily looked in the picture pulled at my heart and wouldn't let me say no. There was nothing in this world that I wouldn't do for her.

"Hey," John said as he opened the door and stepped to the side.

"Hi," I mumbled as I walked inside and adjusted the duffle bag that I had rushed to pack. I didn't even know if I bothered to pack an outfit that matched for tomorrow, but it didn't matter at this point. I was here, and there was no backing out now that I looked up and saw Lily heading my way.

"Aunt Emma!" She ran over and wrapped her arms around my waist, hugging me as tight as she could.

"Hey, sweet Lily," I said softly, rubbing her back.

"Thank you for coming tonight instead of tomorrow," she said excitedly, pulling away to look at me. "I was so excited when dad told me that you're moving in with us, and I couldn't wait for you to start. Plus, I thought maybe you could take me to school tomorrow so daddy can go to work early and be home on time for dinner. And then we can cook for him again like we did today!"

Her baby blue eyes were sparkling with excitement as she talked. I smiled at her while carefully catching John's eye and raised an eyebrow. The last thing that I wanted to do was give Lily the wrong impression of why I was there and my role. She was still in such a vulnerable state right now that I didn't want her to entertain the idea that I could replace what she was missing with her mom.

She was still talking, going a mile a minute, as I tried to listen and keep up.

"You can plan everything out in the morning," John laughed, giving me a reassuring smile. "Let's let Emma get settled in tonight, and then we'll all have breakfast before I have to go to work."

"Okay, fine." Lily's shoulders slumped for half of a second before she turned to face him. "But can we make chocolate chip pancakes in the morning?!"

"Deal," he agreed with a playfully stern tone. "Now, get to bed before I change my mind."

"Alright," Lily sighed, reaching up to hug him. "Goodnight, daddy." She kissed his cheek and then walked over to me. "Goodnight, Aunt Emma."

I wrapped my arms around her, returning the warm hug she was giving me.

"Goodnight, sweetie."

I waited until she went upstairs to her room before turning my attention to John. I folded my arms over my chest and waited for him to talk. His cheeks flushed red for a brief moment before he coughed to clear his throat and turned away.

"Since when do you make chocolate chip pancakes?" I asked after a few minutes of silence. I could tell that there was another reason that he wanted me to come over tonight, and it wasn't just because Lily had insisted.

"It's one of the few things that I've known how to cook for a while now," he laughed. "And thankfully, it's also one of her new favorites. So, I guess it's a win-win."

"So, I gave up my comfortable bed in my apartment tonight for chocolate chip pancakes? You know, I could have come over in the morning and saved everyone the hassle tonight."

He looked down with a sheepish smile on his face.

"I know. I'm sorry that I pushed so hard for you to come over tonight. But honestly, I didn't know what else to do."

He ran a hand down his face and blew out a long breath.

"Why? What happened? Is something wrong with Lily?" I could hear the panic in my voice as I started to worry.

"No, no," he assured me quickly. "Lily is fine. Everything is fine. There's just this issue at—"

"Work," I finished for him, fully understanding what was happening. The only emergencies—other than Charlotte's accident—were related to something at his work.

"I'm sorry. I feel like I've already crossed the line, and it hasn't even been twenty-four hours since I asked you to move in and help me. But unfortunately, there's a deal that I've been working on, and things are starting to go south, which means that I may have to go into the office before Lily is even awake tomorrow. I didn't know what else to do...."

His voice trailed off, and I felt the pull in my heart as I fought the urge to reach out and comfort him.

"It's fine, John. I agreed to help out however I can, and I meant it."

I shoved my hands into my pockets to keep the urge away. He looked so stressed out and overwhelmed. Maybe I had been too lost in my own thoughts earlier that I hadn't noticed the dark bags under his eyes or the way his face looked thinner? Had he been eating? Was he getting enough sleep? I had to remind myself that it wasn't my place to worry about him. I had agreed to help with Lily. To get her to and from school and help her with her homework when she needed it. John wasn't my responsibility, except for the silent promise that I had made to Charlotte that I would take care of both of them. The problem was that the lines were now starting to blur, and I couldn't tell where they were before crossing them.

We didn't bother staying up late to hash out the details on anything; we just went our separate ways and got ready for bed. While I thought it would feel weird to stay in the guest room without having Charlotte here, it was surprisingly more calming than my apartment had been. Maybe it was because this had always felt like home to me? Or because I had pictures of us on the wall to look at? Either way, I felt a sense of peace that I hadn't felt in almost a month since she passed.

The next morning, I woke up to the smell of fresh coffee brewing and the sweet aroma of pancakes floating upstairs. I rolled over and picked up my phone from the nightstand to check the time. It was almost six o'clock, which meant that I had an hour to get Lily up and ready for school. I got out of bed and walked down the hall to her bedroom, surprised to find her already gone.

I made a quick pitstop in the bathroom before going downstairs to find John and Lily in the kitchen. He was standing at the stove, already dressed for work in a designer suit that shouldn't be anywhere near the stove. I leaned against the doorway and watched as Lily sang a song, and he danced while she carefully poured three glasses full of orange juice. Just as I was about to walk in, she turned around and saw me. Her face brightened as her smile stretched across her cheeks.

She was still in her pajamas with her hair in a lopsided ponytail. Thankfully, it wouldn't take long to get ready since her school required uniforms, and she was never fond of fancy hairdos.

"Good morning," John said as he turned around and saw me standing there. "Breakfast is ready."

"Morning," I said with as much enthusiasm as I could muster. I wasn't a morning person, and this was early for me.

"Not good?" he questioned with a quirked brow.

"Good comes after I've had a cup of coffee," I mumbled, padding into the kitchen. Lily pulled a seat out for me at the table and then sat down right beside me. "Maybe two cups," I added as John reached beside me to set the plate of pancakes on the table. He walked off and chuckled as I heard him grab a coffee mug from the cabinet.

A few minutes later, he returned with a hot cup of coffee and set it down in front of me before returning to the stove. I watched Lily serve herself a pancake before adding one to my plate. I smiled and said thank you, wondering what John was doing and whether he was going to join us.

He opened the oven door, and a heavenly aroma filled the room. I turned to see what it was when I saw him pull out a cast-iron skillet, setting it on the trivet next to the stove before reaching down to grab something else. He looked more comfortable in the kitchen than I had ever seen him, and suddenly I questioned whether I knew him as well as I thought I did.

With potholders on his hands, he carried over the skillet and carefully put it on the trivet in the middle of the table. I leaned forward, slightly standing to get a better look as he walked back to grab the other dish. The steam was floating around the perfectly cooked quiche that was making my mouth water. I had been expecting pancakes, yet here he was, pulling out all the stops for a gourmet breakfast.

He came back, setting a plate of bacon down next to the pancakes before he sat at the head of the table. I felt like my jaw was hanging open as I sat there in awe.

"I thought you couldn't cook anything other than hotdogs and pancakes?" I asked in disbelief, scanning the table of food once more to make sure I wasn't dreaming it.

"While I do make a mean wiener and some killer pancakes, I also know a thing or two about cooking. I just never cooked much before because Charlotte always handled it." His face fell after he said it, and he glanced over at Lily. The mention of her name was enough to darken any room because her absence was that terrible.

"Well, thank you for breakfast," I said, clearing my throat as I tried to talk past the stinging pain. I refused to let Lily see me cry if I could help it. "What about work?" I asked carefully, unsure of how much he had told Lily. We both knew that his insane schedule was hard for her, and even though I was there to help out and keep her company, it could never replace the void she felt from him always being gone.

"Thankfully, everything was resolved this morning," he answered as he cut into the quiche before scooping a serving onto Lily's plate. "And, I don't think I'll have to work late tonight either."

This news earned him a bright smile from Lily as she took a bite of pancake.

"That's great," I chirped, handing him my plate when he asked for it. The quiche was too hot to lift, so he was serving everyone. "Just let me know what time you think you'll be home, and we'll get dinner started."

"Sounds like a plan," he replied, his eyes meeting mine before he looked down and took a bite. I turned my attention to my food and enjoyed the meal.

Thirty minutes later, I was helping clean up in the kitchen while Lily rushed upstairs to get ready. John had already left for work, and it felt weird to be in their house alone, without him or Charlotte. I had been here plenty of times to watch Lily while they went out, but it was different now. I was still trying to wrap my head around everything when Lily came downstairs, dressed in her uniform, with her hair brushed and pulled back behind a headband.

I was impressed with how easily she got herself ready without needing any of my help. Then I reminded myself that she would be a teenager soon, which would mean that she didn't want anyone's help. I vaguely remembered those days and felt a stab of pain when I thought about growing up with Charlotte and how much fun we had.

"Are you ready?" I asked, trying to push the thoughts away.

"Yeah, but we still have a few minutes if you want to take a quick shower," she said, eyeing me suspiciously.

I looked down at the t-shirt and sweatpants I was wearing, then held my hands out and looked at her.

"What's wrong with what I'm wearing?"

She gave me a look that all kids give their parents when they're trying to tell them that they're not cool anymore. Then, her eyes wandered up to my hair which had me reaching a hand up to fix it.

"Nothing, I guess. But you can always drop me off by the bus stop if you want to. I don't mind walking."

I could hear the laughter in her voice as I acted appalled that she would say such a thing.

"Just for that, I'm walking you to your classroom," I teased as I walked out of the kitchen and grabbed my purse and car keys from the table by the door.

I heard her groan and mumble something about why I couldn't be a *cool aunt*. I tried to keep the laughter inside as I made a mental note to get up earlier tomorrow to shower and get ready *before* taking her to school. The poor kid had enough problems to deal with, including the shitty mean girls walking past as we drove up. I wasn't going to add to it.

After I dropped her off—by the bus stop—I went back to their house, unsure of what I should be doing. John and I hadn't talked about the plan or what he wanted me to do while Lily was in school. Hell, we hadn't even talked about what he was going to pay me. Not that I wanted his money. Truthfully, I was thankful to have a roof over my head and not have to worry about being evicted from my apartment. It was an added bonus that I got to spend time with the two people who I truly loved and adored.

But that also didn't take care of the monthly bills that I had or the car payment that I needed to pay before they came to repossess it. I hated talking about money, and even more so with John. It felt gross and icky. Like, how do you even negotiate something like this? I was happy to help them for free, but my monthly bills argued that I couldn't afford that price.

I went into the kitchen and finished cleaning up from this morning. The least that I could do while I was there waiting for Lily to get out of school was to clean the house for them. It would be one less thing for him to worry about and more time that he would get to spend with his daughter.

A few hours later, I had already swept and mopped, ran the dishwasher and unloaded it, emptied the trash and took it out to the trashcan in the garage, and finished all the laundry and laid it on their beds. But I wasn't comfortable putting it away, so I left it until I could talk to John about it.

By noon, I sat down to take a quick break and was watching some random soap opera on tv when John called.

"How's it going?" he asked.

"I've gotten a lot done around the house, but we do need to sit down later and go over things in more detail," I said, keeping it vague. I knew that he was likely calling me while on his lunch break, but that could be interrupted and over at any moment.

"Sounds good, we'll talk after dinner. But you don't have to stay there all day if there's stuff you need to do at your apartment. I know that you probably need to start packing soon."

I hadn't even thought about that. I had no idea where I would store my stuff or whether I was even keeping it. Of course, I could always sell the more oversized items—like furniture that I don't need, but then again, I didn't have much of that either. My apartment was small, and I was never one to collect or hoard stuff. If I didn't wear it or use it in a six-month window, I got rid of it.

"That's a good idea. I hadn't even thought about that," I admitted, chewing on my nail.

"Well, start packing what you want to bring over to the house with you, and I'll help you move it later."

Just as I was going to say something, I heard someone come into his office and interrupt.

"I gotta go," he said apologetically. "We'll talk tonight."

I didn't get a chance to respond before he hung up. I leaned back against the couch and took a deep breath, trying to force myself to focus. Everything around me was changing so fast that I could hardly see straight.

<u>Eight</u>

Two weeks flew by, and before I knew it, I was officially out of my apartment and situated in my new room at John's house. The schedule that Lily and I had set up together seemed to be working well, and I had gotten used to getting up earlier in the morning. It was funny how productive I felt when I was already showered and ready to go by six-thirty every morning, even on the weekends.

Lily had stuck to her decision to quit volleyball, so I picked her up every day right after school let out. We usually stopped by the grocery store to pick up stuff to make for dinner on our way home. I found that she was more particular about fresh fruits and vegetables than anyone I had ever met. We would wait in line at the meat counter, so Lily could discuss the options she had in mind for that night's menu. While I thought it would be easier to buy a week's worth of groceries on Monday, she balked at the idea and said that we should focus on putting fresh food into our bodies.

John seemed to enjoy dinner every night and the effort that we put into it. He agreed to restock the wine selection, per Lily's request, when we started running low. She was in love with the idea of having her own kitchen, and that meant gourmet meals and wine for dinner. Granted, I was convinced that she was only pushing for the wine because it meant that she was allowed to have a Shirley Temple filled with maraschino cherries.

I enjoyed cooking and found that it was rather peaceful and not as chaotic as I had found it before when I used to try to cook for myself. Maybe it was because Lily enjoyed it so much and took the lead, or perhaps it was because I found myself desperate to do anything that made her happy.

It was finally Friday, and I was looking forward to the weekend. The weather was supposed to be nice, and I had thought about asking John and Lily if they wanted to go to Santa Cruz for a quick getaway. Lily had spent the afternoon up in her room after I picked her up from school. She seemed to be in a bad mood, so I was trying to give her some space. Unfortunately, two weeks wasn't long enough to prepare me for the mood swings of a pre-teen.

My phone vibrated with a text message from John, confirming that he would have to work late tonight. He asked me to apologize to Lily and suggested that we order a pizza and start our weekly movie night without him. I shot him back a quick reply, letting him know that I would tell her. I didn't bother lecturing him on being late and missing movie night. He already knew how she would take it.

I walked up the stairs and to her room, knocking lightly on her door. I waited a few minutes for her to answer, then banged harder when she didn't. Finally, the door pushed open, creaking a little in the process. I peeked my head inside, trying to make sure that I didn't startle her when I found her sitting on her bed, crying.

"Lily," I said softly, not sure if she had heard me. I walked over to the bed and sat down. I placed my arm on her leg while she covered her face in her hands. "Sweetheart, what's wrong?"

Sitting on her lap was the blanket that she had been working on with Charlotte before she died. The same one that she took to show and tell, even though she insisted she was too old to participate in it anymore.

Her shoulders shook as she continued to cry. I scooted over and crawled up the side of the bed to sit next to her. I wrapped my arms around her and pulled her close to me. I held her while she cried and waited until her sobs softened. She wiped her face with her hands and looked up at me.

I didn't ask her what was wrong. I saw the knitting needle sitting in her lap with the ball of yarn and knew.

"I don't remember how to do it," she cried, covering her face again. "I wanted to finish the blanket, and I don't know how—"

Her body buckled under the weight of her grief as she cried harder. She turned into me and wrapped her arms around me as tight as she could.

"Shhh," I whispered in her ear, rubbing her back as I tried to hold my tears inside. "It's okay, I promise."

I waited for her to catch her breath and continued to rub her back. She pulled away and folded her hands in her lap as she looked down at the partial blanket. Her breathing was ragged as her body continued to shake in response.

"Your mom and I used to knit together when we were your age," I said softly, smiling at the memory. "I can teach you if you'd like?"

Her head whipped up as she looked at me in disbelief.

"You know how to knit?" She sniffled, wiping the tears from her cheeks with the back of her hand. I reached behind her and pulled a tissue out of the box on her nightstand.

"I do," I nodded. "And I'm happy to teach you so you can finish your blanket."

She sucked in a breath and looked down at it as she struggled with her answer.

"It's only if you want me to," I added cautiously, "and whenever you're ready. Just let me know, and I'd be more than happy to help."

I felt my phone vibrate in my pocket and wondered if it was another update from John. There was no way that I could unload the other bad news on her now, not while she was already having a hard time. I ignored my phone and gave her my full attention as she looked up at me.

"I would like for you to teach me. Please," she said with enough sadness to break my heart all over again.

"Of course, sweetie. I would love to."

She reached down and gathered the yarn and needle, passing it over to me. My fingers trembled slightly as I took it from her. I set it in my lap and then lifted the blanket to see what kind of stitch they had been using. While we had knitted a lot when we were younger, Charlotte continued with it longer than I had, and I prayed that she hadn't been using some complicated stitch that I wouldn't know how to do.

I was relieved when I saw how basic it was. My heart warmed with memories of making a blanket just like this when we were little. It was right after my parents had died, and my aunt had given me a giant pile of yarn to keep me busy. In all fairness, she was a single woman who had never been around many kids. She had cats, and everyone knows how much cats like yarn.

Charlotte and I spent so many summer nights together trying to figure out how to knit and would laugh when we made a mess. Eventually, we figured it out and made a blanket that I kept until it fell apart. There was something comforting about it that helped me through my grief, and now it was my turn to help Lily with hers.

I picked up the needle and the yarn and walked Lily through the basic stitches. I felt a tug at my heart when her face lit up, and I knew that the memories of working on it with her mom had come rushing back to her. I handed her the yarn and needle, smiling when she took it and started knitting. I watched her for a few minutes, admiring the pride on her face as she kept going.

I gave her a gentle pat on her back before I carefully scooted down the bed and got up. I was about to walk out of the door when she stopped me.

"I was scared that I forgot," she said sadly, lowering her hands for a moment to talk to me.

"It's okay to forget things sometimes," I assured her. "There's always a way to learn them again."

She shook her head no and lowered her eyes.

"I was scared that I forgot *her.* I couldn't remember what she had taught me, and I was afraid that all of my memories of her would disappear. What if that happens?"

I didn't bother wiping away the tear as it slid down my cheek. I sucked in a breath and held it as I thought of how to answer that question. I walked back over to her and sat on the edge of the bed.

"My mom always smelled like cinnamon. So, whenever I see cinnamon rolls, I get this warm feeling inside me because it reminds me of her. And whenever I eat pizza, I only sprinkle the parmesan cheese in the center of it because that's how my mom did it. She didn't like to get it on her fingers, so she only put it in the middle. I don't like racing, but I sit down with a bucket of fried chicken and watch every Nascar race because that's what I used to do with my dad. And sometimes, I like to look up at the clouds and see what pictures I can make out of them. It was something that the three of us used to do every summer. We would lay in the grass and wait for my dad to burn the food he was barbecuing because he was too distracted with the clouds."

The tears ran freely down my face as I allowed the grief to consume me. It had been so long since I had talked about my parents, I hadn't realized just how much I still missed them.

"No matter how many of the little things you forget, you'll never forget *her*. She will always be a part of you, my sweet Lily."

"I'm sorry your mommy and daddy died," she said quietly, her tears starting again. I nodded and squeezed her hand, unable to find the words to say. I knew that she understood when she squeezed mine back.

We sat there in silence for a few minutes, each of us lost in our own thoughts of sadness. I felt my phone vibrate again and pulled it out of my pocket. I rubbed my eyes, wiping the tears away so I could see the message. My mood lightened when I saw John's message, confirming that he was able to move some stuff around and would be home on time after all. I texted him back and confirmed that I would order the pizza and have it ready.

Lily's face was swollen, and her eyes puffy from crying. I knew that I probably looked like a hot mess at this point too.

"Hey, do you want to go make ice cream sundaes?" I offered, knowing that this was one of her favorite desserts.

"*Before* dinner?" she gasped, her eyes as wide as saucers.

I leaned over closer to her and rested my forehead against hers.

"*Before* dinner!" I pulled back and smiled, feeling like a kid again.

She tossed the blanket and yarn to the side of her bed and jumped up. I was relieved to see how excited she was and almost felt bad that I was such a bad influence on her.

She was about to rush down the stairs when she suddenly paused and turned to look at me. Her brows pulled together as she narrowed her eyes.

"My dad is working late tonight, isn't he? He told you to let me have ice cream before dinner because he's going to miss pizza and a movie night."

She folded her arms over her chest and frowned.

I walked over and stood in front of her, lifting her chin with her finger so she would look at me.

"Your dad is heading home in thirty minutes, which means that *you* better hurry and eat your ice cream *before* he gets here!"

"No way!" she squealed as she ran down the stairs before I could catch up to her. I could hear her shout, *'this is the best day ever!'* as I made my way into the kitchen. I smiled as I sat down at the table, watching her pull out all of her favorite toppings. I pulled out my phone and put in our pizza order. In just a short period, things had already gotten so predictable for us. I would order the pizza and get the snacks ready while Lily picked the movie line up for the night, and John would grab the pizza on his way home.

Lily was finishing the last few bites when we heard the front door open. She gasped and quickly shoveled in the last spoonful before rushing over to the sink to rinse her bowl. John walked in with the pizza in one hand and a paper bag in the other. I eyed it suspiciously, wondering what else he had decided to grab on his way home. He paused in his tracks, looking at Lily as she hurriedly scrubbed the evidence from her bowl.

He looked at me and nodded to her, silently asking me what she was doing. I shrugged and smirked. I wasn't about to snitch on her, especially when it was my idea. Lily set the bowl in the sink and spun around, a look of guilt on her face when she saw John. Her eyes were still a little red and swollen, but it was the streak of chocolate by her mouth that gave her away.

I watched his features change from concern for why she had been crying to playful as he set everything down on the table and put his hands on his hips. He looked from her to me, then back to her again.

"Does someone want to explain what is going on?" he said, raising an eyebrow.

Lily giggled and tried to hide her face behind her hands.

"Lily…" he drawled out. "What are you hiding over there?"

"Nothing," she replied quickly. Too quickly. She immediately turned to me, raising her eyebrows as if she was afraid that she had been caught. I couldn't help myself as I burst into laughter. I laughed so hard that I couldn't catch my breath and snorted, which brought them into hysterics too.

Several minutes passed before the laughter faded, and I was able to catch my breath.

"We decided to indulge in sundaes since it's Friday and officially the weekend," I said with another shrug as if it was no big deal.

"Before dinner?" John asked sternly, even though I saw the green specks in his eyes light up with amusement.

"We're girls. We want ice cream when we want ice cream," I replied with a smug smile.

Lily giggled from her corner, enjoying the snarky back and forth between her dad and me.

"Well, then, I guess *this* will be all mine tonight," John said as he reached into the bag and pulled out a giant gallon of vanilla ice cream. Lily's eyes nearly bulged out of her head as she stared at it, and I fought the urge to laugh again.

"You bought that for tonight?" she asked, her voice cracking with excitement.

"Maybe…" He spun it around on the table, looking at it as if it were some sort of trophy that he was admiring. "But, if you've already had ice cream, then I guess there's no need for this."

Lily looked at me with a look of desperation that made me giggle.

"It's okay, Lily. I can always take you for more later since your *dad* doesn't want to share." I folded my arms over my chest and gave him *the look*.

"Two weeks," he sighed playfully and picked up the gallon of ice cream. "That's all that it took for me to be outnumbered in my own damn house." He shook his head and walked over to put the ice cream in the freezer.

"You never stood a chance," I laughed, patting him on the shoulder as I walked past him to get the paper plates.

"I knew that when the doctor said it was a girl," he mumbled.

I grabbed the box of pizza from the table and followed Lily into the living room, chuckling at how true that was. John joined us a few minutes later, and we started the movie. The night was quiet as we watched a handful of girly movies that Lily had picked before she got tired and decided to go to bed. I knew that it was early for her and that she was worn out from earlier. Grief had a way of silently exhausting and taking everything out of you.

After Lily went upstairs, I got up and carried the empty pizza box and the other trash to the kitchen.

"Did you want to stay up and watch another movie?" John asked as he moved around me to open the garage door. I tossed the empty box into the trash can and thought about it. While I would typically stay up with him and watch an action-packed thriller, I felt pretty exhausted myself. I yawned and covered my mouth to hide it as I walked back into the kitchen.

"I think I'm going to have to skip it tonight, sorry," I said, leaning against the counter. He leaned back against the one across from me and crossed his ankles.

"Is everything okay? Or am I missing something?" he asked with a hint of desperation in his voice. "Because I feel like something is happening with you and Lily, and I have no idea what it is."

I rubbed my lips together and pulled my shoulders back, trying to find the strength I needed not to break down again today.

"Lily had a rough day today. She was trying to finish the blanket that she was making with Charlotte, and she couldn't remember how to knit the stitches. I was able to show her, and everything came back to her. The problem was that she was afraid that she was starting to forget her."

He closed his eyes and hung his head as he exhaled heavily.

"Shit. I didn't see that one coming," he admitted sadly. "I'll talk to her therapist and see if I can add in an additional day for her to go next week since she wasn't available today."

I pulled my head back and looked at him. I wasn't sure if I was more shocked by what he just said or pissed.

"Therapy? Really, John? That's your answer?"

I knew how harsh my tone was, and I didn't care. However, the surprised look on his face showed that he was hearing me, loud and clear.

"What did I do wrong now?" he groaned, lifting his hands in the air helplessly. "She said that she was enjoying her sessions. Why wouldn't I add another one? She's going to deal with the grief she has from losing her mother, and this is directly related. So what am I missing?"

"You, John! You're missing *you*." I paused for a split second to compose myself before I accidentally woke her up if she was already asleep. I balled my fists at my side, trying to force some of the anger to go elsewhere before I said something that I would regret. I loved John. He was the only friend—and family—that I had left, which meant that I needed to tell him when he was wrong. And boy was he wrong.

"I'm right here," he sighed, rolling his neck on his shoulders. "I'm doing the best that I can in a world that I know nothing about, Emma. Obviously."

"I'm not saying that you're not doing a good job, John. You are doing an amazing job at balancing everything and figuring out this new path. But the problem is that she needs you to be her dad and to grieve *with* her."

"I *am* grieving, Emma. Every damn day for almost six weeks, I wake up and feel the loss of my wife. I feel the weight of my daughter not having a mother. It is unbearable, and yet, I push through it every single day! I force myself to be strong for her because she doesn't deserve to see how weak I really am!"

His voice boomed through the kitchen, sending chills up my arms. He didn't scare me, but it was different to see him this way. So open and vulnerable. For a moment, it made me realize that he had been so busy trying to stay positive for Lily that he hadn't been able to grieve with anyone since Charlotte died.

"Your daughter doesn't need you to be strong for her right now. She needs you to fall apart and feel this pain that is so consuming that we all feel like we're being pulled under and don't know when we'll take another breath because the thought of breathing the air in a world where Charlotte doesn't exist is pure torture!" I sucked in a deep breath, replacing the air that I had expelled in that long-winded sentence. My chest was heaving as I felt the energy crackle around us as we stared at each other, unsure of what to say.

Finally, I conceded, realizing that it wasn't my place to tell John how to handle things with his daughter.

"I'm sorry, I didn't mean to overstep," I said quietly. "It's not my place to tell you how to grieve or what to do with Lily. I just think that at some point, she's going to need to see that you're vulnerable too. She needs to know that she can break down in front of you and feel whatever she feels in those moments when life gets too hard. When missing Charlotte is more than her heart can handle. Because it's going to happen, John. No matter how hard you try to prevent it, you can't. But you can be there for her and let her be there for you too. It's an empty feeling to have to live alone in your grief."

I gave him a small, forced smile and went upstairs to my bedroom. I tiptoed past Lily's room and peeked my head in to check on her. She was sound asleep, cuddled up with the half-finished blanket tucked under her arm against her chest. I went to my room and closed the door quietly, making sure I didn't wake her.

I changed into my pajamas and thought about everything that had happened today. My mind was racing as I tried to find something to comfort me. Before, I would call Charlotte when I felt like this and talk me through everything. Even if we didn't address the real issue, she would still find a way to ease my anxiety by talking to me. I walked over to the closet and opened the door, hoping to find what I was looking for.

I pushed the hangers back across the bar, sending the shirts swaying as they moved. In the corner of the closet was the outfit that Charlotte had bought for me to wear to my interview. It still had the tags on it, but instead of sitting in the bag, it was hanging in my closet. I reached out and gently ran my fingers down it, feeling the tears spill over my cheeks as I remembered that dreadful day.

A few minutes later, I forced myself to focus as I wiped the tears from my face. I bent down and picked up the blanket sitting on top of the pile of other linens on the floor. It was tattered and torn and had definitely seen better days. But I wasn't looking for something to keep me warm. I climbed into bed and tucked it under my arm, the same way that Lily had hers, and held the blanket that I made with Charlotte next to my heart. I closed my eyes and let the tears fall as I cried myself to sleep.

Nine

My eyes were swollen when I woke up, a harsh reminder of the grief I had tried to force down last night so I could fall asleep. I rolled out of bed and got ready, not bothering to go downstairs first. I wasn't sure if I was prepared to talk to John about what had happened last night, and I was still debating just how out of line I had been with what I'd said.

I didn't intend to cross the line and overstep when it came to how he was dealing with his grief, but I was feeling overly protective of Lily. We'd gotten relatively close spending every day together for the past two weeks, and then helping her with her blanket yesterday further solidified the bond between us. I felt this new connection to her that I hadn't felt with anyone else before, not even Charlotte. It was this innate urge to protect her, and when John recommended that she go to therapy, my claws were out, and my teeth bared. I wanted—no *needed* him to be there for her and not disregard her grief as another problem for her therapist to handle.

Deep down in my heart, I didn't believe that he really felt that way, but I couldn't swallow down the words as they exploded from me. Maybe it was my own unresolved grief from losing my parents, or perhaps it was because Charlotte's birthday was coming up, and I couldn't handle the thought of not celebrating her.

I leaned forward and swiped at the blob of concealer that I had added to try to hide the circles under my eyes. I rubbed it in as good as I could and pulled back to get a better look. It wasn't terrible, but I definitely looked exhausted. I added some blush to bring some color back to my face and ran the mascara wand through my eyelashes before calling it quits.

That was as good as it was going to get. I had no plans to go anywhere and only bothered with getting ready so I didn't scare Lily with how pale and sick I looked.

I pulled my hair up into a bun and secured it with a hair tie before making my way downstairs. I could hear John and Lily talking in the living room, so I tried to duck into the kitchen before they saw me.

"Good morning!" Lily said happily, stopping me in my tracks. I pulled in a deep breath and turned around, forcing a smile. John was sitting on the couch beside her with a handful of picture albums scattered across the coffee table. I felt the lump in my throat get bigger as I recognized which albums. On the other side of the coffee table, on the floor, was a cardboard box that had Charlotte's name in all capital letters on the side.

"Good morning," I answered, cautiously walking over to where they were sitting. "What are you looking at?" I asked dumbly, given that I already knew. I sat down on the arm of the couch, next to Lily. She reached down and picked up a picture, smiling as she handed it to me.

"Look, this is one of you and mom. It says on the back that you were in—"

"Sixth grade," I whispered, finishing her sentence. I took the picture from her and covered my mouth with my hand as my lips trembled. We were both smiling with one arm hung over the other's shoulder, and our bangs teased up high with an entire can of Aqua Net. It was taken outside of the school, our first day of sixth grade. We were only excited because we had all the same classes together; otherwise, it probably would have been a picture of us crying and holding each other while we felt the anxiety of being separated. Back then, there was rarely a moment when we weren't together.

"It was our first day of school," I added when no one else spoke. "We were so excited to have our classes together that we didn't even worry about being at a new school."

"Did you move?" Lily asked, her brows pulled together.

"No, but starting middle school is like starting a new school because you get mixed in with the older kids."

"I don't want to go to a new school," she groaned, holding her hand in her face dramatically. "But," she paused and thought about it. "I really don't even like the school that I go to now. Can I just drop out and forget about school altogether?" she asked, turning to John.

"I'm afraid that's not an option," he assured her with a smile and a light laugh. "Middle school isn't all that bad."

"It is when you go to my school, and *everyone* follows you to the new school."

I looked over her head at John to see if he was hearing what she was saying. Not just the words but the anguish behind them. I knew from the very first day that I picked her up that she wasn't happy there. I could see it written all over her face when she didn't know that I was there. It was worse when I had seen the reason for it after I got a good look at the girls who had been bullying her. Not much had changed since that day, other than she wasn't subjected to any more of their bullshit after school once she dropped volleyball. Whatever happened during the day, she kept to herself, and I hated that I didn't have a way of knowing.

When John refused to say anything, I decided to push past it and change the subject. I was still feeling frustrated from last night. The last thing that I wanted to do was start another fight in front of Lily. And even if it wasn't a fight last night, I was pretty confident it would be one now.

"What are you doing with the pictures?" I asked, focusing my attention back on Lily.

"It's for a project at school."

"Oh, like the show and tell day you had a few months ago?" I felt the excitement in my tone as I remembered something that had happened without her having to tell me.

She scrunched her face and looked at me as if I'd just grown three horns and smelled like rotten onions.

"What?!" I laughed, leaning back as if she was going to hit me. I handed her the picture and folded my hands in my lap to keep from reaching out to pick up more. I didn't want to intrude on whatever she was doing, especially since they were Charlotte's old photo albums.

"Show and tell is for babies, Aunt Emma," she clarified with way too much sarcasm for her age.

I held my hands up in front of me and laughed.

"Sorry," I apologized playfully. "That's what your mom called it, so I thought that's what it was."

"She always called it that, but I haven't done show and tell since, like—second grade?" She tapped her finger against her chin as she thought about it. "Now we do About Us day and share something special about ourselves or our hobbies. Since school will be ending soon, and we'll be forced into the next prison, we have to share something inspirational about who we want to be when we grow up. I want to be my mom," she said proudly, picking up another picture from the table.

I felt my heart swell and shatter at the same time.

"Your mom would love that," I whispered, unable to say anything more.

She smiled, but I could still see the sadness behind it. She sat on the floor, looking through the pictures that were spread out in front of her.

"I still have to talk about why she's my inspiration and why I want to be her when I grow up, but I also wanted to honor her for her birthday next week. I wanted to find a photo of her where she's really happy—like really, *really*, happy. Because that's what I want to be when I grow up—happy."

"There should be some pictures in there of some of her birthday parties," I offered, lifting off the couch to try to get a better look inside of the box. I didn't know what was in it, but I knew the album that I was looking for and frowned when I didn't see it. "Is that all of the photo albums?" I asked John.

"I think I saw another box marked *Charlotte* in the garage. I'll go grab it."

He got up and went to look for it. I slid down from the arm and sat next to Lily on the floor. She was smiling as she flipped through a stack of photos from Christmas where Charlotte was dressed as an elf for the school play, and I was the Grinch. I was frowning in every single picture, despite her attempts to make me laugh. No wonder I got *that* part out of all of them.

She handed me a small stack of pictures that she had pulled

out of an envelope before grabbing another stack for herself. I felt the twinge of sadness that crept up my back and covered me like a wet blanket. While these memories should be happy, they were now tainted with the sadness of knowing that they would never happen again. I would never hear her laughter. Never see her smile. There would be no more hugs when I'd had a hard day. These memories were now frozen in my mind as the last piece of her that I had left.

A few minutes later, I heard the garage door close as John came back inside with another box. He set it down beside the other one, a cloud of dust floating around us.

"Are there more pictures?" Lily asked, leaning over to look at the box.

"I don't know. I haven't looked inside yet," he replied, running his hands down the front of his jeans. "Shall we look and see?"

Lily nodded yes excitedly and leaned forward as John cut open the box and lifted the flaps. He paused for a moment, caught off guard by something he found inside.

I found myself leaning forward, trying to get a view of whatever it was. Slowly, he reached inside and pulled out two teddy bears that were sewn together to make it look like they were kissing. The girl bear had her leg kicked up while the boy bear held a gift behind his back for her. I saw his eyes water as he looked at it, remembering the night he won it for her at the boardwalk. He had proposed to her shortly after that.

"Teddy bears?" Lily asked, confused by why John was so emotional about them.

He nodded yes, unable to speak. I could see the struggle inside of him as he tried to keep it together. This was a prime example of what I was talking about when I told him to let her see him grieve. She needed to know that he didn't have it together all the time and that he missed Charlotte as much as she did.

"Your daddy won them for your mommy in Santa Cruz," I said, looking over at him to make sure it was okay for me to tell her. He smiled and nodded for me to continue. "Right before he asked her to marry him."

I watched the tear slip down his cheek before he could wipe it away. His fingers gripped the bears tighter as he fought to stay in control.

"Daddy, is that true?" she asked in disbelief, looking from the bears to him.

He looked up at me, his eyes wildly searching for mine as if asking what he should do. It was my turn to nod. I looked away to give him some privacy as he sat down in the chair behind him, clutching the bears to his chest. Lily immediately crawled out from behind the coffee table and rushed over to hug him.

I felt the tears wash down my face, unable to hold them in. John and Lily sat together as he held her on his lap, rocking her as they cried together. It was the first time that I had seen them both openly mourn Charlotte together since she died. This weight felt like it had been lifted from the room and my heart when I saw them together. This was what Lily needed, what both of them needed.

Ten

I was in the kitchen, sitting at the table, drinking a cup of coffee when John walked in. He looked calmer than I had seen him in—who knew how long. Months? Years? It was like the weight of the world was suddenly removed from his shoulders.

"Hey, we were looking for you," he said, walking to the coffee pot to refill his cup.

"I wanted to give you guys some privacy," I said, lifting the mug with two hands to take a sip.

"Thank you, but we didn't need it. Not from you." He poured some creamer and stirred it before turning to face me. "You're family, Emma. There's nothing that we aren't going to share with you. You loved her as much as we did, and you're going through pain, just like we are."

I sucked in a shaky breath and set my cup on the table, afraid that I would drop it.

"Don't say that," I begged softly.

"What?" He frowned as he took a sip.

"That I'm family. That I'm part of you guys." I lowered my eyes to the table and stared at the faded Disneyland image on the mug. "It hurts worse when I pretend that I am, John. I *was* Charlotte's best friend, and I *am* Lily's godmother, but I'm nothing more than that."

He scowled as he listened, his features hardening.

He set his cup down on the island with a little more force than was necessary.

"You're so incredibly frustrating," he bit out angrily. "Do you realize that?"

I pulled back defensively and stared at him.

"How many times do I have to try to convince you that you *are* more than that, Emma? Do I have to spell it out for you that Lily and I would be lost without you? That you're one of the few things that we look forward to when we come home to this house that is filled with constant reminders of what we've lost? Do you not see how Lily lights up whenever you're around and how she can't wait to tell you about her day? Or how I'm pushing myself to get done with work at a decent hour every day so I can come home to eat dinner with you guys? Do you not see *any* of that?"

I tried to swallow back the welling emotions inside, but my throat was suddenly dry.

"I can't make you see how special you are to us, Emma. But I wish that I could. Maybe for once, you would believe in yourself the way I believe in you. You're an amazing woman, and I pity anyone who can't see that." He picked up his coffee cup and walked out of the room.

It took me a few minutes before I could gather myself before walking out of the kitchen and risk facing him again. I hadn't expected him to feel that way, let alone tell me. There was this passion behind his words, a conviction that made me believe them with every fiber of my being. But every time I played them over again in my head, I would hear the ringing alarm bells that screamed that I was crossing the line and thinking more into it than was really there.

I finished my coffee and rinsed my cup before loading it into the dishwasher. I was hoping to sneak past them and go up to my room for the rest of the day. Everything felt weird and awkward now, which made me desperate to find a place to hide until I could figure things out.

Just like before, I was unsuccessful at my attempt to get by unseen when Lily called me back into the living room. I pulled my shoulders back and tried to garner any illusion of confidence I had as I walked in and sat down next to her on the couch.

"Look what I found!" she exclaimed excitedly. "It's a bucket list of all of the things that my mom wanted to do!"

I looked at the journal in her lap and smiled, remembering when Charlotte had made it. We'd stayed up late and laughed for hours as we came up with the most random, impossible list of things. I had completely forgotten about it until now.

"I remember," I said softly, resting my elbow on my knee and my chin in my hand.

"Did you guys ever do any of it?" she asked with even more excitement.

"We were going to, right after we graduated high school. We were going to travel and conquer her list. But then we moved to California, and she met *a boy*. After that, all of her time was suddenly focused on him," I teased, giving John a playful scowl. His smile stretched tight across his face, showing off his perfect teeth.

"Hey, what can I say?" he shrugged cockily. "I was more exciting than her bucket list."

I let my head fall back as I laughed.

"I seriously doubt that," I joked, holding my stomach as I laughed harder.

Lily got the giggles and laughed along with me, while John raised an eyebrow and narrowed his eyes at us.

"Why is that?"

"Because I remember that list. There were some pretty amazing things on it that would be more exciting than *any* boy."

"How do you know?" Lily asked sincerely as she looked at the list again. She picked up the journal and tilted it to the side, then upside down as if she was trying to find some secret code. "None of it makes any sense. It's all riddles and codes."

"That was the fun part," I squealed, remembering how we worked so hard to create the perfect clue for each one.

"Do you remember what all of them are?" She looked up at me with hope in her eyes.

I pulled in a deep breath, not ready to promise her anything that I couldn't deliver on.

"I don't know, honey. It's been a long time since I've seen that list," I admitted sheepishly.

Her face fell, and the excitement that had been there a few minutes before vanished.

"Maybe we could all try to solve them together?" John asked from his chair, sensing the panic that was flooding through me.

"I like that idea," I agreed. "Teamwork always makes things easier."

"Okay," she said with a tiny spark of enthusiasm.

"What's the first one?" John pressed, leaning forward and resting his elbows on his knees as he concentrated. I had to fight the laughter that was bubbling up inside with how serious he looked.

Lily cleared her throat, then lifted the notebook and began reading.

"Go high in the sky, but not faster than the birds fly."

She lowered it and looked between us.

"That's easy," John said proudly, puffing his chest. "It's a plane. She wanted to fly on a plane."

Lily nodded as if that made sense to her. I laughed and shook my head in disagreement.

"Okay, smarty pants," John teased, pointing a finger at me. "Then what is it?"

"Charlotte had already flown on a plane when she wrote this. She went to Florida with her parents when she was ten. They flew there, and that was the first time she went to Disney World."

John's cocky smile faded, replaced with another scowl.

"Shit. I forgot about that."

"*Language!*" Lily scolded and shook her finger at him.

"Do you know what it was?" she asked, looking back at me once she finished giving her dad *the look*.

"I know that your mom always wanted to ride a Ferris wheel. That would be my guess. It's high in the sky and definitely slower than birds." I turned to look at John. "How in the world did you guess plane anyway? What kind of birds have you seen that are faster than a plane?"

I watched as the pink in his cheeks flushed red with embarrassment. He leaned back in his chair, the cocky, confident attitude from a few minutes ago gone.

"I'm going to get a paper and write all of these down!" Lily said before she got up and took off to her room.

Just as fast as she ran up the stairs, she came down even quicker. She plopped down on the floor beside me and opened a spiral notebook, flipping the pages until she found a clean one. I giggled as I watched her write her name and the date in the top right corner, a habit from school she hadn't even noticed she had done.

She numbered the paper and rewrote each riddle, leaving a few lines beneath each one to write her answers.

"Okay," she said when she had them all down. "So, the first one is a Ferris wheel. Are you guys ready to guess more?"

"Let's do it," John said, rubbing his hands together as he leaned forward again. I wasn't sure if he was genuinely this interested in it or if he was just enjoying his time with Lily. I made the mistake of looking over at him and caught him staring at me. I blushed and looked away, trying to focus as she read the next riddle.

"Eat with the ants, but you can't wear pants." She laughed and reread it, unsure of whether she had read it wrong the first time. "Can't wear pants?!" She giggled.

I laughed along with her; the smile that was plastered to her face contagious.

"Why can't you wear pants?" she asked, still tickled by the thought.

"Because it rhymes with ants?" I suggested, not really sure myself. I could imagine us back then, laughing hysterically when she wrote it.

"Okay, so eat with the ants," John said, tapping his finger to his chin. "Maybe a picnic?"

I raised my brows, impressed with his quick answer.

"Eating with the ants does sound like a picnic to me," I agreed.

"So, where can you have a picnic without wearing pants?" Lily wondered, mimicking her father with her chin tapping.

"Maybe you can wear something else?" John suggested. "Like shorts?"

"Or a swimsuit!" I exclaimed, jumping up from my seat on the couch. "You could have a picnic on the beach!"

Lily jumped up next to me and started bouncing with excitement.

"That sounds like so much fun!" she squealed. "Can we go to the beach next weekend and have a picnic with the ants for mom's birthday?" Her energy radiated through the room, but the moment she mentioned Charlotte's birthday, I felt it drain from John and me.

My shoulders slumped as I felt the sadness wash over me. I looked at him and noticed the way his body had stiffened in response as well. It was like being punched in the stomach without any warning. Sensing the change in the room, Lily quickly looked between us, panic washing over her face that she had upset us.

John reacted before I could, thankfully.

"I think that's a great idea," he said with a forced smile. "We can honor your mom by checking something off of her bucket list."

Lily grew quiet and looked down at the notepad on the coffee table. She reached down and picked it up, studying it carefully.

"What's the matter?" I asked, touching her shoulder.

"If I can only do one thing from this list to honor her, I want to make sure that I pick the best one," she explained, still looking at it. "But how do I know what the best one is? How do I know what the one thing was that mom wanted to do before she die—."

I racked my brain, trying to come up with an answer. ANY answer. But there wasn't one because how do you explain to a child that you don't know whether or not their mother got to do everything she wanted to do before she died? I could guarantee that Charlotte had a list of things she wanted to achieve that she had never told anyone. We all did. But how do you help a child pick ONE to honor their mother? Suddenly, I was regretting going through the list with her. It was only going to lead to sadness.

"How about… we do ALL of them?" John asked as he got up and walked over to Lily.

"ALL?" she repeated in disbelief.

He reached down and gently held her head as he rested his forehead against hers.

"All," he confirmed.

"When?"

"This summer," he said, easily as if he had all the time in the world.

I forced a smile as Lily bounced around the room again, filled with excitement at the promise of working on the list of things her mother never got around to doing. I cast a glance at John, hoping that he hadn't just made her a promise that he couldn't keep.

Eleven

The sun was beating down on me as I laid on the beach towel, listening to the seagulls fly above. John and Lily were playing in the ocean before we had our picnic. Thankfully, the beach wasn't as crowded as I thought it would be. Maybe everyone was busy getting ready for the last week of school to end before they flocked off for their vacations. Either way, I was thankful for the peace and quiet as I soaked up the warmth from the sand.

I heard laughing and propped up on my elbow, pulling my sunglasses down a little to see them heading my way. Lily was holding something in her hand, running excitedly toward me. I sat up and smiled, waiting to see what had her so thrilled.

"Aunt Emma, Aunt Emma!" she squealed, dropping to her knees in front of me as she held her hands clasped together. I eyed her suspiciously, wondering if there was some sort of critter that she had caught. Not many things bothered me, but bugs and creepy crawlers of any kind were high on the list. "Look what I found!"

"What is it?" I asked, leaning forward with my hands folded in my lap and my knees pulled into my chest. I glanced up as John joined us, his shadow shading Lily and me.

Lily slowly opened her hands, the grin splitting her cheeks as her blue eyes sparkled in the sun. Tucked inside was a perfect sand dollar. She extended her hand to let me hold it. I reached out and carefully picked it up, admiring it as I placed it in the palm of my hand.

"It's beautiful," I whispered in complete awe. When Charlotte and I were little girls, we would go to the beach at sunrise and scour the sand, looking for them. On occasion, we would find a few, but never any that were as perfect as this one. I could feel the sting of the tears against my eyes and handed it back to Lily before I lost control and had another breakdown.

I had spent the morning crying in bed, struggling with how to handle Charlotte's birthday today. Every year we spent them together, and this year was a painful reminder of what I lost. I avoided John and Lily until the last minute, when it was time to leave. Thankfully, I had my dark sunglasses to hide the red that the eye drops didn't help.

"Mommy told me that you guys used to look for these when you were little," Lily said, examining it in her hand. "She said that they were always broken and that you guys never found a perfect one."

"That's true," I said, swallowing past the burn in my throat.

"Do you know what I think?" she asked, lowering her hand to look at me as she tilted her head and waited.

"What's that?"

"I think that mommy put this sand dollar on the beach for me to find today so I could give it to you."

She extended her hand back to me and waited. I struggled to keep my emotions in, but it was no use. A sob escaped my throat as a tear slid down my cheek. I laid my palm flat and waited while she placed it back in my hand again.

"Bella at school said that sometimes her grandma gives her gifts to let her know that she's still there with her. Usually, she finds pennies, but I think that mommy wanted to use a sand dollar because you would know how special it was."

She paused for a minute and looked out toward the ocean as John folded his arms and listened.

"I also think that she sent you a perfect one because you guys never got to find one together. Maybe it was another thing on her bucket list that you guys didn't get to do?"

I held the sand dollar gently as I lowered my head to my knees and cried. I felt terrible for falling apart in front of them when I should have been the one to stay strong—especially today when all of us were grieving a little harder than usual.

I felt the sand shift next to me as John sat down and wrapped an arm around me. He pulled me into his side and held me as I cried. I hated that I was such a mess and that *he* was the one who was comforting me. I used my free hand to wipe the tears from my cheeks while I attempted to suck in a deep breath to calm down.

"I'm sorry," I muttered, moving my sunglasses out of the way to dry my eyes. I was relieved to see that Lily was sitting a few feet in front of us, playing with the sand, instead of watching me.

"Don't be," John said quietly, rubbing my back before he pulled his arm away. I could smell the soft scent of fabric softener on his shirt. It was so calming that I had to fight the urge to reach over and pull his shirt off him so I could cuddle it. Something about fresh linen reminded me of my childhood and provided a soothing comfort that I had relied on for so many years.

"Can we do our picnic soon?" Lily asked, looking up from the hole she had dug in the sand.

"Sure," John answered happily, pushing himself up. "I'll go grab everything from the car and check with the lifeguard to see if this little guy is still alive or if he's dead," he said, pointing to the sand dollar that was still in my hand. I reached up and handed it to him, feeling a piece of me slip away with it. I knew that we weren't allowed to remove it without checking with them first, but it still stung to have it taken away so quickly.

I smiled the warmest smile that I could, even though my heart felt like it was a crumbled mess of pieces scattered around me.

"Do you want to help me get the blanket set up?" I asked Lily, reaching over to the tote bag that I had brought down earlier. She nodded and got up. I stood and quickly brushed the sand off my body before I dug the blanket out. I unfolded it and gave her one end while I held onto the other, and we gently laid it down. Next, I picked up the giant umbrella that I had convinced John to bring and opened it, laughing when it almost knocked me over. Lily started giggling, the sound lifting some of the sadness sitting so heavily on my shoulders.

I tried getting it in the ground before John came back, but it was bigger than I was and knocked me over a time or two. I was still struggling with it, putting all of my weight into it as I tried to force it into the hard sand.

"Need some help?" John laughed as he set the ice chest down next to the blanket. I felt my cheeks flush as he reached over and took the umbrella from me, carefully moving it away as I ducked and got out of his way. A few seconds later, he had it properly secured and adjusted it to make sure there was plenty of shade for us.

"I could have done that," I muttered, sitting down on the blanket next to Lily.

"I know," he chuckled. "Thanks for waiting so I could do it. I didn't want to be the *unmanly man* on the beach today. I do have a reputation to uphold."

He winked and sat down. I rolled my eyes, the corners of my lips pulling up as I tried to keep from smiling. Thanks to my sunglasses, he hadn't caught the eye roll.

He pulled the cooler closer to him, opened it, pulled the food out, and set it on the blanket between us. Per Lily's request, we packed a lunch made up of all of Charlotte's favorite foods. John handed each of us a sandwich wrapped in saran wrap and then dug inside for the fruit tray we had put together this morning. I grabbed the cans of Pringles and the box of Twinkies and set them next to the giant bag of Sour Patch Kids. I grabbed the other bag that I had packed with utensils and handed Lily a plate before setting one aside for John and me.

I helped Lily fill her plate and then worked on mine. I looked down at the sandwich in my hands, my fingers trembling as I pulled the wrapper off it. Memories of eating peanut butter and syrup sandwiches together flooded through my mind, forcing another wave of sadness to wash over me.

I took a bite and closed my eyes. For a brief moment, I allowed myself to live in my memories and cherished the sound of Charlotte's laughter as we had our own picnics and tea parties.

"So, what's on the agenda this week for school?" John asked Lily, breaking me from my thoughts. "Are they doing anything fun since it's the last week?"

"I don't think so," Lily said, scrunching her nose before

taking a bite of her sandwich. "We have a test on Tuesday, and then I think Ms. Summers is going to have us clean the classroom for the last few days. A lot of kids have said that they're not even going to go to school after the test."

I knew what she was hinting at but didn't know if John had picked up on it.

"Well, at least it sounds like it will be an easy week," he offered, popping a strawberry in his mouth.

I chewed my bite and then immediately took another one. If my mouth was full, I couldn't *accidentally* speak up and tell him what he was missing. Lily hated that school and was making it obvious that she didn't want to go the last few days if she didn't have to.

"I guess. If you count cleaning and doing all of the hard work because the other students don't show up—then I guess it is easy." She set her sandwich down on the plate and looked away.

I took the opportunity to try to get his attention without Lily noticing. While she was still staring out at the ocean, I reached over and tapped his knee with my toes. He looked up at me, confused. I nodded in her direction, raising my eyebrows before realizing that he couldn't see them with my sunglasses on. I set my food down on my plate and took them off.

I tried again, this time making it more obvious with the head jerking and eyebrows, yet he was still oblivious.

"Can I go put my feet in the water?" she asked, not turning to look at us.

John sighed and set his plate down between us.

"Sure. Just stay where I can see you, and don't go in past your ankles."

Lily muttered something under her breath before she got up and walked down to the water. We both sat there, watching her as if she was going to vanish right before our eyes.

"Okay," he said after she was down by the water. "What did I screw up this time?"

He kept his attention on Lily, as did I.

"She doesn't want to go to school," I sighed heavily, leaning back on my hands. "She hates it there, and if she has to go when the other kids don't, she'll just feel left out again. Or worse, her teacher will give her all of the shitty jobs to do. I remember those days in school, and it sucked. I don't blame her for not wanting to go."

"I see," he said softly. "No matter how hard I try, I can't seem to get any of this right."

I turned to look at him, tilting my head to the side.

"Does anyone?"

"What do you mean?" he asked.

"Does anyone ever get any of this right? Granted, I'm not a parent, but I know that Charlotte used to feel the same way. I don't think there's a single parent out there that feels like they're getting it right."

"No one warned me how hard this would be."

I watched his shoulders fall heavily.

"You're doing fine," I assured him. "No matter how much

you think you know what you're doing now, it's going to change as she gets older, and you'll always feel like you don't know what you're doing. It's a vicious cycle, but everyone goes through it."

"So much for wishing that it would get easier," he joked, turning to smile at me before turning back to watch Lily.

"It will. Just give it time. You'll master certain parts of it and learn how to handle the new stuff as it comes. Like boys…" I laughed when he gave me a dirty look.

"She's doing better today than I thought she would," he said, nodding to where she was jumping in the water.

"Yeah, I'm the one who is a hot mess today."

"It's okay to be a mess. I'm a mess every damn day. This week was just a harder week than most, with the settlement and her birthday both happening at the same time."

I swallowed and stared at Lily. We hadn't talked much about the settlements after they happened. Maybe it was because it was the last piece from the accident, and now it was over, or perhaps it was because neither of us wanted to talk about the money that was awarded from the accident that took Charlotte's life. It wasn't anything to be happy about or brag over. Her life was worth far more than any amount of money.

I nodded, unable to say anything.

"So," he said, adjusting on the blanket next to me. "I'm thinking of taking Lily to New Jersey this summer. To go see Charlotte's parents."

I paused for a moment to listen before I responded.

"I think it's important for her to know them and have that

connection with her grandparents. We've made so many excuses for so long about not having the time to visit them, and now I've realized that we don't always have the time we think we do. I'm tired, Emma," he said sadly. "I'm tired of constantly working and never stopping to enjoy life. There has to be more than this."

"You both need a break," I confirmed, smiling as I watched Lily splash in the water with a girl her age that had walked over to play with her. She wasn't an anti-social kid, she just didn't belong at that school with those stuck-up bullies. "How long are you going for?"

I knew that it would mean that I wouldn't have work while he was gone, given that my job was to take care of Lily, and she wouldn't be there. I could always look for a temp job to pass the time until he was back, depending on how long they would be there. The worst-case scenario was that I could use some of the settlement money to live off of, but I didn't want to do that if I didn't have to. Twenty-five thousand was a large amount of money, but I had learned quickly that it wouldn't go far if I wasn't careful with how I spent it.

"A month, maybe two."

I was surprised to hear that John was being so relaxed about missing that much time at work. This was the man who would work 12-hour days just to meet deadlines and had gone in on weekends and holidays when he had to. The last month he had already shown a considerable change with being home for dinner every night, but to miss a few months without worrying about it made me wonder if something else was going on.

"What's really going on, John?" I asked, turning to face him. "It's not like you to be so carefree about missing work, and now you're talking about taking a couple months off?"

"I know, I know," he muttered, picking up a handful of sand and letting it fall through his fingers. He kept his eyes on Lily and smiled when he watched her do a cartwheel in the sand. Whoever her new friend was, they seemed to be having a wonderful time.

"Last weekend was a real eye-opener for me," he admitted, still playing with the sand.

"I'm really sorry about that," I said quickly, feeling bad for yelling at him about how he wasn't grieving with Lily. We hadn't talked about it since it happened.

"Don't be," he said, holding his hand up to stop me from continuing to apologize. "Really—I needed to hear that. You were right. She needed to know that she wasn't alone and that I am still grieving just as much as she is. We all are."

A sad silence fell between us.

"When I was trying to help Lily solve the riddles for Charlotte's bucket list, I realized that there was so much that she wanted to do but didn't. I know that it was a list she made when she was a kid, but I can't help but wonder what else she wanted to do but never took the time to do it. I have this guilt that has been eating away at me all week, forcing me to question whether I was too busy and if that stopped us from living life. If I wasn't constantly at work, we could have been coming to the beach and having picnics with the ants."

We both chuckled as we looked down at the blanket full of food that was barely touched.

"I can't keep working my life away, Emma. I owe it to Charlotte and Lily, and even myself, to do better. To live life and go on adventures and have fun. None of us are promised tomorrow, so we need to start living for today."

I turned and smiled at him, proud of the changes he was planning to make. I loved that he wanted to step back and spend more time with Lily. She needed it now more than ever.

"That's a wonderful plan, John. I think she'll really enjoy being up in Jersey for the summer."

"We're not going to be in Jersey that long, maybe a week or two at most."

I stopped for a moment and frowned.

"I thought you said you were going for a month or two?"

"We'll be gone for a month or two," he said with a grin. "*But,* we're going to drive and work on the bucket list along the way. Go sightseeing and exploring. Just *live* for once."

I felt like I was talking to someone else. Like an alien had taken over John's body and made him into this easy-going man who suddenly wanted to drop everything at work and travel coast to coast to explore with his daughter. What happened to the man I knew?

"She's going to love that," I said with a grin that stretched across my face. "I can't wait for you guys to get back so

I can hear all about it," I laughed, feeling the excitement starting to build.

"Well, I was kind of hoping that you wouldn't have to *hear* about it," he said cautiously. "I was hoping that you would go with us."

I felt my jaw drop open, unsure of what to say. At that moment, Lily came running up the beach toward us with her new friend in hand.

"This is my new friend, Sadie!" she said as she plopped down on the edge of the blanket. We smiled and waved at the little girl with red hair and adorable freckles that dotted her nose.

"Hi, Sadie," I said, smiling as she sat down next to Lily.

"Can she hang out with us for a while?" Lily asked, reaching over to pick up her bottle of water.

"Did you ask her parents?" John asked, scanning the other people around us.

"They're over there," Sadie said, pointing to a couple laying on beach towels with headphones on and their faces covered with their shirts.

"Lovely," John muttered, noticing the parents who didn't seem worried about where their daughter was.

"Of course she can," I said cheerfully. "Would you like something to eat?" I nodded to the food on the blanket and smiled when she shyly reached down to pick up a piece of watermelon.

"This is really good," she giggled as the juice ran down her face.

"We're doing a picnic with the ants," Lily explained, picking up a piece of watermelon herself. I leaned back and listened as she told her new friend about her mom and the bucket list of things she wanted to do.

They laughed and giggled, reminding me of my childhood with Charlotte. I sat back and watched them, feeling the day get a little bit brighter with their innocent laughter floating around us. The day had started out hard, and now I was stuck having to make the biggest decision yet. As much as I had been trying to fight it and carefully avoided crossing the line, it seemed almost impossible not to give in. While I tried to convince myself that I wasn't a part of their family, John was pushing even harder to prove that I was. While a vacation traveling across the country sounded wonderful, I wasn't sure that I could do it.

Twelve

It was almost three-thirty, and I was waiting anxiously at the car for the bell to ring. I don't know if it was the excitement of it being the last day of school or because John was standing next to me, smiling like a goof while we waited for Lily. Other parents were in the parking lot, sitting in their car, head down while playing on their phones. But not us—we were waiting outside of the vehicle, scanning the crowd of kids for Lily as they all made their way outside and celebrated the last day.

I watched as a group of them walked off to the side and bent down, getting something from their backpacks. The smile spread quickly across my face when I saw the cans of shaving cream and knew what they were planning. Off in the distance, I saw Lily talking to another girl before she hugged her and started to walk away. I burst into laughter as the kids began spraying shaving cream and chasing each other as they tried to get away.

John and I had walked over to the fence and were watching them, laughing as they had fun. Lily was oblivious to it all until another girl snuck up behind her and sprayed her with silly string. Lily's eyes went wide as she reached up to touch the cold, gooey substance on her head. When she whipped around to see who had done it, I caught a glimpse of the girl as well.

"Oh my God!" I shrieked and smacked John in the chest. "It's Sadie!!"

"What?" he asked as he leaned forward to try to get a better look.

"She said they went to the same school but that she didn't have any classes with her because she was a fourth-grader. I can't believe it—look at them having fun!"

I was so caught up in the moment that I hadn't noticed when someone walked over and stood next to us, on the other side of the fence.

"Did you forget to check in again?" Her voice was just as bitchy as the last time I spoke to her.

I turned to look at her, a fake smile on my face.

"No. We didn't check in because parents don't need to." I raised a brow and studied her as she looked past me to John. Her eyes traveled the length of his body as she folded her arms over her chest and admired him.

"Well, I don't think I've been introduced," she said, her tone changing to a more flirty one.

I rolled my eyes and ignored her as I looked back to where Lily was chasing Sadie, trying to get her with the can of silly string that she had stolen from her.

"I'm Lily's teacher, *Ms.* Summers," she added when neither of us acknowledged her.

John turned to look at me, ignoring the woman who was practically panting beside me.

"This is *the* Ms. Summers?" he asked. I nodded my head, knowing that he knew plenty about her from the past few weeks of me complaining about how awful she was.

He rubbed his lips together, then made a popping sound as he walked out from behind the fence and faced her. She smiled and pulled her shoulders back, making her breasts look bigger while she extended her hand for him to shake. He ignored it.

"I've heard plenty about you," he said coldly, leaning in closer to her. Her eyes widened as his tall frame towered over her, his face set in stone. "And I can tell you that if you *ever* treat my daughter or Emma with any disrespect *ever* again—I will personally pay you a visit, and we'll have a talk that you will *never* forget. You wanna act like the ring leader of the *mean girls club?* I'll show you just how mean I can get."

She scoffed and pulled her head back in surprise. She lifted her hand to her chest and fidgeted with the necklace that dipped into her cleavage.

"Sir, I can assure you that I have *never* treated either of them—"

"Save it," he snapped, interrupting her. "Lucky for you, today is Lily's last day, so there will not be any problems for me to come handle. However, if I were you, I'd consider my last warning if you ever see them around town."

"Actually, the last day of school is on Thursday," she snapped, switching back into the bitch mode she had when I first met her.

"Lily confirmed that the last test was today. Emma has made sure that all of Lily's assignments were complete and turned in. There's no reason for her to come the next two days," John argued, folding his arms over his chest.

"Every day is an opportunity to learn something new," she countered defensively.

"Like what? How to be a bully? How to clean the classroom while the teacher sits at her desk and watches?" I bit out, feeling relieved when I saw John's smirk after I said it.

"Trust me, she'll learn plenty this summer. No thanks to you," John said coldly, turning his attention to Lily as she and Sadie came running over to us.

"Daddy!!" she screamed when she saw him. He bent down and held his arms open as she ran over and hugged him. He lifted her up and spun her around, her laughter the best sound in the world. Sadie and I laughed along, watching as Lily extended her arms in the air and giggled.

After a few minutes, he set her down, making sure she wasn't too dizzy to stand on her own. Ms. Summers had apparently walked off at some point, not that any of us had noticed or missed her.

"What are you doing here?" she asked, adjusting her backpack and looking up at him.

"I wanted to come pick you up on your LAST. DAY. OF. SCHOOL!"

She rolled her eyes and shook her head.

"Daddy, school doesn't end until Thursday. Remember?"

John tapped his finger to his chin as he looked up, pretending to be deep in thought.

"Hmm. That's funny. I thought you said that today was the last day and that the other days were just for cleaning." He paused for a moment and turned to look at me. "Wasn't that what she said?"

I nodded and scrunched my face, watching her eyes light up.

"That's what she said…"

"But you said that I had to go to school until the last day," she said, suddenly unsure of herself.

"Did I?" He pulled his lips together, making fish lips that made her giggle. "Well, I guess I just figured why stay in school to clean when we can go on a… road trip!"

She covered her mouth with her hand and looked back and forth between us.

"Where?!"

"Everywhere," he laughed and pulled her close to him. "We're going to drive cross country to New Jersey to spend some time with—"

"Grandma and grandpa?" she finished for him, barely able to contain her excitement.

We both nodded, and I felt my heart swell at how happy she was. Hell, at how happy they both were.

"When do we leave?" she asked.

"I was thinking… maybe… tomorrow?"

I felt my stomach tighten, the dread of being by myself for a few months taking hold again. It wasn't that I couldn't be by myself. I just didn't want to. And especially not in their house, alone with memories of Charlotte. I needed to start looking for a job to fill my time and fast. John and I hadn't talked about the trip since Saturday at the beach, and I had avoided him whenever he would start to talk about it. Granted, it had only been a few days, but I didn't think that he was going to get on the road so soon.

Maybe he was worried that if he didn't go right away, something would change his mind? Or perhaps that was just wishful thinking on my end. I wanted them to have this experience together, but I felt so anxious about being alone and not having anyone. It was something that had haunted me ever since my parents died—the thought of truly being alone.

"Tomorrow?" Lily repeated. "Are you coming with us?" She turned to look at me, her eyes full of hope.

"I—" The words caught in my throat, and I looked at John, panic in my eyes. I didn't know how to tell her no.

 "Why don't we go get some celebratory ice cream, and we can talk about everything then?" John offered.

I nodded and walked to the car as Lily grabbed my hand and walked with me. It was at that moment that I realized that my fear wasn't about me being alone anymore. It was that I didn't want Lily to be alone.

Thirteen

I sat on the padded leather barstool and spun back and forth as I drank my chocolate milkshake. Lily and John were at the counter, talking to the owner while he put together their master sundae. It was massive and was overflowing from all the toppings that Lily had picked out. My head felt fuzzy as I tried to think of the best way to tell Lily that I wasn't going. I knew that I would let her down and disappoint her, but it was easier than pretending that I belonged on that trip with them. This was a new adventure that they needed to go on together, and I would only be in the way if I went.

I pulled another drink through the straw, my jaws feeling tight from the thickness of the shake. John and Lily made their way over to the table as he balanced the tray carefully, making sure he didn't drop the massive beast of diabetes in a bowl. I raised my brows and stared at it in disbelief when he set it down on the table with a loud thud. The bowl itself was heavy, but there had to be at least two gallons of ice cream underneath a few pounds of candy and nuts. My stomach hurt just from looking at it.

"You guys are going to be here for *days*," I laughed as he slid it across the table and sat down beside me. He laughed with me before passing a spoon to me and nodding at it.

"Maybe. But lucky for us, you're going to help us." He winked and picked up his spoon. He looked over at Lily, who was grinning like it was Christmas morning as she stared at it. Without taking his eyes off of Lily, he gently nudged my hand with his elbow, holding his spoon in the air as if he was ready to dive in at any moment.

I rolled my eyes, then gave in and picked the other spoon up.

I couldn't help myself. Lily looked so happy and excited that I found myself wanting to join in and be a part of it.

John's smile spread across his face, showing off his perfect white teeth.

"Ready? Set? Go!" he yelled excitedly.

We all dove in, laughing, when the candy started falling onto the table. It was messy but fun. We ate as if we were in a race, never stopping to take a break as we kept an eye on each other. Finally, after a good ten to fifteen minutes later, I leaned back and set my spoon down. There was no way that I could eat another bite. I glanced at the milkshake still sitting beside me and groaned.

"I can't take another bite," I mumbled, checking to see how Lily was doing. The mound of ice cream was smaller, but I still had to look around it to see her. She had chocolate smeared across her chin and a dot on her nose, which looked adorable. Her spoon was lying next to her on the table as she picked at the candy with her fingers.

"Me neither," John said, leaning back in his seat to relieve some of the pressure on his stomach.

"I blame you for this," I laughed, shaking my head at the mess that we had made in our attempt to demolish this monster.

"Hey, it's the perfect way to start a summer vacation."

"With a stomachache from all of that sugar?" I replied mockingly.

"You only live once," he joked before his face dropped at the words he had said.

I turned my head and looked away. It was coming up on two months since Charlotte had died, and it still felt as if it was just yesterday. Every time we would laugh or enjoy ourselves for a moment, it was as if there was a harsh reminder that we were enjoying our lives while she lost hers. I knew that John hadn't meant anything by what he said, yet it still had the same impact.

"So, where are you guys stopping first?" I asked, tucking my hands under the table to keep from fidgeting. I could have waited and talked to John in private to let him know that I wasn't going, but the thought that he would try to talk me into it made me so nervous that I decided to it now, while we were out in public. Not that either of us ever caused a scene, but for whatever reason, I felt stronger with the random strangers around than I would if we were alone at home.

He narrowed his eyes, reading into what I was really saying.

"I thought that *we* could drive down to Santa Monica, get there in the afternoon and have dinner on the beach somewhere."

"That will be fun. I'm sure *you* guys will enjoy it."

"*We* will. It will be nice for *all of us* to check out the pier and maybe ride some rides."

"Well, I know that *Lily* loves rides, so she'll have a blast!"

"Why are you guys being so weird?" Lily asked, looking over the melting ice cream between us.

"We're not," John assured her. "Can you go ask Mr. Willis for some napkins?"

Lily continued to eye us suspiciusly as she climbed down

from her stool and walked over to the front of the counter. There were a few people in line, so she waited patiently behind them while he worked to get their orders together.

"What's the problem, Emma?" he asked sternly, catching me off guard.

"What do you mean?"

"You know damn well what I mean. Why are you being so stubborn about going on this trip with us? Is it because you really don't want to? Because if that's the case, then I won't keep pushing you to go, but something tells me that that's not it."

"It's hard to explain," I sighed, looking over my shoulder at Lily.

"Try."

I looked up at him, his face etched with frustration as he leaned forward, resting his elbows on the clean part of the table.

"This is going to be an amazing trip for you and Lily. I don't want to mess that up."

"How are you going to mess it up?"

"By being in the way." I threw my hands up. "You guys are getting the chance to start over and build an even better relationship together as father and daughter. You don't need me there for that, John."

"Is that what this is about?" he scoffed and looked away, shaking his head.

I stayed silent, pulling my lips together.

"I don't know how many times I have to tell you before you

get it through your thick skull and hear me. We WANT you to be there, Emma. We think of you as our family, even if you don't feel the same way. These new memories that I'm going to make with my daughter this summer—I want to laugh about them years from now when we're all hanging out on our next vacation. You're not just some nanny that comes in and does a job, then checks out for the day—nor have I ever treated you like one."

"I didn't say that you did," I said quietly, looking down at the table.

"Then please, stop acting like it. Emma, we were all best friends before Charlotte died. I can't remember a time in our lives when we didn't all hang out together. You're as much a part of my family as I am yours. I can't figure out for the life of me why that's suddenly changed for you because it hasn't changed for me. I already lost my wife, don't make me lose my other best friend as well."

I felt the tear slide down my face before I could wipe it away.

"I'm sorry," I whispered, feeling suddenly ashamed. "I didn't mean to make you feel that. I just didn't think that there was still a place for me now that Charlotte is gone. She's always been there for me and taken care of me. I didn't want you to have to carry that burden now that she's gone."

"You really think that you're a burden?" he whispered in disbelief. "Emma, you're one of the best things that has ever happened to my family, and I never prayed harder than I did for you to survive that accident. I knew that I couldn't live in a world without both of you, and neither could Lily."

The tears continued to fall, and I was thankful that Lily was distracted up front, talking to a kid that she knew from school.

"I don't have the money to go," I countered, though this time it wasn't an excuse.

"You don't have to worry about that," he said softly, reaching over to pat my arm gently. "I'll take care of everything."

"John, you don't need to do that. I can't stand the idea of going on this trip and you having the added expense for me."

"Emma, I'm renting a motorhome. That's the same cost regardless of whether you come with us or not. The fuel is the same cost either way. If you're worried about the cost of food, then I'll make you a deal. I'll buy the groceries, and you cook?"

I hesitated for a moment, unsure of what to say. It sounded too good to be true. It wasn't like I was going to be a total mooch. I did have some money saved up from working as Lily's nanny for the past month. It wasn't much, but it would cover my share of the food and other expenses. Plus, if I *really* needed to, I could dip into the settlement money if I had to.

John leaned his head to look past me, watching as Lily headed back our way, then locked eyes with me.

"Are you in or out?"

"I'm in!" I squealed excitedly.

Fourteen

"Are you guys ready?!" John called excitedly from downstairs as he banged on the front door with his hand.

I had spent the rest of the day packing once we got home yesterday and had to make a last-minute trip to the store to grab the few things I didn't have. I hated not being prepared, and I was definitely not ready for this trip, but then John reassured me that we weren't going to be stuck in the middle of nowhere and that there would be plenty of stores to pick up whatever I needed.

I pulled the handle up on my suitcase and quickly glanced around the room one last time to make sure I didn't forget anything. I made sure—twice—that I had packed plenty of underwear, my phone charger, and my Kindle. What more could I need?

I grabbed my purse from the top of the dresser and slung it across my chest, letting it hang on my hip as I wheeled the suitcase into the hallway. I heard a loud thud and turned to see Lily in the hallway, dragging a suitcase packed to the brim and bigger than she was. I held back a giggle as I leaned around it to find her face.

"Do you need help?" I asked once she spotted me.

"I got it," she grunted as she gave it a hard push with her shoulder to get it to move. My brows shot up as she shoved into it again, the heavy thing not budging.

"Come on, girls, we gotta get going!" John called up to us.

"We're coming!" I laughed, knowing that it was a lie. "Here," I said, setting my suitcase to the side, out of the way. "Let me help you," I offered.

I walked over to where she was standing and yanked hard to get the handle to come all the way up. The suitcase looked old and worn out, which explained why she was having so much trouble with it—aside from the eighty pounds worth of stuff she must've crammed inside of it.

"What all is in here?" I asked as I used my weight to shift it into the position that I needed.

"Clothes. Shoes. A few games. A notebook. Pens. A scrapbook. My camera. A blanket. And just a few other small things." She shrugged as if this was a normal amount of things to pack for a vacation.

"Well, I guess you've got it all covered," I joked but secretly wondered if she was more prepared than I was when I glanced over at my smaller suitcase.

"I didn't want to forget anything."

"I hear you," I mumbled, knowing that I had already forgotten something. I just knew that I would, but I hated not knowing what it was. Which, if I knew what it was, I wouldn't have forgotten it. I shook my head to clear the unnecessary, never-ending circle that my thoughts were going in.

"I'll take your suitcase if you can grab mine," I offered, nodding over to where mine was sitting. She smiled and shook her head in agreement before walking behind me and grabbing it as we headed downstairs.

I tried to be as careful as possible as I lugged the beast down the stairs, making sure not to damage anything on the way. Once I got to the bottom, I rolled it over to the front door, where I was met with a judgment look from John.

"You know that I wasn't kidding when I said that there would be stores on the way," he asked cautiously. "You didn't have to pack your entire room."

"I didn't," I said breathlessly. "This one is Lily's. That's mine." I gestured to the small one that Lily was standing beside.

"I should have known," he sighed and scrubbed a hand down his face.

We laughed and made our way outside while John locked the doors. I had no idea what to expect when John said that he was renting a motorhome, but I honestly expected some giant, ugly beast of a thing that would be hard to drive and stick out like a sore thumb.

Instead, there was a beautiful one sitting in front of the house, no bigger than a small bus. I started to feel a little uneasy when I imagined how small it was inside and how cramped it would be with all of us sitting on top of each other.

As if reading my mind, I heard John chuckle beside me before saying, "let's go check it out."

He took Lily's luggage from me and loaded it into the back storage compartment. I walked around and took a look inside, amazed at how much room was back there. I waited until he had her suitcase situated before I picked mine up to add it to the pile. He smiled and took it from me, gently setting it to the back, next to what I assumed was his.

I did one last check to make sure that I had my kindle and phone charger in my purse. I wanted to make sure that I had them handy in case I wanted or needed them on the drive.

John talked with Lily for a few minutes as they argued about what she needed from her suitcase from the drive before he closed the compartment and locked it.

John opened the door and stepped to the side, letting us inside first. I heard Lily gasp *wow* as she walked in and knew what she meant when my jaw dropped to the floor when I looked around. It was small inside, but everything was surprisingly spread out to feel comfortable and not cramped.

Immediately to my left was a stove and kitchen sink, which were directly across from a full-size refrigerator. A small table and booth-style seats sat between the fridge and the driver's seat. On the other side, behind the passenger seat, was another chair barely big enough to fit in the small space next to the door. Just from the looks of it, there was plenty of room for us to spread out when we stopped for meals or to rest at night.

I turned around and checked out the rest of it while Lily climbed into the seat behind me. There weren't any walls or dividers to separate the space, other than the bathroom, which was thankfully hidden behind a closed door. The only bed that I could find was butted up against the kitchen sink. There were plenty of cabinets above the bed for storage, but it wasn't very big. I guessed that it was a full-size bed if that.

I swallowed hard, wondering what in the hell John was thinking when he rented this thing. I knew that he had good intentions, but didn't he understand that we needed space? Privacy? I was about to say something when he started talking instead.

"I know what you're thinking," he said quickly. "But trust

me, there's plenty of room."

He walked around me, over to the driver's seat. He reached up and moved a few things around until a bed magically appeared above the seats.

"I'll take this bed, you can have the one in the back, and Lily can have this one," he explained, turning around to pull the table out before creating another bed with the seats.

"It's like magic," I whispered, impressed by the hidden features.

"It really is," he agreed, standing beside me as we stared at the new beds that he had created.

"I can sleep up top," I offered, knowing that it was probably the most uncomfortable.

"It's okay. I don't mind."

"Can I sleep up there?" Lily asked with excitement splattered across her face.

"You want that one?" he asked, studying her. She shook her head faster than the grin could spread across her cheeks.

"Okay, you can have the top bed. I'll sleep on this one," he nodded to the bed that had been made of cushions from the table seats.

"I really don't mind sleeping there either," I countered. He was paying for this thing, so he should have the comfortable bed.

"We're good, Emma. Trust me."

I pulled in a deep breath and tried to keep myself from arguing any further.

"Alright, are we ready to get this party started?!" He rubbed his hands together and closed the doors behind us before getting situated in the driver's seat.

The entire motorhome was one big open space, so I took a seat at the table across from Lily and got situated. I laid my purse on the seat next to me and pulled my phone out to check it. Not that there was anything to check. No one ever called or text me and the only emails that I got were spam. I suddenly felt nervous and didn't know what to do with myself.

John took his seat at the steering wheel and adjusted the air conditioner vents to where he wanted them before checking the mirrors and moving them as needed.

"There's stuff in the fridge if you guys get hungry or need a drink," he said, looking over his shoulder to make sure I heard him.

"Thank you," I smiled back at him, wondering if I should offer to get him something. He reached down and picked up his travel mug of coffee and took a drink. I released the breath that I had been holding and reminded myself that I was here to have fun and help take care of Lily—not John. He wasn't my responsibility, and I had to stop worrying about him.

A few minutes later, we were on the road, and my nerves started to calm down some. Maybe it was the excitement of the trip finally getting underway, or perhaps it was the idea that it was too late to turn back now. Either way, I leaned back against the cool leather and closed my eyes.

Lily and I played a few card games during the first few hours, but we gave up when she refused to let me win one.

I wasn't a sore loser, but I also didn't love getting beat by a ten-year-old. Whoever said that Uno was a game for kids had obviously never played the competitive version with Lily.

Around one o'clock, I started getting hungry and imagined so was Lily.

"Hey, do you want me to fix you something to eat?" I asked loud enough for John to hear, in case he wanted something as well.

"I'm not really hungry," she said with a frown. "My stomach is feeling kinda slushy."

I scrunched my face up, feeling bad that she was getting car sick.

"Sorry, honey. Sometimes my stomach gets that way on car rides too."

"How about we stop for lunch soon?" John offered, hearing our conversation. "We're coming up on Avila Beach in about twenty minutes. Can you wait that long?"

"Yeah," Lily said, a look of relief on her face that we would be stopping soon.

I wondered how she would do on the rest of the trip, given we had only been on the road for a few hours. We had so much ground to cover, and I didn't want her to be miserable the entire time. I remembered my first road trip when Charlotte and I moved to California from New Jersey. It was right after we graduated high school, and my aunt had passed away. I was ready to break free and take on the world, but after the first ten hours on the road, I was miserable and begged her to drive me back to New

Jersey. Granted, when we made the trip, it was in an old VW Bug that didn't have air conditioning. Nothing makes car sickness worse than cramped space and excessive heat. This was a better way to travel, but I could still relate to how she was feeling.

Thankfully, the traffic wasn't horrendous for mid-day on a Wednesday. We pulled into the paid parking lot, and John took care of everything while I got myself and Lily ready. We didn't need much, but I wanted to make sure that we didn't leave anything valuable out while we were gone.

We got out and stretched our legs, the warm salty sea air a welcomed treat. The air conditioning was nice, but nothing beats the fresh air by the water. We walked over to the cute little restaurant that was sitting by the beach and asked for a table on their patio so we could people watch while gazing at the ocean.

The waitress dropped off menus and glasses of water before rushing off to wait on another table. While the traffic might not have been busy, this place was. Servers were rushing around in their khaki-colored shorts and white polo t-shirts. I couldn't imagine being a server at a fancy restaurant like this. There was no way that I would keep either piece of clothing from being covered in food by the end of my shift.

I looked over the menu, my stomach knotting at the prices. I suggested we come here because it looked fun and laid back, which meant that they would probably be reasonably priced. However, I failed to remember that anything on the beach is always expensive. I considered getting a salad, but when I saw that it was the same price as the cheeseburger and fries, my decision was made.

The waitress came back a few minutes later, plucking the pen from behind her ear as she held the notepad out in front of her.

"What can I get you guys?" she asked, glancing over at a table behind us that was being seated.

We gave her our order—three cheeseburgers, three fries and sent her on her way.

I slowly sipped my water, feeling thirsty but not wanting to drink too much and having to pee all day before I remembered that we literally had a bathroom in the motorhome with us. I laughed and rolled my eyes, drawing the attention of John and Lily.

"What's so funny?" he asked, already amused as his crooked smile pulled at his cheeks.

"Nothing," I waved my hand in the air. "I was trying not to drink too much water, so we didn't have to make too many pitstops, and then I remembered that I didn't have to worry about that because we have a bathroom." I felt the blush pinch my cheeks as John watched me, continuing to smile. I had only seen this look from him a few times in my life, and it was always given to Charlotte.

"I keep forgetting too," Lily admitted. "I thought I was going to have an accident earlier when I was trying to hold it, and then I remembered that I didn't have to." She pressed the palm of her hand to her forehead and shook her head.

We all laughed about it, and things started to feel like normal between us. The stress and anxiety that I had been feeling earlier were already melting away.

The waitress came back with our food quicker than I had expected. The smell immediately sent me over the edge, the corners of my mouth dotted with drool as my stomach grumbled while it waited for that first bite.

I closed my eyes and chewed, the flavor exploding in my mouth. It was a simple meal, yet it was one of the best ones I had had in a while. I opened my eyes to find John and Lily staring at me, their burgers inches away from their faces.

"You guys need to try this burger—it's amazing!" I said, pushing my food to the side as I covered my mouth with my hand. They laughed and finally focused their attention on their food.

We must have been hungrier than we thought we were because it was completely silent around us for a solid ten to fifteen minutes. Who knows? I had already lost track of time by that point.

It also looked like we had come in at the tail end of their lunch rush as the noise started to die down and tables cleared out around us. There were only a handful of people on the patio, most of them scattered around. I couldn't help but notice the little old man sitting a few tables away from us. I was about to ask John and Lily if I could invite him to sit with us when he looked up and scowled at me.

I lowered my eyes and looked away. So much for that idea.

And then it happened.

Out of nowhere, he sneezed. Loud. So loud that it startled our table and caught Lily by surprise. Her eyes went wide as she covered her mouth with her hand. I could see her lips twitch as she fought to keep from laughing.

"NO!" I whispered, my eyes going back and forth between her and the grumpy old man behind her.

Just when I thought that everything was under control and Lily was able to control herself, he sneezed again. This time it was louder and accompanied by a fart that echoed off the patio around us.

Lily's eyes were as big as saucers as she dropped her burger to her plate. The laughter erupted out of her quicker than I could try to stop it. He looked over at our table and gave us a dirty look as John, and I lost control and laughed along with her. I was bent over, slapping the table as I snorted. John joined me, the sound so loud that I almost missed it when the old man got up and left, mumbling for us to *grow up* as he walked past our table.

Fifteen

Our stomachs hurt after lunch, and it was hard to say whether it was from eating too much or laughing too hard. Either way, it was a great start to our trip. Once we were back inside the motorhome and on the road, Lily decided to lay down for a while, so I sent her to the bed in the back to make sure she had plenty of room and was comfortable.

It felt weird to sit at the table by myself and read or listen to music, so I grabbed a couple of water bottles from the fridge and climbed into the passenger seat next to John. I set them down in the middle consoles and buckled my seatbelt.

"Thank you," he said before taking one and opening it.

"I thought you might need it," I said dismissively, trying to work past the obsessive thoughts in my head that I needed to stop worrying about him. I reminded myself that it was just a kind gesture, nothing more.

The last stretch of the drive wasn't terribly long, aside from the construction that we got stuck in that added an extra hour. I glanced back plenty of times to check on Lily, even though it felt silly since she couldn't go anywhere without us hearing her.

Soon, we were following the signs for Santa Monica Pier and found a parking lot that was open. John paid at the kiosk and then searched for a big enough space to park the motorhome without taking up two of the compact car spots. Finally, another motorhome left in the back of the lot, so we waited and took their spot.

Lily was still sleeping, so we didn't wake her up. We got

out and stretched our legs, leaning against the back bumper.

"It's so nice out here," I said, tilting my head back and letting the sun kiss my skin.

"I can't remember the last time that I was down here," he said softly. "You would think that we would have made more time to travel and do more, but we never did."

"Life gets busy," I sighed, knowing that it was more of an excuse than anything. Hell, I had used it more times than I could count.

"Yeah, it does. But you have to stop and make the time."

I didn't say anything. It felt pointless because he was right. You do have to make the time, and we were both guilty of never bothering to.

"So, what made you choose Santa Monica Pier?" I asked, changing the subject.

He chuckled and shook his head.

"There was an item on Charlotte's bucket list that I thought might be related."

"What was it?" I asked, not able to recall half of the stuff that we had discussed. I was emotionally drained that day and shut down at one point.

"You might get a tummy ache from the funnel cake. But if you sink a ball in, you might just win," Lily said happily, walking around the side of the motorhome to where we were standing.

"Hey! You're up," I exclaimed, surprised to see her.

"You guys were talking loud. I could hear you through the window." She looked up at the back window that was cracked open above the bed.

"Sorry," I apologized, rubbing her back. "But that riddle does sound like a fair of some sort. Though, I already had the tummy ache," I laughed.

"Well, lucky for us, we have funnel cake and games to find!" John squealed. "Let's get going!"

I laughed and realized that I loved seeing this side of him, and I was thankful that he was sharing it with his daughter.

After walking for what felt like miles, we spotted a stand with funnel cake and other greasy, fried foods. John ordered one for us to split, thank goodness. I couldn't imagine eating more than that, given how massive this thing was. We found an empty bench and sat down, the sun starting to set and casting a warm glow on the water.

The temperature dropped quickly, and I watched Lily shiver as we walked. We were on a mission to find a game where Lily could sink a ball in but had yet to come across one. Maybe it was because we had been distracted several times already with riding the rides and eating dinner, but there didn't seem to be any games that matched what we were looking for.

Lily yawned, and I knew that she was getting tired. The walk to the car was going to be long and tedious, given that we were at the other end. I was about to tell John that we should turn around and start heading back when I saw it. I reached down and grabbed Lily's hand, pulling her with me to the table off to the side of the sidewalk.

There were easily two hundred small fishbowls lined up on several tables. A young kid, maybe sixteen or seventeen, waited for us to decide whether we wanted to play or not. I watched the way John's eyes narrowed as the kid checked out Lily, probably completely unaware that she was only ten, going on eleven. She was beautiful and looked older than she was.

"Hi," I said cheerfully, walking up to the tables that separated us from the play area. "How much is it to play?"

"Um, it's five dollars for ten balls," he stuttered, unsure of himself. "But I'll give you some extra," he added with a wink.

I raised an eyebrow, unsure who he was actually trying to flirt with as he kept looking between Lily and me. I reached into my purse and pulled out a ten-dollar bill, handing it to him.

"Both of us are going to play," I said when he tried to give me change.

"Unless you want to join us?" I added, looking over at John, who was still glaring at the freckled face kid.

"No, I'm good just *watching*."

I bit the inside of my cheek to keep from laughing.

"Suit yourself," I chuckled. "Okay, Lily. Are you ready? We're going to throw these balls and try to sink one in a bowl. Got it?"

She nodded and picked up a ball, looking like she was getting ready to play professional softball. She looked at the table, analyzing it, before glancing at me. I winked at her and waited for her to toss the first ball. It missed and bounced off the rim of one bowl before falling to the floor.

We both tried after that, missing each time until we were down to one ball.

"Alright, it's all on you," I said, smiling encouragingly. "You got this."

She closed her eyes and took a deep breath. When she opened them, there was a look of determination on her face that reminded me so much of her mother. She bent her knees and lowered herself a tad before gently tossing the ball. We all held our breath as we watched it bounce off a few bowls before it spun around the top of another. Slowly, it finally stopped spinning and got stuck in between the bowls.

Lily sighed heavily and hung her head. I was about to reach into my purse for more money when I heard John.

"I'm gonna play after all," he told the kid, slipping him a five-dollar bill. The kid grabbed a bucket of balls and set them down before moving out of the way.

Lily and I watched as John's eyes laser-focused on the bowls, studying every move the way Lily had done just a few minutes before.

He bent down and checked again, looking for the right angle. I was so focused on what he was doing that I hadn't felt Lily squeezing my hand.

John picked up a ball and gently tossed it in the air. I watched in horror as it completely missed the table and flew off to the side. I turned to look at him, questioning what had just happened, when he shrugged.

The kid muttered under his breath before lifting the wooden tabletop and stepping out to get the stray ball. Once he was out of sight, John picked up another ball and tossed it onto the table, making it into the bowl on the first try. He repeated it with the next eight balls, sinking each one into a bowl. The kid came back a few minutes later after he tracked down the other ball and stared open-mouthed at the table.

"Um, so, how many fish do you want?" he asked, looking at John then back to the table. I hadn't noticed until now that some of the bowls had goldfish in them.

"*Fish?*" John asked in disbelief. "The prize is a *fish?*"

"Yeah, or I guess you could have a stuffed animal," he agreed, looking up at the ones that were hanging on a wire above our heads. He glanced back at the table and counted how many balls had been sunk. "Or, like, eight animals, I guess."

Lily danced excitedly, clapping her hands.

"Which stuffed animal do you want?" John asked her, rubbing a hand across the back of his neck.

"I don't want a stuffed animal. I want a fish," she replied, jutting her chin out.

"A fish?" he questioned again.

"I think it's official that they have *fish*," I teased, feeling the smirk pull across my face.

"We can't take a fish on a road trip with us," he said to Lily, avoiding eye contact with me.

"Why not?"

"Because we don't have anywhere to put it. And we don't have food for it."

"Then we'll buy it a tank and get some food. You said that there wasn't anything that we couldn't find in a store along the way," she lectured, folding her arms.

I pressed my lips together to keep from laughing as John's brow wrinkled in frustration. But she was right, and he had promised both of us that before we left.

"Fine. ONE fish. That's all."

Lily cheered and turned her attention to the kid who was helping her pick which fish she wanted. A few minutes later, she had a plastic bag filled with water and a chubby-looking goldfish. The top was tied tightly with plenty of air at the top, but it was only a temporary home, and John knew it.

"Did you want to pick the stuffed animals, or do you want me to just get some for you?" the kid asked John.

I could feel John's eyes on me as he answered the kid. I looked away, trying to avoid him.

"Lily, pick a stuffed animal that you want. The rest can be whatever, but I want that donkey right there," he said, pointing to a bright pink one above my head.

The kid worked on getting them down and tossed them into a bag before handing them to John. Lily was too focused on her fish to care about the stuffed animal. As we started to walk off, John gave me the pink donkey and waited for me to take it.

"What's this for?" I asked.

"That's for being a smart ass and suggesting that game," he said playfully, with more than a touch of sarcasm. "Now I have to figure out what to do with a damn fish," he muttered.

"His name is Samuel," Lily said as she walked in front of us, holding the bag up to look at it. "Sammy the fish, for short."

"That's actually longer," I said, feeling like an ass afterward. "But I like it," I added.

We had made it to the main entrance when I noticed the Ferris Wheel.

"Hey, Lily, isn't there something on the list that involved a Ferris Wheel?" I asked, knowing that there was. We could check another item off while we were here, but I wasn't sure whether fish were supposed to go on rides or be that high up in the sky.

"Yeah, I think so! I have to check my list, though," she said as she stopped and turned around, handing the fish to John.

"We're not going to do the Ferris Wheel here," he said, looking at the fish with a scowl on his face.

"Why not?" I asked, hurt in my voice.

Lily didn't say anything, just looked up at him with sad eyes.

"Because we're going to a BIGGER and BETTER one!"

"Where?" I asked, unsure of what his plans were. He hadn't mentioned anything to me about it, yet this seemed like something big that he had planned.

"Las Vegas!"

Sixteen

We started the morning later than I had expected, but when we added in a last-minute pitstop to buy a fish tank and food for our newest family member, it put a slight delay in the plans. Not that we were on a strict schedule or anything, but I was on pins and needles, excited to get to Las Vegas. I hadn't been there since Charlotte, and I celebrated our twenty-first birthdays, and that was a trip that I would never forget, what I could remember of it anyways. Tequila had a funny way of making memories and reality disappear.

John had grabbed us breakfast from McDonald's and was eating his while he drove while Lily tended to Sammy's new tank. She wanted to make sure that it was fun and safe—something that I didn't quite understand but insisted that he had plenty of rocks and a castle that he could hide in if needed. I wasn't sure how she even knew that it was a boy, but I wasn't about to argue about it. I also didn't want to be the one to break her heart by telling her that its life expectancy was going to be relatively short.

I sat back and ate my egg McMuffin, wiping my face with my napkin as I watched her. It was quiet in the motorhome, other than the soft sound of the road beneath us. We had spent our first night in it, and I was pleasantly surprised by how comfortable it really was. John never budged and ended up sleeping on the bed where the table goes, and Lily took the one at the front of the motorhome above the chairs. That left me with the big bed in the back, all to myself. It was kind of nice to have them so close, yet there was plenty of room between us. I found myself waking up a few times to check on Lily, worried that somehow, she would just vanish into thin air.

A few minutes later, Lily was satisfied with Sammy's home and let him be in the new tank that had been decked out with all the extras that she purchased. I was worried about it sliding around or getting knocked over if John took a turn too hard, but luckily, the tank fit perfectly in the kitchen sink where it was safely tucked in.

She smiled and sat down across from me, pulling her breakfast over to her.

"You made a nice home," I said, nodding to Sammy.

She looked over her shoulder, still smiling. I could see the pride on her face from a job well done.

"Thanks. Once we get home, I'll see if we can get a bigger tank and maybe another fish to keep him company. I bet he would like to have a girlfriend. Everyone needs someone," she said with a hint of sadness in her voice.

"Are you okay?" I asked softly, keeping my voice low to keep John from hearing too much.

"Yeah," she sighed heavily. "I've just been thinking."

"About boyfriends and girlfriends?" I pried gently, wondering if she was getting to the age of *the talk*.

She looked up in surprise, her eyes darting past my shoulder to look at John. I noticed the music up front got a little bit louder and realized that John was trying to give us whatever privacy he could in the small space.

"Not for me," she said wearily, taking a bite out of her hash brown. She waited while she chewed, thinking about how to say whatever it was that she was trying to say.

"For my dad."

I pulled back, surprised by what she had said. It wasn't something that I was expecting, and I didn't know how to respond.

"Does your dad want a girlfriend?" I asked quietly, unsure of how to navigate this.

"He says that he doesn't. And I know that he misses my mom. But my friend at school, her dad died before Christmas, and her mom is already starting to date again. She said that her mom is happier than she's ever been before. And I don't want to forget my mom, but I want my dad to be happy again, so maybe he needs to have a girlfriend."

We weren't in Las Vegas yet, but I was willing to bet everything that John had heard everything that Lily had just said. How could you not? Maybe it was just in my head, but it felt like her words were so loud that they ricocheted off the walls of the motorhome and slapped me in the face.

"I think that each person is different," I said uncomfortably, trying to ease into the conversation. "There's not really a timeframe for how long it takes before someone is ready to start dating again. I know that your dad is happy to be spending so much time with you, but I'm not sure that he's ready to start dating someone yet. I think that when he is ready, you'll know because he'll sit down and talk to you about it beforehand."

"That makes sense," she replied around a mouthful of pancakes. While she seemed okay with what I had said, something still seemed off with her.

"Lily, do you think your daddy wants a girlfriend and that he won't tell you before he starts seeing someone new?"

"No. I think he will tell me when he's ready."

"Are you afraid that *you* won't be ready?"

Her face fell, and she dropped her hands to the table.

"What if he tries to replace my mom?"

"Oh honey," I rushed out, my heart breaking for her. "No one, and I mean *no one,* could ever replace her. I can promise you that your daddy won't try to either. She was an amazing woman and meant so much to him. Even if your dad does find someone else that he wants to spend time with, it won't be to replace her."

She nodded her head, her eyes filled with tears.

"I know that you want him to be happy, but you don't have to be scared that his happiness will mean that he forgets about her. That's not how it works, sweetie. And I'm sure your friend's mom hasn't forgotten about her dad either."

Lily seemed to be better after that, but I had a knot in my stomach the size of Mars. I knew that I would have to talk to John about my conversation with Lily, but I also didn't want to break her trust. Maybe, if I was lucky, he would have heard it all and know what to do from here.

The hours passed by quickly, and the next thing I knew, we were looking at the Welcome to Las Vegas sign as we approached the strip. I got up and sat in the passenger seat, taking in the rush of excitement that was pulsing through me as I took everything in. Things had changed so much since I had been here—almost twenty years ago—that it felt like being here for the first time again.

"Do you remember the last time we were here?" John asked

as if he was reading my mind.

"The penny margaritas at our hotel that got us drunk off our asses the first night we got here," I laughed, remembering how drunk we were. "And the guy who tried to marry you and me when he thought we were a couple—only because he was trying to get with Charlotte."

"Shoot, we were all so wasted that we probably did get married and didn't even know it," he laughed.

I swallowed hard, unable to laugh naturally at his attempt at a joke, with my conversation from earlier so fresh in my mind. There was no way that John and I had been accidentally married, but Lily's concern about someone replacing her mom ate at me in a weird way that I couldn't put my thumb on it.

"It was a crazy trip, that's for sure," I said to fill the silence.

I watched the people walking along the sidewalk in masses, looking around at everything around them instead of paying attention to where they were going. I remembered that feeling, being so in awe that you couldn't focus on anything other than the wonderment around you.

The traffic was heavy with cars lined up, bumper to bumper, waiting for the light to turn green. Lily came and sat in the chair behind me, leaning around to look at the strip. It was a lot to take in, and I loved the look on her face when she tried. Soon, we had made our way to the hotel and checked in. I was surprised when John told me that we were staying for a few days and that there would be plenty of time for shopping, sightseeing, and catching a few shows. The bigger surprise was when he told me that he had rented me my own room, which adjoined theirs. This way, I could have privacy without being too far away from them.

I sat down on the pillow-top queen-sized bed and looked around the room. There were two beds, which made me excited to have Lily stay with me one night and give John a break if he wanted it. I imagined us staying in and having a total girl's night with manicures and pedicures and junk food galore! I got up and walked over to the window, pulling back the sheer curtain to take a look at the strip below. It was still daylight, so the real magic wouldn't happen until the sun went down and the neon lights created the real Vegas vibe.

I grabbed my suitcase and set it down on the other bed, unzipping it to find an outfit to wear. I didn't know what the plans were for the day, but it was definitely too hot to wear what I had on. When we left Santa Monica this morning, it was a little on the chilly side, so I had thrown on a pair of leggings and a tank top, with a hoodie over it until I warmed up.

Las Vegas was a whole different beast, and it was already over one hundred degrees. I sent John a quick text to let him know that I was going to take a quick shower and freshen up, then I would be ready if they wanted to do something. He confirmed that they would clean up too and said that they would be ready in an hour. That gave me plenty of time to get ready.

I unpacked the bottles of shampoo and conditioner that I had packed and took them with me to the bathroom. I turned on the shower, waiting for the water to get hot, while I looked through the pile of samples sitting by the sink. Once the water was steaming over the shower curtain,

I grabbed the bottle of coconut-scented body wash that I wanted to try and hopped in.

The shower was refreshing and gave me a nice burst of energy. I blow-dried my hair to keep the frizz away, thankful that it was still relatively short, even though I could use another trim. Since it was barely longer than my chin, it didn't give me too many options to pull it up off of my head. I grabbed a few bobby pins and pulled half of my hair up into a ponytail, pinning my bangs back with it.

I didn't bother putting much makeup on since I would end up sweating it off anyway. I ran the mascara brush through my lashes, pulling up to make them look longer. It wasn't much, but I loved the way it made my eyes look. I opened my make-up bag, looking for my lipstick when I felt that something was missing. I dumped the contents out on the counter next to the sink and went through each item, separating them by the order I used them.

In one pile were the two eyeshadows that I brought, an eyeliner, an eyelash curler, mascara, blush, and two lipstick tubes. Next to that was my bottle of foundation, my pressed compact, and the makeup brushes that I used. The only other items were the things that I used at night when I was getting ready for bed. I had a pack of makeup-removing wipes, a moisturizer, my toothbrush and toothpaste, and some floss. Then I realized that the one thing that was missing was the one thing that I didn't want to forget—my birth control.

Not that I was planning to need it while on vacation with my best friend's husband and their daughter, but I hated not being on the pill. I couldn't remember a time when I hadn't been on them, so it felt like a huge problem not to have them.

I tried to force myself not to think about it or let it ruin my trip. There were worse things that could happen, and I wasn't going to die from not taking my pills for a month. Granted, I was getting ready to start a new pack on Sunday, and now I wouldn't have them. I thought about what the likelihood was that my doctor would be in the office at four o'clock on a Thursday, but it was worth a shot. I could call her and ask if she could call in a one-month supply to a pharmacy out here, and then everything would be okay.

The only problem was that I had no idea where there was a pharmacy close by, and the last thing that I wanted to do was explain this to John or Lily. It would be mortifying to talk to him about birth control because I didn't want him to think of me having sex. I had been on it since I was a teenager and needed it to help me regulate my cycles, which is why I felt so stressed over not having it.

I pulled on a pair of cutoff denim shorts and a loose cotton tank top, hoping that it would be cool enough for the unbearable heat outside. I loved the summer, but only in California, where it wasn't this dry heat that they had in the desert. I preferred the cooler temperatures of the bay area, where you could cool off with a quick dip in the ocean.

I was sitting on my bed, googling pharmacies near me, when I heard a knock on the adjoining door. I got up and unlocked it, smiling when I saw John on the other side. There was still twenty minutes before we were supposed to go, so I wasn't sure if they were ready early.

"Hey, are you guys ready?" I asked, opening the door to let him into my room. His door stayed open on the other side, and I heard the shower running.

"Not yet. Lily is taking a quick shower and then has to get ready. I just thought I would check and see how you like your room."

"It's great, thank you. You didn't have to book a separate room for me, but I do appreciate it."

"I thought it might be nice for us to all have some room to spread out for a few days before we're back on the road in the motorhome. Lily is excited to have her own big bed," he laughed, looking back into the room where her suitcase was overflowing onto her bed.

"She really needs a new suitcase," I commented. "Maybe two."

"She's as bad as her mom," he muttered, sitting down on the edge of my bed.

I laughed, knowing that it was true. Charlotte was a horrible packer and took more than she needed. Always be prepared was her motto, and she definitely lived by it.

John looked over at my suitcase that was open on the other bed and laughed.

"I can't imagine a woman who packs that light," he said. "It seems unreal that you don't have a whole house in there."

I looked at the suitcase and laughed. It wasn't all that small, but not the biggest compared to what they had brought. It was twenty-five inches, which was more than enough for me. If I had the larger ones, like they had, it would probably overflow with a bunch of random crap that I didn't need.

"I only bring what I think I will need," I said with a shrug.

"And forget the things that I actually do need," I muttered under my breath, frustrated.

"What did you forget?" he asked.

"Nothing," I said dismissively. I still needed to find a pharmacy and get in touch with my doctor before she left for the day.

"Emma."

I rolled my eyes and blew out a heavy breath.

"My birth control."

He pulled his head back in surprise, his cheeks flushing with embarrassment.

"Oh. I didn't realize you were planning to—"

"John!" I shrieked, stopping him from finishing his sentence. "I'm not planning to get with anyone while on vacation with you guys," I said quickly to stop the thoughts that were running through his head.

"Oh," he replied nervously.

"I need them to regulate my cycles," I explained, turning to face the window to avoid looking at him.

"I wasn't judging if you wanted to—"

"John—please stop. We are not going to talk about birth control or me getting with any guys while we are on this trip. Okay?"

He laughed and put his hands up, almost relieved that I put a stop to it.

"Is there a way that you can get a prescription for them while you're here? Do they do that?"

"I was getting ready to call my doctor to ask her. I have no idea whether or not she will do it, but it's worth a shot. I just have to find a pharmacy close by first."

He got up from the bed and started to walk back to his room.

"We have a car, Emma. Just have them call them in to whatever pharmacy they can, and we'll go pick them up." He tapped his knuckles against the doorframe before he walked inside and closed their door.

I exhaled heavily and sat down on the bed. I picked up my phone and called my doctor, chewing on my nail while praying that she would do this for me.

Seventeen

Lady Luck was definitely on my side when the pharmacy got us in and out with a brand new pack of birth control. I laughed at how quickly my doctor was willing to write me another prescription when she heard that I was on vacation and had forgotten to pack mine. I had been seeing her for years and had never taken a trip that she knew of, despite her constantly telling me that I needed to get out and see the world.

By the time we had finished, it was already after six, and we were starting to get hungry. John and I agreed that it would be too chaotic on the strip and that we didn't want to wait for an hour or more for a table which ruled out everything around our hotel. Luckily, we spotted a cute little restaurant on the backside of the strip that was relatively busy but didn't have a line out the door. Twenty minutes later, we were seated at a booth in the back, watching an older couple belt out their rendition of I Honestly Love You by Olivia Newton-John. We had picked a lively place for karaoke, which was fine by us.

We placed our order and watched as a group of young girls- slightly older than Lily, went up to sing as a group. It was hard to make out what song it was supposed to be through the giggling and whispering about how nervous they were. Next up was a group of guys who looked like they belonged on Jersey Shore, who tried to serenade the group of girls that were sitting at the table beside us, part of a bachelorette party.

I smiled at the waitress as she brought our drinks and set them on the table. My stomach growled, wanting food as another server passed by carrying a plate of nachos.

Lily picked up a stack of papers from the middle of the table and looked at them.

"What are those?" I asked, wondering what had her attention as she focused intently on them.

John looked over her shoulder and smiled.

"Signup sheets for the karaoke," he confirmed, taking a drink of his iced tea.

I turned my attention back to the DJ, who was looking through the stack of papers on the table next to him.

"Alright, folks, we're going to take a quick break, and then we'll be back for more," he announced before turning the microphone off and setting it beside him. He pressed a few buttons, and a Justin Bieber song started playing through the speakers behind us as he walked away.

I could feel the excitement building as the waitress made her way over to our table, carrying a tray with sandwiches that almost toppled over. I covered my mouth with my hands as I stared at them in disbelief. I guess the sign outside wasn't lying when they said they had the *biggest* sandwiches on the strip.

She set our plates in front of us and dropped off a handful of napkins before checking to see if we needed anything else. Aside from an extra stomach, I couldn't think of what could possibly be missing from this massive sandwich. Now I wished I had offered to split one with John or Emma as there was no way that I could eat all of this.

I studied the mighty club, with its layers of bread, meats,

and bacon, trying to figure out the best angle to dive in. Finally realizing that there wasn't one, I gave in and smashed it down the best that I could, the toast crumbling around my plate. I opened my mouth as wide as it would go and tried to take a bite. I heard giggling from the other side and lowered my hand to see Lily laughing at my attempt.

"There's no other way to eat it," I complained, lowering it back to my plate. I looked over at John, who sat there with a smug look on his face, trying to contain his laughter, as he pulled the toothpick out and separated it into four very manageable-sized sandwiches.

"Oh," I said quietly, feeling a little silly and embarrassed. "I guess there is another way after all."

John and Lily laughed, much to my expense, as I pulled the toothpicks out and copied John. The waitress came by again, refilling drinks. She stopped by Lily's side of the table and bent down as she whispered something in her ear. I didn't know what she was up to, but the waitress nodded and gave her a light pat on the shoulder before she walked away.

I finished separating my sandwich and popped a sweet potato fry into my mouth, desperate to finally eat. John was already through half of his food by the time I took my first bite. It wasn't like we were in a rush, but I still felt silly for attempting to eat the whole thing in one bite.

Lily dipped her french fries in ketchup and bounced excitedly in her seat when the DJ came back and sat down. The waitress went over and gave him a handful of papers that had been collected while he was gone.

"Alright, let's get this competition started! It's officially seven o'clock, which means that it's time for the Sing for Bling contest. Only, I don't have any bling to give you, so the winner will walk out with one hundred dollars! How this works is each contestant comes up to sing, and whoever gets the crowd going the loudest wins. Easy peasy." He looked around, making sure everyone was paying attention and listening.

I lifted my pickle spear to my mouth and took a bite. The place was busier now than it had been when we first got here, and I wondered how many people had come for the contest. By the looks of it, that's what the majority of them were here for as they eagerly watched him as he shuffled through the papers in front of him.

"Alright, first up we have, Emma and John! Come on up!"

It was at that moment that I choked on my pickle, causing a scene as John leaped forward to see if I was okay. I beat my fist against my chest, trying to stop the coughing as I prayed the pickle would set itself free. I took a drink of water, followed by another one before it finally dislodged and slid the rest of the way down my throat.

I was beet red, mortified as everyone stared at me.

"Emma and John, you guys ready?" he asked, looking directly at us as Lily so kindly pointed at her dad and me. Now I knew what she had been up to, and she was lucky that she was cute.

I narrowed my eyes at her and then looked at John. He just shrugged helplessly and got up, extending his hand out to help me.

"I'm gonna kill her," I muttered under my breath, getting a chuckle from him.

We walked over to the makeshift stage area and stood behind the two microphone stands.

I looked at Lily, who was still bouncing excitedly in her seat, her dad's phone in hand as she got ready to take pictures—or worse—video.

"Whenever you guys are ready," the DJ said, waiting for us. It would be great to know what song it was, but John just nodded anyway, deciding we were ready.

A few seconds later, the music started playing, and I felt the nerves begin to wear off. I recognized the song immediately as one that John and I had done at karaoke more times than I could count. I was surprised that Lily remembered it and wondered if maybe John had been in on this without me knowing as well. I had been a little distracted by the nachos earlier, so it wouldn't surprise me if I missed them planning this right under my nose.

I closed my eyes for a second as John started singing, the crowd going wild as he sang Kid Rock's part in Picture. It was a song that we did well together, and John had an incredible voice. Mine wasn't bad by any means, but John had the attention of every woman in the room, and I was waiting for the panties to start flying toward us at any moment.

He turned his head slightly and winked at me, watching as I did Sheryl Crow's part. The crowd continued to cheer for us, likely impressed that I didn't sound like cats that were being murdered. Maybe it was just because we were the first ones to go up, but the energy in the room was electrifying, and I found myself putting on a show for everyone as I sang to John like the wounded woman in the song.

Before I knew it, the song was over, and everyone was still cheering for us. We walked back to the table and sat down, feeling on top of the world. I turned my attention to Lily and shook my finger at her.

"You little troublemaker," I pretended to scold.

She put her hands up in the air and looked shocked that I would say such a thing.

"I didn't do it, I swear," she insisted with a giggle.

"Then what were you whispering to the waitress about?"

She looked behind me and tucked her chin to her chest, looking overly guilty. I turned around just in time to see the waitress standing there with a birthday cake, covering the flame of the candle as the air conditioner threatened to blow it out. Several other servers joined around us as they sang happy birthday as loud as they could.

I waited for her to set the cake down in front of me before I blew out the candle. I thanked them and was relieved when they all scattered off to wait on their tables, leaving us alone. The DJ continued calling the next contestant up to the stage while I fished the candle out of the cake.

"It's not my birthday," I said gently, pulling in a deep breath. I had hoped that they forgot about it, but obviously, they hadn't.

"I know, but if I didn't tell them tonight, then we wouldn't get to celebrate your birthday," Lily complained, pouting with her arms over her chest.

"That's not true," I lied.

"Yes, it is," John laughed. "You would insist that you didn't feel well just so you could avoid going anywhere or doing anything, and you know it."

I scrunched my face and thought about it. They were right. I hated celebrating my birthday, and this year it was even harder without Charlotte. Our birthdays were one week apart, and I had hoped that we would be on the road for mine. Instead, John confirmed that we were staying in Las Vegas until Sunday morning, which meant that I was celebrating another birthday in sin city on Saturday.

"Alright, alright, you're right. But I know that you did the karaoke thing too. You can't lie to me," I teased, looking at her.

"Actually, that was me," John admitted sheepishly.

"What?!" My jaw dropped. I would never have imagined him volunteering us to do karaoke. Maybe when we were younger because that's what we used to do, but not now. We were way more serious than we used to be, and this wasn't something that we would typically do anymore.

"Hey, we're on vacation," he laughed. "It sounded like fun, so I figured why not?"

I grinned as I studied him, not sure who he was anymore. I had to admit that I really liked this version of him, and I was glad that he was sharing it with Lily too.

We all shared the cake, and John ordered me a glass of wine while we watched the rest of the performers. Finally, they had reached the end, and I got nervous again while we waited for the results.

The DJ had each performer stand up and had the audience cheer for whoever they liked best, but this time he went in reverse order, so we were last. Some really great singers had gone after us, and I was sure they were going to win. When it got to us, we both stood up, and the entire room filled with clapping, whistles, and cheers, which decided that we were the winners.

We collected our prize money and were surprised when our meal was paid for by the restaurant for winning. We piled into the motorhome and made it back to our hotel, exhausted. John and Lily said goodnight, and I went to my room alone, plopping down on the bed, too tired to bother with changing into my pajamas.

The next day, we got up early and had breakfast before waiting in line to ride the High Roller. It was the largest Ferris Wheel that I had ever seen. Lily and I were both bouncing around with excitement, while John seemed less than enthused.

"What's the matter?" I asked when Lily turned her attention to watching the giant wheel stop as people got out and new passengers boarded. It was a different setup than any Ferris Wheel I had ever seen, mainly because it didn't have the baskets that most of them had. Instead, it had cabins that you walked into that could hold up to ten people. I had looked up the information yesterday when I knew that we were coming.

The line slowly moved, and soon we were almost at the beginning.

"Nothing, I just don't like heights," he admitted quietly.

"Then why did you decide to do this?" I asked in shock, nodding at the giant beast beside us. "You could have gone on the one at the boardwalk instead—it was like half the size of this thing."

"I wanted it to be special for Lily," he said sheepishly, guiding me by my lower back as we walked forward to the man who was directing us to our cabin. Lily led the way, walking over and standing by the window. John and I joined her and waited for the other passengers to get in before we felt it move while they continued loading the rest of the cabins.

Finally, it started moving, and we had the perfect view of the strip from all angles. I glanced over at John, who was rigid as a board and slightly pale. I placed a hand on Lily's shoulder, talking to her about the sights below while using my other hand to gently hold John's. I didn't want to draw attention to his fear, especially since he was doing this for her.

Thirty minutes later, John had survived, and we were waiting our turn for our cabin to reach the ground so we could exit. I checked on John a few times as we made our way over to Planet Hollywood. He assured me that he was fine and happy to be back on solid ground again.

Lily and I were excited to go shopping while John was content to sit in the room and wait for us. In the end, we dragged him along with us and laughed when he ended up buying more stuff than we did. I popped into a convenience store along the way and picked up a few bottles of nail polish and some supplies for my girl's night with Lily. I hadn't talked to John about it yet, but I couldn't imagine that he would say no.

We stopped for lunch, and people watched for a while before walking the other half of the Miracle Mile. By the time we were done, our arms hurt from the bags that hung off them, and our feet had blisters from too much walking.

We made it back to our hotel and decided on room service for dinner.

We sat in their room, eating and watching tv, when I decided to ask John about having Lily stay with me.

"Hey, I was thinking," I said quietly, leaning closer to him while Lily watched her show on tv. "Can I have a girl's night with Lily tonight?"

"Girl's night? Like go out and have drinks and pick up boys?" He raised an eyebrow and took a bite out of his cheeseburger.

"Is that what you think girl's night is?"

"I guess," he shrugged. "Every time Charlotte had girl's night, she always came home tipsy and flirted with everything, including the mailbox."

I laughed and snorted, remembering when she told me about that night. She had been out with some moms from the PTA and had too much to drink. When she got home, she thought that the mailbox out front was John and had been hugging on it for a few minutes before he found her and had to pry her off of it.

"No, that's not girl's night," I laughed. "Our night will consist of girly movies—which we're going to rent, by the way. Junk food, manicures and pedicures, and maybe some soda if we get the wild hair for it."

"No boys?" he asked with narrowed eyes.

"No boys," I agreed.

"Good, I don't need to worry about that with either of you," he said quietly before taking another bite.

I wanted to ask him what that meant but thought better of it and ignored it instead.

"So, can she stay the night with me?" I asked. "I have the extra bed, and we are right next door if you need us."

"Are you sure you don't want to go downstairs and gamble or something?" He set his food down and looked at me.

"I'm not a big gambler, and I think it would be fun for us to hang out. Plus, it'll give you a break to go play poker if you want to."

He used to play poker often before they had Lily, and he got his big promotion at work that tied up any free time he used to have. After that, he stopped going to the poker nights with his friends, and some of the joy that he used to have seemed to disappear as well.

"Okay, if you're positive," he said, reluctantly as if he was waiting for me to change my mind.

"I'm positive!"

Lily turned to look at us, confused by my outburst.

"What's going on?" she asked.

"We're having a slumber party in my room tonight! Just you and me!" I squealed.

Her face lit up as she looked to John to make sure it was alright. He nodded yes and smiled at her.

We finished our dinner and cleaned up before packing stuff for Lily to take over to my room. It wasn't like we couldn't come back if she needed something, but I wanted to give John some space for the night without having to worry about us barging in.

He cleaned up and went downstairs for the night while Lily picked which movie she wanted to watch in my room. We spent the night painting our nails and eating junk food before crashing out in a food coma. I went to bed feeling happy and content for once as Lily slept beside me instead of in her own bed.

Eighteen

I woke up Saturday morning to Lily singing happy birthday to me. It was so sweet that I wanted to live in this moment forever. She placed a quick kiss on my cheek before jumping out of bed and opening the door to John's room. I sat up on the bed, looking around at the mess that we had made last night. The tv was still on, and there were empty bags of chips from the vending machine scattered along with bags of candy on the other bed.

"Happy birthday!" John said warmly as he walked in, taking in the mess. "Looks like you girls had quite the party last night."

I laughed as Lily came back over and sat down next to me on the bed.

"It was sooo much fun, daddy! You have *no* idea!"

"I'm glad you had a good time, honey."

"How was your night?" I asked, covering my mouth as I yawned. I was still in my pajamas that we had changed into before we did our manicures last night, and I was pretty sure that my hair was a knotted mess, but it wasn't like he didn't see me like this most mornings at his house anyway.

"It was good. I played poker for a bit and walked away with a nice payout."

His eyes sparkled for a moment, and I wondered just how *nice* it was. John was a diehard poker player but hadn't played in years. Apparently, it was a skill that didn't fade away for him.

"I'm glad you had a good night, too," I said, meaning it.

My night with Lily had been as much fun as she said, and I was glad that John was able to go enjoy himself for the night as well. I had no idea what time he got back in, but he looked well-rested and fully energized this morning.

"So, what does the birthday girl want to do today?" he asked, sitting down on the other bed after moving some of the mess away.

"Ugh, don't remind me," I groaned playfully, covering my face with a pillow. "I'm too old to do anything. Let's just forget that it's my birthday. Maybe I should go buy some wrinkle cream and Metamucil."

"Oh please," he snorted. "You're younger than me, and you look gorgeous."

"I'm forty. The big FOUR-O. My life is downhill from here."

"Well, given that I'm *forty-four*, I'm going to tell you that your forties aren't that bad."

"Yeah, but you're a guy. You age well. It's not fair. A woman turning forty is different. Men see her as *aged*."

"What kind of men are you trying to date? Twenty-year-old college punks? Men your age would love to have someone like you. You're beautiful, smart, kind, and just a wonderful person. Age isn't anything to be this stressed over. You're not old, so stop thinking that you are."

I pulled my mouth to the side and glared at him. Maybe he was right. Maybe I was just making a big stink out of it for nothing. I had been looking forward to my fortieth birthday for a while— shocking, I know! But ever since we found Charlotte's bucket list, I had been thinking about all of the things I hadn't done yet and felt like I was starting to run out of time.

"Fine, I guess it's not that bad," I conceded. "But that doesn't mean that we have to devote the day to it. We can do whatever you guys want to do."

Lily was lying next to me, twirling her blonde hair around her finger as she listened to us.

"Is there anything that you wanted to do today, Lily?" I asked, drawing her into the conversation.

"Not really," she said, not engaging beyond that.

"I had an idea for tonight if you trust me?" John said cautiously.

That immediately made me wonder what he was planning. He looked so excited about it that I didn't bother to fight him on whatever he had planned.

"Alright, I trust you. Even though I'm not sure that I should after the karaoke surprise last night," I joked.

"Hey, you made a hundred dollars from that!"

"I told you to keep the money," I insisted. "It was your idea. You should have taken the money."

"I wanted you to have it. Consider it an early birthday gift from Sin City."

"Why do you call it Sin City?" Lily asked, looking over at John as she waited for his response.

I laughed as he blushed, realizing that he didn't want to explain this to his daughter.

"Just let me know what the plans are for tonight so that I

can get ready."

"I think we should do a little shopping, and then we can spend some time at the pool before we get ready to go," he said with a wink.

"What kind of shopping do we need to do?" I groaned, my feet still sore from yesterday.

"We're going *dress* shopping. And maybe a pair of heels."

I felt my jaw drop, wondering even more now what he was going on.

"I didn't take you for a high heel kind of man," I teased.

"They're for you," he laughed. He got up and walked back to his room, calling to Lily over his shoulder, "come on, we need to get ready. We have lots of fun stuff to do today."

Once they were gone, I closed the door and jumped in the shower. I had no idea what we were doing tonight or where we were going, so that left me clueless about how to do my hair and makeup. I decided to hold off until I knew more, especially since John mentioned hanging out at the pool for a bit.

I pulled my hair back into a low ponytail and pinned my bangs back. I found another pair of shorts, this time cotton, and put them on with a flowy tank top. This was a comfortable outfit for running around in, and half the time, I used it as pajamas because it was so soft and breathable. I was sitting on the bed, grabbing the stuff I needed out of my purse, when I heard a knock on the door.

I opened it and found John and Lily on the other side with a bouquet of roses that had been delivered.

"These were supposed to come to your room, but they

delivered them to mine instead," he explained, handing me the vase with pink and white roses.

"Oh my goodness, these are beautiful!" I brought the vase to my nose and smelled them. "Thank you guys so much!"

"You're very welcome," John said, his face lit up with happiness. "Are you ready to get going?"

"Yeah, let me set these down and grab my phone, and then I'm ready." I found a safe place for the flowers on the dresser next to the tv. I figured it was as safe of a place as any given that it was where Lily had put Sammy's tank when we first checked in, and he seemed to be doing just fine.

I grabbed my phone and shoved it into my pockets, slinging my clutch across my shoulders. I hated carrying a big purse and had bought this small, cute clutch yesterday that held all my credit cards and license. It was more expensive than I would have liked to pay, but it was name brand, and you paid for that.

We went downstairs, and I was relieved that John had picked a store close by instead of making us walk far. It was a small boutique and had plenty of cute dresses to choose from, including some that were fancier and more formal.

I still had no idea what the plan was or why I needed a dress, but John walked through the store like he was Richard Gere, and I was the beautiful prostitute that he was trying to domesticate. Okay, so maybe not a prostitute, but he was oddly comfortable talking to the saleswoman about the dress selection she had and the need for something fancy but not over the top.

I followed them through the store, watching as they discussed different options. Apparently, she knew where we were going because she insisted several times that I would need something more comfortable and not so restricting. After sorting through several racks, and her trying to figure out my size by looking at my body, she helped me to a dressing room and hung up the handful of dresses that she thought would work best. I waited for her to come back with the assortment of shoes that she wanted me to try as well before I bothered trying anything on.

My stomach knotted as I thought back to the last time I had tried clothes on in a store. It was with Charlotte before the accident. I still had the outfit that she had bought me for my interview hanging up in the closet at home, never worn, with the tags still on it. I wiped away the tear that had escaped and picked up the first dress.

It was a black spaghetti strap dress that had a plunging neckline and barely covered my ass. This was Las Vegas, but I had imagined that she would find something that *didn't* make me look like a prostitute. I shimmied out of it and hung it up on the hanger before grabbing the next one. I didn't bother going out to show them the dresses, mainly because I felt too naked in all of them.

"How's it going in there?" John asked from the waiting area outside the door.

"I feel like Julia Roberts in Pretty Woman," I replied as I slipped out of another one. There was only one dress left that I hadn't tried on, and I was doubtful that it would be any better than the others.

"Spoiled by a rich man with too much money on his hands?"

"More like the prostitute that is showing her ass in every single dress. And if my ass isn't hanging out, then my boobs are about to pop out. Don't they believe in clothes that cover you?"

"Do you want me to order a pizza?" he offered with a chuckle.

I pulled my brows together, confused, as I pulled the satiny red fabric over my head.

"Are you hungry? We just had breakfast."

"No," he laughed. "It worked in the movie. They ordered her a pizza, and then she was happy and bought all sorts of clothes and shoes and stuff."

"I'm not sure if I'm impressed by how well you remember the movie or worried," I teased, smoothing the fabric down over my hips and turning to the side to get a better look in the mirror. This one wasn't bad, and surprisingly, it covered the parts of my body that I wanted to hide. It was short, but not too short, hitting mid-thigh. The fabric was soft and light, making it feel like a summer dress, even though it was far from casual.

The straps were thin but thick enough for me to wear a bra and not have it be noticeable. The waist was tapered, creating curves that I didn't remember having before now. I reached up and ran a finger along the neckline, admiring how it dipped low enough to show some cleavage without putting the girls on full display. As much as I had hated the idea of trying on dresses, I was suddenly in love with this one and knew that I had to have it.

I sorted through the boxes of shoes that she had brought me—surprisingly, in my size. How did they do that? Just look at someone and know what size they were? They were all heels with at least a five or six-inch heel. How I was going to walk in those and not fall was beyond me. Maybe Charlotte would send me some sort of superpowers to get me through the night without falling on my face. I was torn between the red stilettos and the black leather shoes with a slightly thicker but taller heel when there was a knock at the door.

"How's it going? Do you need more dresses to try on?" the saleswoman asked.

I stepped back and pulled the door open enough for her to see me without letting John have a look. If he was going to surprise me with a night out, then he was going to have to be surprised with what I was wearing.

"I can't decide on which shoes to wear," I said shyly, pulling at my dress as she stared at me.

"You look beautiful," she said sweetly. "I would go with the red ones."

"Thank you," I said with a nod. She turned and walked out, giving me privacy to change.

I hung the dress up and got dressed. When I walked out of the fitting room, I found John talking with her at the register as she showed him a handful of ties. I swallowed hard, hoping that she didn't think that we were together. It would be an easy mistake to make, but I couldn't stand the thought of anyone assuming that, let alone saying something where Lily could hear.

She stood next to John, pointing at the different ties, before turning around and spotting me.

"Emma! Did you pick a dress?" she asked as she ran over to me.

"I did, and it's gorgeous," I said, hugging her shoulders. "But your dad can't see it, so I'm waiting until he's done, then I'll pay for it."

John laughed and nodded his head. He pointed to a tie and slid his credit card over to the saleswoman.

"I'll be outside," he said before adding, "She's not to pay for anything. Add her items to my purchase."

I was about to object as he walked off. Once he got to the door, he stopped and turned back to us.

"And give her the other pair of shoes that she couldn't decide on."

He walked out the door, and Lily followed him, jumping around with excitement. I walked up to the counter, the woman grinning from ear to ear.

"Are you ready, dear?" she asked, not prying into what had just happened. Maybe it was common here for men to do things like this for women, or maybe it was the look of shock on my face. Either way, I appreciated that she didn't push for information.

I waited while she rang everything up and handed me the bags.

"Do you want me to go grab him so he can sign for the purchase?" I offered, knowing that I couldn't sign for him.

"No need for that. Mr. Wright is a valued member and has asked that we charge these items to his room."

She handed me the receipt and a smaller bag that I hadn't seen before. I took it and wandered outside to where John and Lily were sitting on a bench waiting for me.

"What was that about?" I asked, nodding to the store behind me. "Since when do they just let you drop hundreds of dollars in a store and charge it to your room?"

"I told you that I had a good night," he said with a shrug. "I'm glad that you found something that you liked."

I pulled in a deep breath and held it for a few seconds before I spoke.

"Thank you, John. For all of this. But it's too much. You didn't need to go through all of this effort."

He got up from the bench and stood in front of me, so close that I could smell the hint of aftershave on his collar. I found myself holding my breath again, but this time, for a different reason.

"Emma, when was the last time that you got dressed up and went somewhere special?"

I paused, thinking about it, even though I already knew the answer.

"Exactly."

He ran a hand down the stubble that dotted his jaw.

"We don't get many opportunities to do things like this. To live as if we don't have a care in the world. We're on vacation, and we're filling items on a bucket list that someone else never got to do. So, I want to live in the moment. I want to pretend, just for a little while, that we don't have a damn care in the world. Can you please stop fighting me on this and trust me when I say that I *want* to do this for you?"

He reached out and gently grabbed my elbows as I had my arms folded across my chest. When he said it like that, I couldn't be mad at him. I understood where he was coming from, but I hated that he was spending money on me, knowing that I could never pay him back.

"Okay, I'm sorry. It is a very nice gesture. I just feel bad with how much you're spending on me."

"Emma, I wouldn't spend it if I couldn't afford it. Trust me, I'm very good with money and know my budget. Now, are you ready for the next part of the day?"

I was starting to feel a little less stressed and overwhelmed, which made the idea of lounging by the pool for a few hours sound even more appealing.

"Yes! I could go for a cold drink while I lay by the pool," I said excitedly, looking past him to Lily, knowing that she was probably just as excited.

"I actually had something else in mind," he laughed, turning and steering me by my elbow as Lily joined us. We walked back into the hotel and toward the elevator that went to our rooms. I was confused when we kept going past it and ended up at a dead-end where the spa and salon were.

"Here we are," he said, opening the frosted white glass door and holding it open for me.

"What are you talking about?" I asked, looking around at

the room full of women wearing crisp white aprons who were staring at me and smiling.

"I booked you a spa appointment. They're ready to pamper you for the day with a facial, a haircut and color, and a ninety-minute massage. If there's anything else that you want, just let them know, and they'll add it in for you." John winked and gave me his best smile, probably knowing that I was about to complain about him spending money again.

"I thought we were going to the pool?" I replied dumbly, at a loss for words.

"Oh, yeah, Lily and I are going to the pool while you relax and let them spoil you. I'll meet you in the room around four? Four-thirty?" He looked down at his watch, checking the time.

I couldn't speak if I tried. John and Lily walked out and left me to a team of very friendly, very eager professionals ready to pamper me.

I spent the first half of the day getting a massage and a real pedicure, not like the one I attempted last night with Lily. Not that it was even a pedicure, just a couple of coats of nail polish. After that, I succumbed to the magical feeling of Claud's hands as they worked the knots out of my shoulders and made my body feel like I was twenty again. I've had plenty of massages in my life, but I could honestly say that nothing had compared to this one.

Once I had rinsed the massage oil off my body and soaked in the hot tub for an hour, I decided to go see what John had set up for my hair. I had been talking about getting a cut and color recently, but I hadn't expected him to listen or pay attention.

I sat in the chair, watching Helena use her fingers to style it. I hadn't realized how much my hair had grown since the last time I had cut it, but it felt great to have it short again. I stuck with the same chin-length bob that I had before, enjoying how easy and simple it was to maintain. I decided to go a shade darker than the honey brown color that I had before, this time settling on a chocolate brown.

I looked at myself in the mirror, barely recognizing myself. It felt like I had been renewed and refreshed, which was definitely not what I imagined I would feel on my fortieth birthday. I thanked the team for everything they did for me and tried to leave a tip, which was quickly denied based on their direct orders from Mr. Wright.

I went back to my room and got ready, leaving ten minutes to spare before John knocked on my door. I pushed the silver hoop earring through my ear and quickly fixed my hair before I walked over and answered the door. John was standing there in a fitted black button-down shirt and dress slacks, with a red tie that matched my dress snug around his neck. I knew that he would be burning up as soon as we stepped outside, but I appreciated him making an effort for me.

Lily came to stand beside him, wearing a beautiful blue summer dress with pink flowers all over it. Her hair had been combed; a small portion braided on top to keep it out of her face. She looked adorable, and I covered my mouth to keep from squealing and gushing over it.

"You guys!! You look amazing!" I said, stepping back to let them in the room.

John's eyes widened when he saw the dress and shoes that I

had chosen, and immediately I panicked, worried that I had spent too much.

"You… look." He stopped and shook his head. "Gorgeous. Just absolutely gorgeous, Emma."

If it was possible, he took my breath away again in less than sixty seconds. But this time, it was because of his sincere reaction. He was still looking at me, his eyes slowly traveling the length of my body as he took it all in when Lily cleared her throat.

"Dad, the gift," Lily coaxed.

"Yes, thank you," he said, his voice scratchy. He reached into the pocket of his jacket and pulled out a small box. My eyes went wide as I tilted my head to give him *the* look.

"Before you say anything," he warned with a laugh. "This was a gift that was bought long before this trip."

He handed me the box and stepped back. They watched as I opened it, slowly lifting the beautiful silver locket necklace out and held it in my hand.

"Charlotte had bought it for you months ago," John explained, a crack in his voice as he said her name. "She found it at an antique store and thought you would love it."

My fingers trembled as I opened it. Inside was a picture of her and me from our senior year in high school. I closed my eyes, willing the tears to go away, so they didn't ruin my makeup.

"I do love it, thank you."

I set the box down on my bed and lifted it to my neck.

"Here, let me help you," John offered.

His fingers lightly grazed the back of my neck as he clasped it in place.

"I like the new hair, by the way," he said softly, barely loud enough for me to hear.

"Thank you," I said again, running my fingers over the necklace.

"Alright, shall we get going?" he asked, turning to look at Lily, who was smiling brightly at us.

"We shall," I said, feeling my nerves all over the place.

A quick—quick for Las Vegas, drive later, we boarded a three-level paddle wheeler on Lake Mead for a dinner cruise. The scenery was beautiful, and Hoover Dam was stunning at night. The food was delicious, and the dessert divine. But the best part was spending this moment with John and Lily.

We were cruising back when John came and stood next to me by the railing. I closed my eyes and enjoyed the fresh air. Lily was standing between us, watching the water as we moved.

"You know, Lily, this trip was partly for you tonight too," he said, looking down at her. "There was a bucket list item that we checked part of it off."

"Which one?" she asked, looking up at him.

"I don't remember it word for word, but it was the one about being in three different bodies of water," he replied.

"You might need more than a breeze to travel across all

three of these," she recited, grinning cheekily, proud that she had remembered it.

"Are you happy that we're getting some of the things on your mom's list done?" I asked, looking down at her.

"Yeah, but I don't know if we'll get all of them. Some of them were really hard."

"We'll never know if we don't try," I reminded her gently.

"And, tomorrow is a new day with new adventures," John said with a wink that told me he had more things planned that were being kept secret.

Nineteen

The drive to the Grand Canyon was short- a whopping two and a half hours. Checking out of the hotel and fighting traffic was more time-consuming than our actual travel. Lily was quiet most of the trip and laid on the back bed, complaining that she didn't feel well. I wondered if it was too much junk food and made plans to cook a few meals over the next few days to get us back on track with healthier eating.

I had checked on the supplies that we had when we packed up the motorhome this morning. Sammy was doing *swimmingly* well and seemed to be enjoying his home. I added fish food to the list of items that we were going to need soon. Toilet paper and food were the other items that we needed to replenish, and soon. There were a few rolls that would last us through today and probably tomorrow, but not much food other than a few boxes of crackers and some half-empty bags of chips.

I was starting to feel weighed down and gross from all the greasy food I had been eating and decided that a nice, clean salad would be beneficial for all of us. While Lily rested in the bed, I climbed over into the passenger seat next to John, setting my notepad and pen on my lap while I buckled my seatbelt.

"How's she doing?" he asked, nodding back to Lily.

"I'm guessing that maybe all of the junk food is making her sick. I know that I'm starting to feel the effects of it," I laughed and rubbed a hand across my stomach, convinced that I had already put on ten pounds in less than a week. Maybe *this* was why I shouldn't go on vacation.

"Me too," he said, patting his stomach. I rolled my eyes at the thought of him thinking that he had an ounce of fat on his body. He was probably one of the healthiest and leanest humans I had ever met. Even though he was a dad, there was no dad-bod for this guy.

"Oh, please," I snorted. "You could live off of cheeseburgers and fries and not gain an ounce. The rest of us, well, we need to eat a few salads to balance out these carb-heavy meals."

"A salad sounds delicious," he commented, turning to look at me. "I was planning to stay in Williams, Arizona tonight, but since Lily doesn't seem to be feeling good, I doubt she's up for a long trip there. Maybe we stop and look at it, then head on to New Mexico?"

"That's fine with me," I agreed. "Hopefully, her stomachache will pass soon, but it wouldn't be terrible to get some of the travel out of the way while she's sleeping it off. I can drive for a bit too if you want. Give you a break."

"That would be nice, thank you."

I smiled, pleased that he was ready to let me help out.

"Where in New Mexico were you planning to stay?" I asked, looking down at my list of things that we needed. It would be best to stop in a big city with a Walmart or a decent grocery store.

"It's a little out of the way— a couple of hours—but I was planning to go up to Taos. From what I've researched, it's beautiful up there, and I thought we could go check out the Rio Grande Gorge. It's the tenth highest bridge in the US and sits six hundred feet above the Rio Grande river. They have boat tours that I thought about signing up for if you girls are interested. We can rent a boat and hang out in the calm part of the river, or we can do the tour, which includes white water rafting."

"Do you think Lily can handle that?" I asked, feeling a little nervous and uneasy about it.

"They say that it's fine for children six years and older, but I'll admit, I feel a little nervous about it myself."

"Well, we can always decide once we get there," I sighed heavily, feeling the weight of responsibility sitting square on my shoulders. Lily wasn't my child, but that didn't stop me from wanting to protect her.

"Are we going to stay in the motorhome tonight?" I asked, going back to planning dinner.

"I was thinking about it if that works for you? I didn't rent a hotel and don't know if we could get one with this late of notice...." His voice trailed off.

"No, that's perfect. Sorry, I wasn't suggesting that we get one. I wanted to make dinner tonight, so I was checking to make sure we weren't going to be on the go again."

He nodded his head in understanding as he pulled off at the turn to the Grand Canyon.

"I want to at least see it before we pass by. Maybe we can stop by again on our way back home when Lily is feeling better?"

"I'm sure she would like that." I looked out the window, excited and anxious to get out and see it. I had never been to the Grand Canyon before, and it was one of the few things on my bucket list.

"Do you want me to go wake Lily up?" I asked as John found a parking spot.

"Sure, I think she should see this."

I unbuckled and got up, surprised to find that Lily had just woken up.

"Where are we?" she asked sleepily, running a hand over her face.

"The Grand Canyon," I said, sitting down next to her on the edge of the bed. "How are you feeling?"

"I still don't feel well," she said sadly.

"Do you want to get out and go look at it before we get back on the road again?"

She nodded and scooted off of the bed as I got up. We walked outside to join John, the heat immediately pounding down on us. It was barely ten o'clock in the morning, and it felt like it was easily over a hundred degrees outside already.

We walked over to where a crowd of people were standing, and I felt myself reaching over to grab Lily's hand. She wasn't a small child, but I had this immediate fear when I saw the steep edges and sharp drop-offs just below the railing. Either she didn't feel good enough to care, or it just didn't bother her that I was holding her hand. We made our way to the railing and stopped. The view was breathtaking and unlike anything that I had ever seen before.

The canyon was painted in shades of red and orange with purple highlights depending on where the sun was beating down on the rocks and trees. I leaned forward slightly, one hand holding onto the rail while the other held onto Lily. My stomach dropped as I looked down, the ground beneath us barely extending a few inches past the railing. There was a sharp drop that would be certain death if this railing wasn't in place, and someone took one wrong step.

I pulled back, feeling John's eyes on me, filling with a hint of curiosity and concern.

My heart was racing, the blood rushing loudly in my ears. I wasn't a daredevil and didn't enjoy living life on the edge, but there was something about the adrenaline coursing through me that made me want to do it again. I pulled in a slow and steady breath before I leaned forward again, feeling the same rush that I had a few minutes ago. This time though, it was different. Instead of the fear overruling everything, it was the tingle in my body as I flirted with danger.

"Can I go back to the motorhome now?" Lily asked, looking up at John as she let go of my hand.

"Sure, sweetie." He squinted his eyes and studied her face before lifting a hand to her forehead. "You feel a little warm. Are you still not feeling well?"

She shook her head no, not having the energy to answer him.

"Well then, let's get you back inside so you can rest."

I took one last opportunity to lean forward and face my fear as I stared into the vast darkness beneath me before turning and walking back with John and Lily.

Once inside, I asked John to give us a few minutes for her to get comfortable so she could rest. He studied the map, making sure he planned the stops that he wanted to make on the way. According to Google maps on his phone it was at least an eight-hour drive to Taos.

Lily changed into her pajamas and laid down in the bed. I pulled the curtains closed around her and hung up a few towels to further block the light from her. She had already fallen asleep by the time I was done, so I quietly climbed off of the bed and pulled the covers up around her.

I did a quick check on Sammy as he hung out in the sink, still living his best life. I was honestly surprised that he was still alive, but thankful, nonetheless. I had checked online and found that he should be fine without needing his tank cleaned for two weeks. By that time, we should be in New Jersey, and it would be easy to do at Charlotte's parent's house.

I grabbed a couple of bottles of water from the fridge and took them up front, setting them in the cup holders.

"Do you want me to drive now or later?" I asked, taking a swig of water.

John turned to look, smiling when we saw me.

"Which do you prefer?"

"It doesn't matter to me."

"Well, I was planning to head to Albuquerque and stop there. It's about six and a half hours from here. That's the next big city that we'll hit before Taos, which isn't a big city by any means. That will put us there around dinner time, and if you don't feel like cooking tonight, we can always stop and eat while we're there. It's only two and a half hours to Taos from there."

"How about I take this stretch and get us to Albuquerque, then you can take the last one to Taos?" I offered.

"Sounds like a plan." He smiled and got out of the driver's seat. "Are you getting hungry? It's barely ten-thirty, but I don't know if there are many places to stop for food once we leave here."

"I'm not, but we can grab some stuff at the gas station when we fill up if that works for you?"

"Deal."

I smiled and climbed into the driver's seat, feeling on top of the world.

Twenty

While I tried to stay focused at the gas station and *not* buy junk food, it seemed to make its way back into the motorhome with us anyway. I had grabbed a handful of coffee drinks and a bag of ice that I was able to shove into the small freezer portion of the refrigerator. There was a paper bag sitting in the middle console, filled with bags of mixed nuts, a couple of granola bars, and a package of chocolate donuts. Those were for John, not me.

The drive went by quickly, with only a few delays from construction at the Arizona-New Mexico border. Otherwise, it was fairly easy and light traffic through to Albuquerque. I followed John's directions and got off on one of the first few exits. A few minutes later, we were in the parking lot of a very busy Walmart.

"Do you want to wake Lily and we can all go shopping? Or do you want me to go grab what I need, and then you can go grab what you need?" I asked, turning in my seat to look at him. It had been a long ride, and I imagined that he wanted to stretch his legs as much as I did.

"We can make separate trips. I don't want to wake her if we don't have to. She must not be feeling well if she's slept the entire day," he noted.

"I can look for some Gatorade and medicine if we need it?" I offered, unsure of what to get since I didn't know what symptoms she had other than a stomachache and fatigue.

I heard movement in the back and turned to see Lily getting up.

"You okay, sweetie?" I asked, noticing the look of concern on her face.

John turned, his face immediately catching the tone in my voice.

"What's wrong?" John questioned when she looked down at the bedding in horror.

"I'm… bleeding," she whispered, looking up at me with fear in her eyes.

I felt a sigh of relief, knowing exactly what was going on and why she hadn't been feeling well.

"Bleeding? Do we need to get to a hospital?"

I could hear the panic in his tone, knowing that he was already starting to freak out as he got up and starting walking back to her. I got up and followed, patting him gently on the back.

"She's fine. We don't need to go to the hospital," I assured him gently, trying to pull him back some so Lily didn't get even more embarrassed or scared.

"She said that she's bleeding—what if she has internal bleeding or a hemorrhage that—"

I raised my eyebrows and pinned him with a look waiting for him to stop. He snapped his mouth shut, it finally dawning on him what was happening. I could see the thoughts running through his head as he tried to figure out what he needed to do.

"Hey, why don't you go inside and get started on the list?" I suggested, reaching over to grab the notepad from the table. I tore the top sheet of paper off and shoved it into his chest. When he tried to object, I gave him another look and pushed harder.

"But—"

"We'll meet you inside in a few minutes," I said quickly as he stepped backward down the steps and bumped into the door.

"Okay," he sighed and gave in, turning around and closing the door behind him.

Once we were alone, I walked over and sat down on the edge of the bed beside Lily.

"Am I going to die, Aunt Emma?" she asked quietly.

"No, honey," I shook my head and kept from laughing. I knew that she was worried, and that Charlotte likely hadn't spent much time talking to her about this, given how young she was. "You're going to be just fine, sweetie."

"What's wrong with me?"

"Nothing. You're becoming a woman." I looked at her with a sense of pride that I was the one who was getting to share this moment with her. To teach her the things that she needed to know and guide her on this journey.

"I am?"

I nodded.

"Yes, ma'am. You just got your first period."

"Is that why my stomach has been hurting and cramping so much?"

I nodded again, this time more sympathetically. I should have considered this earlier when she was complaining about having a stomachache.

"Those are cramps. And they stink, but we can get you some medicine to help make them feel a little better."

"Okay," she said, dropping her hands into her lap.

"Do you have any questions about it?" I asked carefully, trying not to overwhelm her. "I don't know how much your mom talked to you about it, but if you have questions, you can always ask me."

"She covered the basics but said that I would probably be older when I got mine."

"Everyone starts at a different age," I assured her, remembering that Charlotte didn't get hers until she was almost fourteen. "I got mine at your age."

"You did?" Her eyes widened in surprise.

"It was actually on my first day of school, in sixth grade."

"That had to be rough," she giggled.

"It was," I sighed. I didn't bother to mention that I had just lost my parents. Thankfully, my aunt stepped up right away and taught me how to take care of myself and explained what was happening in my body. It was one of the rare few times that I had been able to help Charlotte with something when she got hers a few years later.

We sat in silence for a few minutes, and once I was sure that she didn't have any questions, I helped her get cleaned up and offered her a panty liner that I had found in my bigger purse. We went into the store and made our way to the feminine hygiene section to get the rest of the supplies that she would be needing. I stocked up on pads and panty liners, explaining the different options based on how heavy her flow was. We bypassed tampons when I realized that I wasn't any more comfortable talking about them than she was hearing about them.

I made sure to grab a couple of bottles of Tylenol and some Midol. I also grabbed a few heating pads of different sizes, one for her stomach to help with the cramps, and the other was a full-length one for your back that plugged in.

We found John while we were shopping in the clothes section. I wanted to make sure that she had enough underwear to wear without having to worry if she accidentally leaked. I had just tossed a pack into the basket we were using when John glanced down at its contents and grimaced. Lily was looking at pajamas and out of earshot.

"It's not as bad as you think it is," I said playfully, adding another pack of underwear to the cart. We would have to find a laundry mat soon so I could wash my clothes before I ran out; why not stock up for Lily too?

"Isn't she too young for this?" he whispered, pointing to the cart.

"No," I shook my head. "I was her age when I got mine. It's just her body being ready." I shrugged and pulled my mouth to the side.

"*I'm* not ready," he groaned.

"*You* don't have to do anything but be supportive and buy her the stuff that she needs. She has the truly hard part in all of this."

He raised a brow and considered what I was saying.

"Her body is going through so many changes right now,

and she doesn't know what they are. You can help her through it by *not* acting like this is the end of the world. It's just a period."

He flinched at the word, and I laughed.

"What else does she need?" he asked, calmer this time.

"Some loose shorts might be nice. Nothing too tight on her tummy."

"Okay, add some clothes for her, and we'll stop to do laundry soon."

I nodded and pressed my lips together, trying to fight the laughter that threatened to spill over at how uncomfortable he was with all of this.

"I'm going to the sporting goods section. I'll meet up with you guys in a little bit," he said, his voice suddenly a little deeper. I rolled my eyes at the macho attempt to try to be manlier and not have to hear about his daughter's period.

I helped Lily find more clothes to wear, as well as a cute makeup bag that she could store all of her stuff in, so she didn't have to be embarrassed with having it sit out on display in the bathroom. We wandered over to the women's clothing, and I found a couple of clearance racks with tank tops and loose shorts. I piled some into the cart and smiled, knowing that I would love to be a little more comfortable on the long car rides than I had been.

Twenty minutes later, we found John looking at inflatable rafts. I pulled my brows together, wondering what in the world he was going to do with this giant inflatable boat raft when it dawned on me that it was for the river ride in Taos tomorrow. I smiled and nodded, loving the idea that he had. I was about to point out that we didn't have an air compressor or anything to inflate it.

"Is that going to be big enough?" I asked. "And how are you going to blow it up?"

"It says right here, it can fit three people, up to four hundred pounds. And it comes with a pump!"

I felt the excitement radiating from him and smiled. I glanced down at my cart, eyeing the new bikini that I had bought to wear tomorrow. Usually, I stuck to one-piece swimsuits, but something about this trip had me wanting to live on the edge and try new things, even if that meant flaunting my body for everyone to see in a two-piece.

We wrapped up the trip and grabbed a few more snacks— and a giant bag of assorted chocolate candy bars for Lily and made our way to the register. It was already getting late, and we still had to figure out dinner before we got back on the road to drive the last few hours to Taos.

"Is there anything you girls feel like for dinner?" John asked as if reading my mind again. It was eerily creepy how he could do that lately.

"I feel like a giant cheeseburger, fries, and a chocolate milkshake," Lily said, looking up at him with her bright blue eyes.

He tried to fight the smile from pulling across his face but failed.

"And so, it starts," he mumbled, running a hand down his face.

We paid for our stuff and packed everything inside the

motorhome where Lily and I were going to sort through things once we were back on the road. John made a quick stop at McDonald's for dinner, and then we were on our way again. *So much for eating healthy tonight,* I thought as I took a bite of my quarter pounder and wiped the ketchup from the corner of my mouth with a napkin.

There was always tomorrow, and I had made sure that we bought plenty of stuff to make breakfast, lunch, and dinner for the next few days. I had even stocked up on juice, tea, and a six-pack of Coors, knowing that it was John's favorite. After we finished eating, Lily took all the tags off her new clothes and added them to the laundry basket that I had purchased to keep all of the dirty clothes in. It was way too hard to know what was clean and what was dirty when everything was living in our suitcases. There wasn't much room for the basket, but I made it fit in the small space under the bathroom sink, so it was out of the way.

I helped Lily change the sheets on the bed with the new ones that we had bought. I tossed the other ones into the hamper and made a note to soak them in cold water later to get the blood stain out of them. Once we finished, I stopped and gave Sammy some fresh food before I got to work reorganizing the fridge and the cabinets next to it. Everything was packed full, but I was excited to cook again, which was odd because I had never enjoyed it much before I started cooking for John and Lily. It was amazing the things that I suddenly loved now that they were a huge part of my life.

Twenty One

By the time we made it to Taos last night, it was already after ten o'clock. John found a safe place for us to stay close to the river, which was nice. Lily was already asleep by the time we got there, but I felt energetic and not ready for bed.

John got out and stretched his legs. I debated whether to follow him or not because I didn't know if he wanted time to himself or preferred the company. After fifteen minutes, I decided to grab a couple of beers and went out to join him. While at the store, he bought some folding camping chairs, which now came in handy.

He reached into the back, where our luggage was kept and grabbed two for us to sit on. Once the chairs were situated, I handed him a beer and sat down while he dug into his pocket for his keys, looking for the bottle opener he'd had since college.

"It's a beautiful night," I said, looking up and admiring the clear sky. When I was little, I loved to lay outside and look at the stars, waiting to see if I could spot a shooting star, but the city lights always clouded the skies and made it near impossible.

"Yeah, it is," he replied, taking a drink.

I lifted my bottle to my lips and parted them, the cold liquid tickling my tongue before sliding down my throat.

"Thanks for taking care of Lily earlier," he said, turning to look at me. "As you can tell, I'm a little lost in that area."

"It's not a problem. I don't mind."

"I know that she appreciates it too. It's hard for her not having her mom here to help her with these things, but I'm glad that she has you. She needs a woman in her life to teach her the things that I can't."

I debated for a moment whether I should talk to him about what Lily had told me the other day about him finding someone new. Now felt like as good of a time as any, and we were already on the subject, so I figured I might as well go for it.

"Do you plan to start dating again?" I asked nervously, looking forward, so I didn't have to look at him when he answered.

He paused and waited before responding as if he was looking for the right answer.

"I don't know. There's a lot that goes into making that decision, and it won't be an easy one."

"Because of Lily?"

"For starters."

Now it was my turn to pause and question what he meant by that.

"Sorry, I shouldn't have pried," I apologized. "Lily had talked to me about it the other day, and I didn't know if she had talked to you yet."

He turned to look at me, surprised. He took a long drink and sighed.

"Does she not want me to date?" he asked, taking another drink. I felt the need for the same liquid courage, so I took one before I answered.

"She has a friend at school that lost her dad before Christmas. Her mom recently started dating someone, and her friend said she's the happiest she's ever been. Lily wants you to date someone, so you'll be happy again, but she's afraid that it means that whoever you date will replace Charlotte."

"It won't," he snapped.

"That's what I told her," I said quickly, feeling mildly attacked. "I told her that I imagined that you would talk to her *before* you started dating anyone, and I assured her that no one will ever replace her mom."

John got up and walked away, the door to the motorhome closing behind him. I leaned back against the soft fabric of the chair and closed my eyes. I was sitting outside, by myself, in the middle of the woods. All I needed now was for a bear to come and attack me and put me out of my misery.

Why had I decided to talk to John about this tonight? I should have known that he wouldn't take it well, given how he reacted to his daughter starting her period. He was under a lot of stress and pressure, and it wasn't fair for me to add this to his plate. It wasn't like he had started bringing someone new around, and we had to worry about him dating anyone. I had just taken a made-up problem and blew it up into a real one that he didn't need.

A few minutes later, he came back, closing the door quietly behind him. He stopped in front of my chair and popped the top off a new beer, handing it to me without speaking. I took it and set it down on my thigh, holding it with my left hand while I finished the other one with my right. I set the empty bottle down between us, moving the new one to my other leg.

"I didn't mean to upset you," I said quietly. "I shouldn't have said anything. It wasn't my place."

"It's fine," he replied coolly, taking a sip. "It's been on my mind a lot lately, and I was hoping that I had a little while longer before I had to really think about it. I had no idea that Lily would start worrying about whether I was going to start dating again."

"I don't think she thought about it until her friend brought it up."

"It's only been two months since she died. I haven't been thinking about other women—not even once. But dating, that's a different beast, and it's messing with my head," he admitted. "How do you know when is the right time to move on? It's not like I'm waiting for Charlotte to come back, but when will I stop feeling this guilt every time I think about the future and try to picture my life with someone new in it? Will I ever get there?"

I could feel the pain in his words. I had no idea how to answer him because I had never experienced a loss like this before.

"I don't know," I whispered sadly. "I guess when you find someone that you know you want to spend the rest of your life with again, you'll just know. It'll feel right for you and Lily. It's okay to move on, John. No one is going to judge you for doing that."

I swallowed, trying to push past the lump in my throat when I realized that I was telling a huge lie to him and myself. I wasn't going to judge him for moving on and finding someone else, but it stung in my heart to think that she would replace me. Not that we were dating, but she would be the one to help Lily with the new things that came up in her life. She would be the one to make them dinner and worry about whether they were eating too much junk food. She would do all of the things that I had come to enjoy doing for them these past few months.

We finished our second beers and sat quietly. It was a heavy subject that neither of us wanted to push any further. I got the feeling that maybe he was already interested in someone else by the way he talked about it, but I wasn't stupid enough to ask. Doing so would undoubtedly ruin the rest of the trip for me when it turned into a ticking bomb, waiting to explode as I was replaced by a new woman in their lives.

"It's getting late. We should probably turn in soon," he said, breaking the silence.

I nodded and stood up, turning to pick up the empty bottles at the same time he did. We bonked heads and laughed, rubbing the sore spot where we had collided. I went to move out of the way and lost my balance when I stepped onto an uneven part of the gravel beneath me. John reached out and grabbed me, his arms wrapped around my waist as he caught me.

I looked up, my breathing quickening from his touch. I could feel the heat of his body so close to mine, the smell of his shampoo, still fresh from this morning. His fingers dug lightly into my hips as he stared at me, fighting something in his mind. I was about to make some sort of sarcastic remark about how clumsy I was when his head dipped low, and his mouth covered mine.

I gasped at the contact, but then my fingers reached up and ran through his hair, pulling him closer to me as we kissed. He pulled me tighter, and my body pressed up against his muscular chest. I wanted more, to get lost in this moment, but as quickly as it started, it stopped.

He pulled back, running a hand over his face as he turned away. I wiped my mouth, my lips slightly swollen in the best way. I was still trying to catch my breath while I processed what had just happened.

"I'm sorry, Emma," he said, his tone thick with disdain and regret. "That shouldn't have happened."

He bent down and picked up the empty bottles, carrying them between his fingers as he walked over to the trash can and threw them away. I took the opportunity to sneak inside and put some distance between us. When he came back a few minutes later, I was already up on the bed above the seats since Lily was still in mine, with my back turned to him.

I heard the door close, followed by the locks clicking in place. He quietly pushed the table down and set up his bed, not saying another word to me while I pretended to be asleep.

The next morning, I woke up in a crabby mood but tried to put everything behind me. I wanted to blame it on the beer last night but knew that two beers weren't enough to make John lose his mind and kiss me out of nowhere. I also didn't want to beat myself up about it any longer than I needed to, so I went about making breakfast as if nothing had happened.

Lily got up and used the restroom, making me a little sad

that I no longer had her as an excuse for avoiding talking to him. The second she closed the door he stood and walked the short distance to where I was standing by the stove.

"About last night," he started.

"Don't—" I held my hand up to stop him. "We're fine. Just let it go."

"Emma, will you please let me explain?"

The door opened, and Lily walked out, saving me once again.

"Breakfast is ready!" I said cheerfully, transferring the bacon to a plate lined with a paper towel to capture the excess grease. I moved the food to the plates and set them on the table. I gave Lily a quick kiss on her head before grabbing a piece of bacon and walking to the bed.

I didn't bother to sit and have breakfast with them. It was pointless with my stomach still tied in knots and the nausea that threatened to ruin my day. Instead, I dug through the pile of clothes that I had bought yesterday and found the bikini. I grabbed it and a change of clothes and went to the bathroom to get ready.

I took a quick shower and shaved my legs. I didn't bother to put makeup on since we were planning to be on the river, and it would just come right off. So instead, I applied a heavy layer of sunscreen and looked down at the bright pink swimsuit that I was certain would draw attention to me. Unfortunately, the only mirror was above the sink *outside* the bathroom, and John would see me before I could get to it.

I pulled my shoulders back and tried to rock the confidence

of a toddler having a dance party with no music. I pulled on the cotton shorts and tank top that I had bought yesterday and opened the door, not bothering to look at them. I reached into the cabinet above the bed and pulled out my purse, fishing my sunglasses out of it before grabbing one of the beach towels we had bought yesterday as well.

"I'll see you guys outside when you're done," I said passively and walked down the steps, letting the screen door slam behind me.

There were a handful of people who had joined us since last night, most of the space around us filling up quickly. I walked down the warm sand, thankful that it was still early in the day and not blistering hot and found a spot to lay my towel down. I spotted a group of guys a few feet over who looked like they were getting ready for some wild adventure. I looked at the water, noticing how calm it was, and wondered what they could be so excited and pumped up about, given there didn't seem to be any excitement nearby.

I pulled my tank top off and shimmied out of my shorts, kicking them to the side as I slid my sunglasses up higher on my nose. Nervously, I dipped my fingers under the thin string that was responsible for keeping my bikini bottoms on and adjusted it. This earned the whistles and a few catcalls from the guys who had now taken notice of me.

Feeling the confidence that I needed, I laid down and closed my eyes.

The warm sun kissed my skin, melting me into a pool of oblivion when I heard a low voice directly above me.

"What the hell do you think you're doing?"

I lifted my hand and shielded my face as I opened my eyes. John stood over me, his hands on his hips with a scowl on his face.

"I'm sunbathing," I replied dryly. "Which would work better if you weren't towering over me, blocking the sun."

"You realize that there's a group of guys over there, staring at you—right?"

I turned my head in their direction and smiled. I knew they were still there because I had heard them the entire time I'd been out here. I gave a quick little wave before turning away and lifting my chin to the sun.

"I know that you're mad at me about last night," he stammered angrily. "If you would just let me explain—"

"John, you said that it was a mistake. I took you at your word. What else is there to discuss? I'm single. You're single. We're not dating—so why do you care if other guys check me out?" I pushed up off the towel and brushed the sand away. My relaxing soak in the sun was quickly getting ruined by his misplaced jealousy.

"You're impossible," he mumbled under his breath.

"I'm not the one making things difficult. You are." I poked him in the chest with my finger, surprised to see him wearing a new tank top and swim trunks. At that moment, Lily came out of the motorhome and joined us.

"Are you ready to go?!" she asked excitedly.

"Where are we going?" I tilted my head, confused. I thought the plan was to hang out on the river today.

"On the boat!! Daddy got us a big boat so we can float

on the river and check off another body of water from the bucket list. After this, all we have left is the ocean."

"I think we'll need a bigger boat for that than the one your dad got," I joked, returning her smile.

"Yeah, there's no way I'm going out in the ocean in *that* thing," she added, looking up at her dad with arms crossed.

"What? It's a great boat! Not for the ocean, but I bet you're going to have an amazing time on it today."

"I can't wait!" She bounced excitedly, waiting while he grabbed it from the motorhome and unpacked it. He was busy pumping it full of air while Lily and I talked about how she was feeling. Some Midol and a hearty breakfast had her feeling better and ready for another adventure.

As John continued working on the inflatable boat, I took my towel back to the motorhome and made sure everything was locked and secure. When I went back, they were waiting for me with the giant boat and two sets of oars. I still doubted that this thing was going to hold all three of us, but I was taking John's word. Plus, I had read the side of the box to confirm that he wasn't lying.

We pushed it into the water, and John held it steady while Lily and I climbed in. Once we were settled with me on one end and her in the middle, John climbed into the other end and almost tipped us over.

We all laughed hysterically while trying to move our bodies quickly to keep it from flipping. Finally, a few minutes later, the water around us was calm and the boat steady. I handed John a set of oars and got mine ready as we began moving. We didn't go too far, and luckily the water was calm, even with the abundance of other rafts in the water. Lily loved every minute of it, and for once, we just relaxed and played in the river with no worries in the world as John and I continued to pretend that something major hadn't shifted between us last night.

Twenty Two

It was hard to believe that we had almost been gone a week, and this time last week, Lily was celebrating her last day of school. So much had happened as we went on so many fun adventures already. Today was another travel day as we headed to Fort Worth, Texas, from Taos. Since John insisted on driving, I pretended that I had a tension headache and spent most of my time in bed, as far away as possible.

I was being childish and petty about the kiss the other night, and I knew it. It wasn't something that I had expected to happen, but I was confused about why it did in the first place. John was an attractive man, and under different circumstances, I would probably consider him date-worthy material. But given that he was my best friend's husband, that automatically put him off-limits. The part that was really eating away at me was *how* I had felt when he kissed me. It didn't *feel* like the mistake it should have been. It felt different but in a good way.

I realized that part of my childish reaction toward John didn't have much to do with him but rather with my frustration at myself. I should have stopped it from happening in the first place. Instead, I found myself pulling him closer to me and regretting the moment that it stopped. I was a terrible person and, even worse—a terrible friend. If Charlotte were still alive, she would immediately turn her back on me and never speak to me again if she knew what I had done. But then again, if she was still alive, I could guarantee that it wouldn't have happened in the first place.

She would be here with them on this vacation, not me. She would be helping Lily with her first period, not me. She would be kissing her husband under a beautiful starlit sky, not me. There was so much that she should be here doing, and it killed me that she wasn't. Survivor's guilt was a real thing, and I hated that I had all the experiences that she never got to have. It wasn't fair, and regardless of how much everyone tried to convince me that it wasn't, it was still my fault.

I rolled over on my side, letting the sun warm my face through the small crack in the curtains. It felt good just to lay down and not have to worry about anything. Maybe it gave me too much time to think and make a mess out of things in my head, but then again, maybe that was the real problem—I *hadn't* been thinking lately.

Lily sat up front in the passenger seat next to John. She was excited to be his co-captain today and assured him that she was up for the task, even after he told her that it would be close to a ten-hour drive. She had packed a picnic basket full of snacks and bottles of water, which she then placed on the floor behind them, so she had quick access if they needed anything. I giggled at how serious she was taking her role, promising to never take her eyes off the road.

I closed my eyes, not tired enough to sleep, and listened to their conversation.

"Daddy, can you tell me the story again?" Lily asked.

"Which one?"

"The one about how you and mama met. It's my favorite."

I smiled, knowing how much she loved hearing it. I had heard it at least a dozen times over the past few weeks while I had been staying there.

"Well, your mom and I met at a party. She was there with

Emma and kept trying to set her and me up, pretending that she wasn't interested in me. She avoided me all night, and every now and then, I would catch her checking me out. I tried to make small talk, but she wasn't interested. Finally, I offered her snacks and a drink, but she had already beat me to it. She was impossible to win over!"

"So, what did you do?" Lily asked with a giggle, already knowing what was coming next.

"I won her over with my incredible dance moves!"

Lily started laughing. Full belly laughter filled the motorhome with the most beautiful sound. I smiled and turned my head into my pillow, trying to keep the tears from falling. I knew the story after hearing it plenty of times, but this was the first time that I had heard him mention that Charlotte had tried to set me up with John. I was thankful that Lily seemed to miss that part.

"No, daddy, no!" She laughed even harder, and I looked up to see him dancing at the steering wheel, his weird jerky movements making her giggle even more.

"Hey, these moves are what got your mom to agree to go out on a date with me," he laughed. "That and the fact that Emma convinced her to go on a double date with her because she was nervous about going on a date with this guy she really liked. He was a loser, by the way," he added. I didn't have to look up to feel his eyes on me from the rearview mirror.

"He was *your* best friend," I blurted out, getting up out of bed. There was no way that I was going to let him off that easy. I walked over and opened the fridge, looking for something to make Lily for lunch.

"*Was* my best friend. I grew up quickly after that and stopped being his friend," John said matter-of-factly.

"Well, I still blame him and *you* for my lackluster love life since then. If we hadn't met you at that party, I wouldn't have met him, and I would probably be with the love of my life by now," I groaned dramatically.

"Wait—did you say that *mom* tried to set you up with *Aunt Emma*?" Lily asked, looking between us.

"She did," I confirmed, pulling out a loaf of bread, some lunch meat, and the sliced cheese. "But in all fairness, your mom would have offered up a vacuum if she thought your dad would go for it."

John's eyes darted up to catch mine in the mirror. There was something dark in them, something that I hadn't seen before. I turned my attention away and opened the fridge. I grabbed the head of lettuce and a tomato, then temporarily moved Sammy to the side so I could wash them. He swam around in fast circles, in what I assumed was his version of yelling at me for disrupting his home. I get it, Sammy, I get it.

"So, if it hadn't worked out the way that it did, does that mean that Aunt Emma could have been my mommy instead?" she asked innocently.

I dropped the knife that I was using to cut the tomato and hung my head. The air passed through my lips quickly as it rushed out of me.

"No, sweetie," John assured her. "It doesn't work that way, my love. You're who you are because your part me and part your mommy. God decides how we get here and who our parents will be. Nothing can or will ever change that."

"Okay," she said quietly. "But just for the record, I would have wanted Emma for my mommy if I didn't already have a mommy."

I finished slicing the tomato and turned around to set the plate on the table. I could feel John's eyes on me again, piercing me with an 'I told you so' look. I quickly went to work making the sandwiches, desperate for them to have something else to keep their mouths occupied so this conversation could be over.

After lunch, we stopped for a quick break so John could stretch his legs. Or at least that's what we had told Lily when we stopped at the border of New Mexico and Texas and pulled over on the side of the road. Lily and I got out with John, standing off to the side away from traffic, just in case anyone passed by us.

"Okay, Lily, are you ready?" John asked excitedly.

"For what?" She scrunched her cute little button nose in confusion.

"Another bucket list item!"

"What?!" She looked between us, waiting to hear what it was.

I grabbed the piece of paper that I had written it down on after John and I had talked about it the other night. It was the perfect moment for this one.

"Just when you've crossed the line, take a step back and go back in time," I read, looking up at her when I was finished.

John was standing at the sign in the dirt, looking over where the "Welcome to Texas" sign was standing across the road. He moved over some and motioned for us to join him.

"Okay, are you ready?" he asked as we stood on the New Mexico side. "Three. Two. One—Jump!"

We jumped over the line that he had drawn in the dirt with a stick.

"Alright, now we're in Texas, so we're in a new time zone," he said, looking down at Lily. "BUT, we can go *back in time* by jumping back to New Mexico. Ready?"

She nodded her head, clearly enjoying it as we all jumped back to the other side.

"Now you can say that you've gone back in time!" John exclaimed happily.

Lily smiled and wrapped her arms around his waist, hugging him, before she came over and hugged me. It was something fun and silly, but I could see how much it meant to her. We climbed back into the motorhome, ready to get back on the road again.

Since I had spent the morning resting, I offered to drive the last five hours to Fort Worth. John agreed and decided to lay down for most of the trip, while Lily kept me company up front. We laughed and talked about the journey so far and what our favorite parts were. While I had loved the dinner cruise on the lake for my birthday, Lily loved that I had decided to come with them. That single sentence wrapped itself around my heart so tightly that I felt like I couldn't breathe.

We made it to Fort Worth shortly after eight o'clock and found our hotel. John went inside to check in while Lily and I packed up the stuff that we needed. It wasn't going to be a long stay, just tonight and tomorrow night, and then we would be heading to Little Rock, Arkansas, on Thursday. I grabbed my suitcase and pulled a few outfits out, along with a pair of pajamas and my toiletry bag. We had been so busy that I hadn't had a chance to read much and debated whether to take my Kindle to the room with me or if it was better to leave it in my suitcase in the motorhome.

Lily had her bag packed and was going through the snack options when John came back to let us know our rooms were ready. I went ahead and tossed the Kindle into my tote bag and followed them to the rooms. We didn't have adjoining rooms this time, but they were right across the hall from each other. I thought about asking Lily if she wanted to stay with me again, but I was feeling mentally exhausted and needed some downtime.

Once inside my room, I set my bag down and went to the window, looking at the beautiful view around me. We were staying by Sundance Square—less than a mile away, and I had the perfect view from my eleventh-story room. I was excited to have the day tomorrow, to go shopping again, even though Lord knows that I didn't need to spend any more money. I found that it was a really fun experience for Lily and me, and I cherished those moments with her.

My head was still reeling from John's comment earlier about Charlotte trying to set us up at that party. I doubted that it was true and wondered if John had just said it to mess with me. Maybe his own way of trying to get back at me for the little tiff we were having. If it had really happened, Charlotte would have told me. Wouldn't she?

I decided to ignore the obsessive thoughts that were still lingering around the subject and decided to take a hot bath. A good soak would surely help at this point. My body was a little stiff and sore from the boat ride yesterday—mainly trying to fight to keep it from tipping over, as well as the long drive today.

I plugged the drain and turned the water to hot. There were a handful of sample items by the sink, so I took a look and settled on an orange blossom body wash. If I were back home, I would have added some Epsom salts and maybe a bath bomb, but I didn't think to bring any of that with me. I stripped down, tested the water to make sure it wasn't too hot, then went to the bedroom to grab my phone.

It had been a while since I had checked my email or been on social media, so I figured now was a great time to catch up. I climbed into the tub, wincing a little bit when the hot water bit at the sunburn I had on my lower back from yesterday. Once settled, I swiped my finger across the screen to unlock my phone, surprised to see a text message from John.

John: Are you okay?

I reread the message, wondering why he was asking me that. Did I not look okay? I had tried my hardest today to act as if nothing had happened the other night while I forced the memory as far out of my head as possible.

Me: I'm fine. Why?

Almost immediately, his message came through.

John: Because I know you well enough to know that you're lying.

Me: What exactly do you think that I'm lying about?

John: Lots of things. Pretending to be okay for one.

Me: It seems I'm not the only one who has been telling stories.

John: What do you mean?

Me: Why did you lie and tell Lily that Charlotte tried to set you and me up that night? That never happened.

John: I didn't lie. Charlotte did try to set us up when you were in the bathroom, right before you met Tanner.

Me: I've never heard that part of the story until now.

I couldn't help the overwhelming emotions that were bubbling up inside.

John: Charlotte was a wonderful woman, but she had plenty of secrets that she kept well-guarded.

Apparently.

John: Lily is settled in for the night. She said she wants to go shopping tomorrow if you're up for it.

Me: It's a date!

I froze when I saw the words displayed on the screen after hitting send without thinking it through.

Me: I mean with Lily. It's a date with Lily.

John: I knew what you meant.

John: Call if you need anything. We'll be ready to go by eight.

Me: Okay.

I set my phone down on the towel by the edge of the tub and closed my eyes. Things were getting so awkward between us, and I hated it.

The following day, I was up earlier than expected. I jumped in the shower and got ready, taking the time to do my hair and makeup even though I knew it was pointless with the Texas humidity. I used the waterproof eyeliner and mascara that I had picked up the other night at Walmart, hoping they would hold up today. My hair dried quickly, allowing me to skip the blow drier. I combed through it, using the skinny point at the end of the comb to part it to the side before using my fingers to style it.

It was barely seven o'clock which left an hour before they would be ready. So, I made some coffee in the small pot by the sink and sat on my bed, ready to read for an hour when my phone rang.

My stomach sank when I saw the name on the caller ID. BayView Advertising.

"Hello," my voice squeaked into the phone, my nerves getting the better of me.

"May I speak with Emma Monroe?"

"Yes, speaking."

I held my breath, biting my fingernail, wondering why on earth they could be calling me.

"Hi, Emma. My name is Meghan, and I'm calling from BayView Advertising."

I swallowed hard, unable to say anything.

"The reason for my call is to see if you're still interested in a creative marketing position with our company."

"Um, yes, I am." I had no idea what else to say. It was my dream job that I had wanted for so long, but I knew that I had already committed my time to John by helping with Lily.

"There's been a change internally, and our current director has decided to retire in August. Because this is such an important position within our company, we have decided to start interviewing in July. Would you like me to add your name to the candidates that we will be reaching out to schedule, starting next week?"

There was no way that this was happening. I had to be dreaming it. It was like the universe was playing some sort of sick joke on me, offering this opportunity after I had already given up and moved on.

"Yes, please."

I covered my face with my hand, feeling terrible for it. It felt like I was betraying John and Lily by doing this. I had to remind myself that it was just an interview. It didn't mean that I would get the job. I was likely going up against a handful of more qualified people, so there shouldn't be anything to stress over. I could go to the interview and say that I tried.

"Wonderful. Alexis, our recruiting director, will be in touch next week to get you on the schedule."

"Thank you."

The phone went silent, and I was left sitting there in a numbed state of confusion.

By the time John and Lily were ready, I had tried to push the call out of my mind and enjoy my time with them. I had sat on my bed and wrote down the rest of the stops that John and I had discussed. We were leaving tomorrow morning and heading to Arkansas, and then after that, we would make a stop in Tennessee. Saturday, we would travel from Tennessee to Virginia and stay the night, and then Sunday, we would hit the last few states before we made it to New Jersey. I could finish the first half of the trip, spend a few days with Charlotte's parents and finish the last few things on the bucket list in New Jersey before catching a flight back to San Francisco.

I felt like a jerk for cutting the trip short, but I was also starting to worry that maybe the lines were blending too much now, and I didn't know what would happen when they were completely gone. I loved the bond and the relationship that I had with Lily, but when she said that she would want me to be her mom if Charlotte wasn't, I knew that we were already crossing into new territory. Add in the kiss between John and me the other night, and things were getting even messier.

"Do you have any arm left?" John joked, laughing at the string of bags lining mine and Lily's arms.

"In all fairness, they didn't pack them very full. That's why it looks like there's more than there is," I grunted, shifting my weight to try to get the bags to slide back up.

"Give me those," he sighed, reaching over and taking the bulk of the bags from my arm.

"I got them, thank you. Help Lily. She needs it more."

He quickly narrowed his eyes at me before turning to her and taking the three bags that she had.

"Okay, now give me yours," he said, turning to me and waiting.

I rolled my eyes and gave him a smug smile while I reluctantly handed him a few.

"I can carry the rest," I assured him, moving them up my forearm. "Thank you," I added, not wanting to be rude when he offered to help.

We finished shopping, and John made a quick trip back up to his room to drop off our bags. Lily and I hung out on a bench, and people watched for a few minutes until he came back. I was impressed with his speed and stamina and then reminded myself that he runs for fun every chance that he gets. I've never been athletic and don't have a single bone in my body that wouldn't protest if I tried to run. My body and I have a very clear understanding that I don't run unless something is chasing me. Like a bear.

After the recommendation of a few locals, we walked over to the Fort Worth Water Gardens and cooled down for a bit under a cypress tree by the blue mediation pool. The sound of the water on the towering walls around us was so tranquil and relaxing that I could spend all day there. Lily had fun walking the steps of the active pool while I felt like a mother hen, watching to make sure she didn't slip and fall as she walked ahead of us.

By five o'clock, we were hot, tired, and sticky from the humidity, so we decided to head back to our rooms. I took a quick shower to cool off, not bothering to wash my hair or makeup since it had actually held up today. We had dinner in Sundance Square, and then John surprised Lily with another item from the bucket list.

When we pulled into Coyote Drive, Lily looked around, confused by where we were.

"Be entertained while under the stars. It's even better if it's in the car," I read out loud, answering her question. "We're at a drive-in movie theater."

Her eyes widened with surprise, followed by excitement. John found a place to park by the speaker, and once we were situated, I helped him get the camping chairs out of the back. It was a warm night, but I still grabbed a blanket from my bed for Lily to use to cuddle up with for the movie. I knew that's how she liked to watch them at home, so it just felt natural now.

John and I sat on opposite sides of her, watching the movie and eating the popcorn that he had made before it started. It helped having the motorhome, so we didn't have to go far for snacks, drinks, or a bathroom break. Once it was over, Lily yawned and climbed back into the motorhome, making her way to my bed.

We got back to the hotel, and I helped John carry their stuff up while he carried Lily, who was still asleep. It was a long and busy day, and I couldn't help but feel sad that I would soon miss all of this.

Twenty Three

We woke up Thursday morning and loaded up the motorhome before grabbing breakfast in Sundance Square. I slept terribly last night, and the weight of my decision to take the interview with BayView Advertising felt so heavy that I couldn't shake the guilt away. I knew that I needed to tell John, but I didn't know how. If I didn't get the job, then none of it would matter anyway. However, if somehow fate finally decided to take pity on me and give me this opportunity, then John would need time to find a new nanny for Lily before school started in August. Either that, or he would have to cut his hours at work back even further, which I wasn't sure he could do.

I poked at my poached eggs on my plate, not having an appetite. My mind was overwhelmed with the excitement of possibly getting everything I've ever wished for and the dread of having to walk away from everything that I had come to love.

"What's wrong?" John asked quietly, nodding to my plate full of food. I shook my head and shrugged my shoulders. There was no way to avoid him when he had that look on his face. He was going to keep pressing until he got it out of me. I already knew that. I just hoped that I could stall as long as possible.

We were sitting outside on the patio at a bistro table, enjoying the warmth before the day heated up beyond our comfort levels. We would already be back on the road, on our way to Arkansas, before that happened.

I turned my attention to Lily, who was devouring the chocolate chip pancakes on her plate, sliding the pieces around in the syrup before popping them into her mouth.

"So, Lily, what's left on the bucket list?" I asked, ignoring the way his intense glare bored into the side of my head with a heat so extreme that my brain should be fried.

"Let me see," she said around a mouthful of pancakes while she reached into her back pocket and pulled out a folded-up, worn-out piece of paper.

I cut into my sausage link, trying to force the small bite into my mouth, so it looked like I was eating.

"There are six left that we haven't done yet," she confirmed, looking over her list. There were giant checkmarks in the boxes she made beside each one that we had completed.

"Okay, let's hear what they are," I suggested, desperate to keep the attention on her and away from me.

She set her fork down, using both hands to hold the paper up in front of her.

"Keep your eye on the night sky, and you just might see one pass by."

I smiled, remembering when Charlotte had written that one down. She felt lovesick over a boy at school and was convinced that making a wish on a shooting star would make it come true.

"Shooting star," I confirmed. "We're staying in Virginia tonight, at a campground. We can sit outside and look for one if you want? The sky will be clear without any city lights nearby."

She nodded excitedly and pulled a pen out of her purse as she made a note.

"Okay, the next one is, if you are what you eat, make sure you pick something sweet."

I scrunched my nose and nibbled on my toast.

"We can see if your grandparents have a garden. Or maybe one of their neighbors?" I offered, feeling a little bit lost on that one.

She shrugged and kept on down the list, buying me the time that I needed. I noticed the tension in John's neck and hands as he clasped them together under his chin, resting his elbows on the table. Once she was finished, he was quick to take over the conversation.

"Lily, can you go inside and find our waitress. I'd like to get our check so we can get back on the road." His tone was curt, and she flinched for a second at it. I narrowed my eyes at him, giving him a dirty look for taking his anger and frustration out on her.

Lily pushed away from the table, her plate empty, as she went to find her.

"Was that really necessary?" I huffed out, turning my head to look at him.

Our backs were turned to the door that Lily had gone inside, so I had to turn around fully to make sure she had made it in. It was weird how overly protective I had gotten over her, but the thought of anything bad happening to her crushed my soul in a way that I couldn't begin to imagine.

"We need to talk, Emma, and you keep pushing me away. So yeah, I'm a little frustrated about it."

"So that means taking it out on your daughter? Real mature, John."

"I didn't mean to," he growled, the frustration ready to burst out of him. "I can apologize to her later, just like I've been trying to do with you, but you won't let me."

"Because I don't want to hear it," I snapped, immediately hating the anger in my tone. "The kiss was a mistake that should have never happened, and it's best that we just forget it."

"You guys kissed?" Lily said, suddenly standing behind us.

I whipped around in my chair, covering my mouth as my eyes nearly popped out of my head. I had no idea that she was there and didn't know how much of that conversation she had heard. She hadn't been gone that long, but then I also didn't hear her walk up on us.

"It's not what you think," John said calmly, reaching out to touch her arm.

She jerked away from him angrily, tears in her eyes as she turned and ran away.

I pushed away from the table and tossed my napkin on the plate. I grabbed my phone from the table and took off after her.

Twenty Four

The drive to Arkansas was painstakingly awkward. I had found Lily in the restaurant's bathroom, crying in the stall, and had to beg her to talk to me. She refused—which I couldn't blame her. After all, I was supposed to be helping her family, not wrecking it. We walked—in silence—to the motorhome. She climbed into the bed, not speaking to either of us.

John drove the eight hours it took for us to get to Little Rock after getting stuck in construction along the way. He didn't seem like he wanted company, and it wasn't like we could continue our conversation from earlier with Lily right there. Not that I even wanted to continue it. I wished that he had just forgotten about it and pretended like it had never happened. If he did, we wouldn't be in this mess right now. Just one more reason why I needed to remove myself from their lives and let them live happily ever after without me.

I took the time to sit down at the table and read the book I had started before we left last week. While reading was usually a stress reliever for me, I couldn't get attached to the characters, making it less enjoyable. I gave up after an hour and decided to clean up around the motorhome.

The fridge was relatively clean, though there were a few things that were almost empty and could be condensed. I worked on organizing everything that was left and made another list of things that they would need to replenish before their trip back to San Francisco. A trip they would be making without me.

I walked over and checked on Sammy, making sure he was still doing okay. He eagerly swam to the top of his tank, waiting for me to feed him. I rolled my eyes and gave in, dropping a few flakes of food in for him. I knew that Lily had already fed him this morning, so he wasn't starving, just acting like it.

My stomach grumbled, reminding me that I hadn't eaten much for breakfast and had completely missed lunch. John had stopped to grab something but I declined, still not feeling like eating. Finally, deciding that I needed to eat something, I opened the cabinet beside the fridge and found an unopened box of strawberry Pop-Tarts.

Knowing they were Lily's favorite, I gently tossed a pack on the bed beside her, giving her a soft smile before sitting down at the table. I heard the crinkle of the wrapper, knowing that she had opened them. I ate mine, looking out the window, wondering when I should break the news to them that I wasn't planning to stay long.

Meghan at BayView Advertising said that Alexis would start reaching out to the candidates next week to schedule them but that the interview wouldn't be until July. It was barely the first week in June, so I still had a few weeks before I would have to be back for the interviews. Unless something changed at the last minute, I *technically* could stay a little while longer.

But what would that do anyway? Give me more time with them before I left and ripped their worlds apart? It was a selfish thing to consider, and I hated myself for it. It was best to get back to San Francisco as quickly as possible and start looking for an apartment. Even if I didn't get the job with BayView, I still needed to give John and Lily the space they needed without having me complicate things.

I knew that John said he was planning to stay in New Jersey for a few weeks to let Lily have time with her grandparents. That meant that they would be there until the last week of June, then they would start heading back home. So, I had until July first to find a new place and prepare myself for the interview of a lifetime.

By the time we got to Little Rock, it was already dark and hard to find a campsite to stay for the night. After driving around aimlessly, John finally stumbled upon a remote site and parked the motorhome.

I got out, needing some fresh air to clear my head. A few minutes later, Lily came out and stood beside me. She looked up at the night sky, not saying a word.

Thankfully it was clear without a cloud in sight. I walked around to the back of the motorhome, where John was grabbing our luggage. I waited until he stepped to the side, then grabbed the camping chairs, setting them up in front of the door to the motorhome.

I didn't know the area and given that we got here after it was already dark, I wanted to make sure that we could get to safety quickly if an animal approached us. John closed the back door, startling me, before going inside with the bags he pulled out.

I sat down next to Lily and looked up, feeling the warmth of childhood memories floating back to me.

It was a relatively warm night, though a little too much on the humid side for my liking. I pulled at my tank top, adjusting it as I shifted in my seats. I could already feel the cotton shorts stick to my butt.

The door to the motorhome opened and closed again. John came and sat down in the empty chair beside Lily, not saying a word. We all sat there quietly, watching the night sky, looking for a shooting star to grant our wishes.

We had been sitting out there for an hour, maybe longer, when Lily started to get restless. She was about to get up when she looked off to the side and gasped. Her hand quickly reached out as she pointed at the shooting star that had flashed across the sky, gone within seconds.

I didn't have to look over to know that John's grin was stretched across his face, ear to ear. I could feel the happiness radiating from her and wondered what she had wished. Was it something silly that all kids wanted when they made a wish? Or was it the same thing that I found myself wishing for after my parents died—for one last wish?

Back then, I was convinced that if I could have just *one wish,* I could wish them back to life, and then I wouldn't ask for another wish ever again, in my whole entire life. I was desperate for a second chance and didn't realize that I had been given one until it was almost taken again.

Lily pulled in a deep breath and looked at me. There was a look of liberation on her face, and I knew that she had a lot of faith in whatever she had asked for with her wish. I winked at her and smiled. Without saying a word, she walked inside the motorhome and let the door close behind her.

I got up and folded my chair, noticing John do the same. I reached for hers at the same time he did, our fingers brushing against each other. I pulled back as if I had been burned by a fire that was raging out of control.

"I'm sorry," he muttered.

"It's my fault," I said quickly, stepping around him to put

my chair in the back of the motorhome.

"I mean for earlier," he said, standing right behind me with the other two chairs.

I inhaled slowly, the smell of pine trees overwhelming my senses.

"I'm sorry too. I didn't mean for Lily to find out."

"Me neither," he said, setting the chairs down on top of mine. I stepped back, making room for him to close the door.

I stood there with my arms wrapped around my chest, shielding myself from his rejection. I knew that it was a mistake and that he regretted it, but it still hurt to keep hearing about it.

"I've been trying to apologize to you, but you won't listen," he added when I refused to say anything more.

"You don't need to keep apologizing, John. I get it. We don't have to keep beating a dead horse."

"You don't get it. That's the problem. You can't get it because even *I* don't get it. I have no idea what any of this means, and I'm sinking in quicksand, trying to make it right when I don't even know that it's wrong."

He threw his hands up in the air and looked at me. I could tell that he wanted me to say something. To reassure him that it wasn't wrong and that we could figure it out.

"I've been offered the opportunity to interview for the creative marketing director position at BayView Advertising. I'm catching a flight back to San Francisco on Thursday and will find a new place to live before you get back in July. I think that it's best that you have the conversation with Lily so she can help you find a replacement for her nanny."

I swallowed down the acidic bile that was rising in my throat and walked away from him. I didn't look back or give him the chance to try to stop me so we could talk about it.

But the part that hurt the most was that he didn't try to. Instead, he let me walk away without a fight, and that alone told me everything that I needed to know about the future between us.

Twenty Five

I had no idea what day it was, and time was irrelevant at the moment. Sometime after we got on the road from Arkansas to Tennessee, I came down with a terrible cold and laid miserable in the bed for the majority of the nine-hour drive it took for us to get there. Or at least that was how long John assured Lily it was when she complained that we had been driving for hundreds of hours already.

The few times that I got up were to use the bathroom or to get more tissue. I kept a few plastic bags beside me that I used as a trashcan before they filled up quickly. When we stopped for gas earlier, John went inside and bought a handful of Gatorade, assorted medicines, and an endless supply of tissue. Only, it turned out that the end came quickly as I stared at my last box.

We were almost to Great Smoky Mountains National Park when John made another quick stop for more supplies. I felt terrible and imagined that I looked even worse every time he grimaced when he looked at me. This time when he came back, he had a thermometer that he insisted on using to make sure I wasn't running a fever and nighttime medicine to help me sleep off whatever this was.

Lily had sat at the table most of the day, from what I remembered, and didn't talk much. I imagined that she was still upset with finding out that we had kissed. If I had any energy left inside of me, I would have made an effort to check in with her and make sure she was okay. Instead, I had to pray that John was already taking care of it. I also had to keep reminding myself that this would no longer be something for me to worry over. Lily was John's daughter, not mine, and I needed to remember my role in all of this.

"Emma," John said softly, gently shaking my arm to wake me. "I need you to take some more medicine. Can you wake up?"

I tried to roll over, but it felt hopeless. My body ached in more places than I could count. I felt terrible that he was having to take care of me and wished that I could just curl up in bed and not bother them. I knew that I was putting a damper on the trip, and I hated it.

"Come on, Emma. I know that you're tired, but I need you to take more Tylenol. Your fever is climbing again."

I felt something cold on my forehead and looked up to find him sitting on the edge of the bed, pressing a cold washcloth against my feverish skin while holding the pills in his other hand.

"There you go," he said encouragingly. "Just go slow, take your time."

I tried to roll over onto my side, groaning when it hurt more than anything. Finally, I laid on my back, giving up for the moment.

"I would ask how you're feeling, but I can see that you've only gotten worse." The worry in his voice was thick, and even though it shouldn't, it warmed my heart that he cared so much about me.

"Where's Lily," I whispered, trying to talk around the dry ache in my throat.

"She's sitting up front, looking for fireflies."

"I feel terrible," I croaked, turning to the side to cover my mouth as I coughed. "I know how bad she wanted to watch them."

The next item on her bucket list was sit and be still; maybe they'll come. When they light up, it's even more fun.

It bummed me out that she had to miss out on it because I was so sick, and John was stuck taking care of me instead of sitting outside with her to watch them. When we talked about the list yesterday at breakfast, John had a cheeky smile when he told her that he had picked the Great Smoky Mountains National Park for us to stay at tonight because it was supposed to be the *best* place to see them. I was rather impressed by how much research he had done in advance and that he was taking everything on the bucket list seriously, knowing how much it meant to Lily.

"Don't worry about that right now," he said gently, leaning over to help me as I tried to sit up. "I'll take her outside to look at them in a few minutes, but I need to tend to you first."

"You don't have to take care of me," I muttered, swatting my hand around in the air. I felt drunk and completely out of it.

He handed me the two pills in his hand and waited for me to pop them in my mouth before passing me the bottle of Gatorade that was sitting next to me.

"Is it really that bad to have me take care of you?"

"It's not your job, John. You take care of Lily. I can take care of myself."

"Well, I hate to break it to you, but I don't think you *can* take care of yourself right now. Besides, I'm fully capable of taking care of both of you."

I took a drink and swallowed the pills, wiping my mouth with the back of my hand when I was done. It wasn't my fault that the mouth to the bottle was huge and hard to drink out of without making a little mess.

I laid down and turned to look at him. He placed the cold rag on my head again then his knuckles gently caressed the side of my cheek.

"I'm not yours to take care of," I mumbled, already falling back asleep. "I'm hopelessly in love with you, but you're not mine either."

Twenty Six

I woke up to the sun glaring at me through the curtain. I rolled over and found Lily sitting at the table, her head down as she watched something on her tablet. She looked up, surprised when she saw me awake.

"What time is it?" I asked, hoping that I had more strength than I did last time. I guess I should have started with what *day* it was instead because it felt like several had passed by already.

"It's a little after three," she said, getting up to come over to me.

"How long have I been asleep?"

"All day yesterday, last night, and then all day today."

"What day is it?" I asked, feeling the pain as I sat up.

"Saturday."

"Are we still in Tennessee?"

She shook her head no.

"Where are we?"

"Virginia. We just got to the hotel a few minutes ago. Dad's inside checking in."

"Hotel?" I croaked, my throat still sore. It was turning into a game of twenty questions, but I felt so lost and had no idea what had been going on.

"Daddy didn't want to push it today, so he thought we could stay in Virginia today and then get on the road again tomorrow. He said that he knew you wanted to get to New Jersey before you leave on Thursday, so we'll drive all day tomorrow and get to nana and pop's house in the evening."

The look on her face almost killed me. She was sad that I was leaving, and I hated that I had created this pain for her. I couldn't be mad at John for telling her about it—hell, I had been the one who told him that he needed to. I just wished he would have given it a little more time before he ripped that band-aid off.

"I'm sorry that I have to leave early and go back," I said softly, trying to force the corners of my mouth up into a smile.

"It's okay. Daddy said that the job you've always wanted finally opened up, so you need to go back to interview for it."

"That's right." I kept my words short and sweet, unwilling to add any more turmoil to her beautiful face by telling her that I wouldn't be her nanny when she went back either. I wanted her to enjoy the rest of the trip without having that weighing on her mind.

"Did you get to see any fireflies last night?" I asked, hoping to change the topic.

Her face lit up as she started telling me about their adventures and how she tried desperately to catch one but couldn't. John, on the other hand, was the hero who caught *two* in a mason jar for her. They let them go and watched as they flew away. She also told me about how John had created a story for them and told her that they had found their soulmate and were flying off to spend forever together because they were *hopelessly in love.*

The words struck a chord somewhere deep down inside

of me, and I felt the heat tingle up my spine as I started to panic. Those sounded like the same exact words that I had heard last night, too, only I couldn't place where.

Part of me thought that maybe it was on one of the shows that Lily had been watching on her tablet, but when the door opened and John walked in, I knew that wasn't it. He looked at me in a way that I'd never seen him look at me before—guarded. I cringed as I imagined the worst things going through his mind as he tried to figure out how to deal with this *situation.*

It's not like it's an everyday thing for your dead wife's best friend to confess her love for you while she's delirious from a dangerously high fever.

"How are you feeling?" he asked, leaning against the table, one ankle crossed over the other.

"A little better, but still weak."

He nodded in understanding.

"I was just telling Emma about our fireflies last night and how they were in *love!*" Lily giggled, making kissing sounds.

I watched John's Adam's apple bob up and down as he swallowed. This wasn't a conversation that he wanted to have. I could tell by the tension radiating through the room the moment he stepped inside.

"Well, our room is ready. Why don't we go get settled in?" He pushed off from the table and fished the keys out of his pocket to go grab the luggage from the back. He paused for a minute before walking down the steps to the door. "I'm sorry, I tried to get two rooms so you could have your own.

Unfortunately, they were completely booked, but they did give me a room with two queen beds and a sleeper sofa. I'll sleep on the couch, and you girls can take the beds."

"It's okay," I rushed out, not wanting him to go out of his way for me. "I can stay in here. I don't mind."

"You're going to stay in here?" he asked as if it was the most ridiculous thing he had heard.

"Sure, why not? I have a bed. A bathroom. Food and water." I looked around, trying to find more to justify me staying in here. "Sammy the fish. Someone's gotta keep him company," I said with a wink to Lily.

"The fish will be fine," he grumbled, his hand hovering over the door handle. "Please come stay with us in the room."

I couldn't tell if it was an offer or a demand, given the way that he said it. But the look on Lily's face with her beady little blue eyes staring up at me convinced me to give in and go.

Thirty minutes later, we were in the room. Luckily, we had a room on the first floor this time, so I didn't have to worry about climbing the flight of stairs to the second story. It wasn't a terrible hotel, but not as fancy as the other ones that John had chosen so far. Overall, we were lucky to even get a room, so I guess there was no need to complain.

It was a little after four, and my stomach was finally starting to wake up and feel hungry. Apparently, it was so hungry that it growled loud enough for John and Lily to hear. She laughed hysterically while I tried not to, sparing my ribs the pain.

"Well, it sounds like we should start looking at dinner

options," John announced. "Does anything sound good to you?"

I knew that the hotel didn't have room service because of how small and outdated it was. That meant that he was going to have to go out of his way to get food for us.

"I'll just grab something light from wherever you guys go," I said nervously, feeling the weight of his look.

"Emma," he scolded with a sigh. "What do *you* feel like? You're the one who hasn't eaten anything in over twenty-four hours. I want to get you what you think you can handle. So please, tell me what you would like for dinner."

I leaned slightly closer and noticed the exhaustion in his tone and the faint bags under his eyes. I wasn't trying to make things harder for him. But it seemed like the more I tried to keep him from doing things for me, the worse I made them.

"I would love some chicken noodle soup if you can find some," I replied softly.

"Thank you," he said and got up from the bed. "Lily, do you want to go with me to get food? I might need your help carrying it back."

"Sure!" She climbed off the bed and put her shoes back on.

After they left, I stretched out on the bed, hoping to relieve some of the achiness that I was still feeling. For the most part, I was feeling better, but definitely not 100%. I looked over at Sammy as he swam around in his tank next to the tv and thought about how simple his life was and how I wished mine was like that.

I was in the bathroom when they got back and hadn't heard the door when they came in. As I walked out of the bathroom and washed my hands, I glanced in the mirror above me and jumped when I saw John standing right behind me.

"Oh my God, you scared the shit out of me," I said breathlessly, holding the towel in my hand as I clutched it to my chest. "What are you doing there?"

"I thought you heard us come in. Lily let the door slam hard enough that I'm sure the neighbors at the other end of the hallway heard it."

My heart rate was slowly starting to come back down to normal as I dried my hands and laid the towel on the edge of the sink.

"My ears are still kind of plugged, so I can't hear much. Plus, the bathroom has a fan that turns on with the light, so I couldn't hear anything."

"Sorry," he said, pulling his mouth into a crooked, side smile. "I didn't mean to scare you. I was just coming over to grab the cups." He pointed at the stack of paper cups lined up next to the coffee maker.

I moved out of the way and walked to the bed where Lily had a picnic set up with the take-out bags they brought back. Everything smelled delicious and was making my mouth water.

I was still standing there when John came up behind me, gently touching my lower back as he stepped around me. He set the cups down on the nightstand that separated the two beds and took the clear wrappers off each one.

"Sorry, I couldn't find chicken noodle soup anywhere," he apologized, twisting the cap on the 2-liter bottle of Seven-Up. He turned slowly, letting the bubbles fizz to the top before he opened it the rest of the way. "The only thing close by was a Chinese food place, so I grabbed you some egg drop soup. I know that it's your favorite, but if you're not in the mood for it, you don't have to eat it."

I felt my heart swell inside of my chest, completely touched by his gesture.

"Thank you, that was really sweet of you to remember."

"No problem," he shrugged as he filled each cup before putting the cap back on the bottle. "I also ordered family-size portions of everything, in case you felt like eating more than soup. We got chicken fried rice, pot stickers, kung pow chicken, sweet and sour chicken, and my favorite—beef and broccoli."

I laughed when Lily made a face at the broccoli. She loved pretty much *any* vegetable *except* for broccoli.

It didn't take much to notice that he had ordered *all* of my favorites. I was surprised that he had remembered everything and even more so that he had ordered all of it, not even knowing if I would be able to eat it. This wasn't their usual order. It was mine when I would stay for take-out.

"Everything looks and smells delicious," I said, taking a seat on the bed across from Lily, making sure I didn't spill anything. John was sitting against the headboard, cramped in the little space that he had left after all the food and plates were spread out between us.

Even though I still felt terribly under the weather, at that moment, I felt the best that I had ever felt. It was the same feeling I had every time I was with *them*.

Twenty Seven

"Right there," I whispered as John's lips slowly trailed kisses down my neck. I tilted my head to the side, allowing him full access as he pulled his arms around my waist. I still couldn't believe that we were doing this. I leaned back against this muscular chest, allowing my body to give in to the pleasure that he was providing.

"Tell me what you want, Emma," he coaxed, running his tongue along the side of my ear before playfully nipping at it.

"You," I confessed. "It's always been you."

I heard a low growl in this throat before he spun me around, wrapped me in his arms, and lowered his mouth to mine. His kiss was as sweet as it was urgent. Both of us were desperately moving our hands over each other's bodies, afraid that we wouldn't get enough.

I felt his fingers on my back as he unzipped the red dress that he had bought me for my birthday. Our lips continued their dance, never bothering to break the kiss as the dress fell to the floor. I was standing in front of John for the first time, wearing nothing but the black lace bra and panties set that I bought for tonight—in case something ended up happening.

I quickly unbuttoned his shirt, pushing it down his broad shoulders until it landed in a pile next to the dress. My hands reached for his belt, ready to unfasten it, when he reached down and grabbed my wrists, stopping me.

Our lips finally parted as he stepped back and looked at me. His eyes slowly traveled the length of my body, drinking in the sight before him like a stranded man in a blazing hot desert.

He licked his lips before pulling the bottom one between his teeth. I could see the desire on his face and felt the swarm of butterflies in my stomach, knowing he wanted this as much as I did.

His eyes stayed locked on me while he took off his belt, then his jeans, stepping out of them as he watched me. I felt the blush flaming up my neck and onto my cheeks from all the undivided attention he was giving me.

"I've waited for this moment for a while now," he said, stepping closer to me.

"Me too," I whispered, closing my eyes as he reached me and ran his hand behind my head, holding it in place. His lips hovered over mine, the anticipation of what was about to happen electrifying.

"Everything is perfect again, Charlotte."

I gasped, my eyes flying open to look at him. Surely, he said her name on accident, right?

I slowly stepped back, feeling the guilt well up inside of me.

"What's wrong?" he asked, tilting his head.

"You called me Charlotte," I replied quietly, wrapping my arms around my body.

He stopped for a moment, pulling his shoulders back as he contemplated what I had said.

"You're my one true love. Always have been, always will be."

"But I'm Emma," I said uneasily, unsure of why he was being so weird about it.

"You're right. You are Emma. Not Charlotte. Not the woman I'm in love with, I was wrong."

He turned and walked away, leaving me exposed and vulnerable on numerous levels. I quickly grabbed my dress from the floor and slid into it, desperate to cover myself up.

I turned around, ready to leave when I stopped in my tracks. I felt my heart crash hard against my chest, nearly knocking the breath out of me.

"What are you doing here?" I asked, staring at Charlotte's beautiful face. Everything about her was perfect, from her silky blonde hair to the breezy white dress that adorned her evenly tanned body. I knew that she was an angel, but I was desperate to hug her. To feel her one last time and pretend that she was really there.

I reached forward to grab her hand, but she yanked it back quickly, a scowl on her face.

"Charlotte, it's me. Emma," I pleaded for her to understand. "I've missed you so much. I can't believe that you're here," I whispered as a tear slid down my cheek.

"I have so much to tell you, so much to catch you up on." I was starting to ramble, but the scowl on her face didn't fade. She crossed her arms over her body.

"Please, talk to me, Charlotte. I need to hear your voice. I need to know that you're okay…."

I could feel the tears washing over my face as I begged her.

"I trusted you," she said, catching me by surprise. "You let me down."

"What?" I gasped, clutching a hand to my chest. "What are you talking about?"

Just then, John and Lily appeared behind her. They were scowling too as they took their place beside her.

"I trusted you to take care of my family, and instead, you tried to replace me. You want my husband. You've overstepped with my daughter. You're not the friend that I thought you were."

I felt my world crumble around me as I stared at them. I sobbed harder as I realized that what she was saying was true.

"No, no, no. Please, let me explain," I pleaded. I took a step toward her, my hands folded in prayer in front of me. "Please, Charlotte. Please. You have to let me talk to you. Please."

With each step I took toward them, they moved even further away from me into the bright white light behind them while I was left in the shadows of the darkness that was falling around me.

"Please…"

"Please…"

"Emma, wake up."

I felt strong hands as they shook my arm repeatedly.

"Come on, Emma. I need you to wake up."

The words hit hard in my chest, remembering the last time that I heard them when I was in the hospital after the accident. I was afraid to open my eyes and look around, for fear that I was reliving that moment again.

I felt cold hands on my forehead, followed by a muttered string of curse words. My eyes slowly flickered open, everything blurry from the tears clouding my vision.

"Hey," John said, gently turning my head to face him. Worry was etched onto his face as he studied mine. I reached up and wiped the tears from my eyes, embarrassed that I was crying in the first place. My heart felt like it had been ripped open as the sadness spilled out of it.

I looked around the room, spotting the empty Chinese food containers from last night, and remembered that we were in a hotel room in Virginia.

"You gave me quite the scare," John said quietly, shifting on the bed next to me.

"What happened?"

"I'm not sure. I woke up to use the bathroom, and when I was coming back, I heard you crying in your sleep. I thought maybe it was just a bad dream and didn't know if I should wake you."

I nodded, my heart still hammering in my chest. It was definitely a bad dream, to say the least. However, I could still feel the realness of it, the desperation that I felt to talk to Charlotte. The look of betrayal on her face when she saw that I was trying to replace her.

"When you started pleading in your sleep, I knew that I needed to wake you up. You scared me when I couldn't. I was worried that your fever had spiked again and that I was going to have to rush you to the hospital."

"I'm sorry, I didn't mean to worry you."

I sat up and scooted over, so he didn't have to hang on the edge of the bed anymore. He moved up and sat beside me as we leaned against the padded headboard. I could feel my heart rate starting to come down, the cold sweat fading away. I looked over at the bed next to me, making sure that Lily was still sleeping peacefully. The sofa bed had been pulled out, and I felt bad that John had to sleep on it when I could see that it wasn't very comfortable.

"What time is it?" I asked, feeling completely disoriented still.

John leaned forward and checked the clock on the nightstand.

"Two-thirty."

I knew that there was no way that I would be able to go back to sleep any time soon. The dream had really messed with my mind, and I needed time to sort everything out. I hated being alone with my thoughts. Charlotte was always good at helping me work through them, but she wasn't here now. I also didn't trust that she *wouldn't* be upset with me if she were here. The guilt of thinking that I had subconsciously been trying to take her place was eating away at me quickly.

"Do you want to talk about the dream?" he asked quietly, making sure not to wake Lily.

I shook my head and looked away, unable to make eye contact with him.

"I won't push," he added, resting a hand on my knee. "But I know that you get too far into your head sometimes and need someone to pull you back out. I'm happy to do that for you if you'll let me."

I knew that he meant well and that as friendly as his offer was, it struck something deep inside of me. I felt the tears spilling down my cheeks faster than I could stop them. I pulled my knees up to my chest and tucked my head down, hoping that my sobbing wouldn't disturb Lily.

John reached over and gently wrapped an arm around me, pulling me closer to him. I let go of my knees and gave in as he held me against his chest. I cried as quietly as I could while I told him the quick summary of my dream—aside from the part where we were crossing the line of our friendship.

I didn't know how hard it would be for him to hear me talk about Charlotte, but surprisingly, he didn't react negatively. Instead, he continued to hold me the entire time, except for the few minutes that it took for him to run to the bathroom to grab a box of tissue. When I was finally calm and able to catch my breath, I pulled away from him and leaned against the headboard again.

"I'm sorry," I apologized. "It's late. You should try to get some sleep. We have a full day of driving tomorrow."

"I'm not worried about any of that," he said, sighing heavily. "I'm worried about you."

I looked up at him, finding his green eyes studying me like they were in my dream.

"Why?"

He paused while he thought about how to answer the question.

"Because you're so hard on yourself. You've been a tremendous help with Lily and me, yet you constantly worry about replacing Charlotte. You live in this guilt of doing something wrong, and I worry that it will eat you alive if you let it."

I could feel my voice get shaky as I started to speak.

"It was just a dream, and I know that. I'm fine." I waved dismissively, hoping that he would buy it. Lord knew that I didn't. I was the worst liar and always sounded like a squeaky mouse when I told a lie.

He arched a brow, calling me on it.

I chewed my nail nervously, not sure what to say. It wasn't like I could just outright confess to him that I had been feeling something for him and that it scared the crap out of me because I didn't know what those feelings were. I just knew that I shouldn't be having them for *him*.

"I don't know what's going on in that beautiful head of yours," he muttered, running a hand down his face. "But I don't want whatever *this* is between us to end. So, I think we need to be open and honest with each other."

I sucked in a ragged breath, trying to prepare myself for whatever it was he was about to say. I could see the look on his face and knew that it was going to be heavy.

"It's only been two months since Charlotte died," he started, a slight strain in his voice when he said her name. "I don't know that I will ever really get used to a world without her in it, but I know that I have to try. There's not a single day that goes by that I don't miss her. I want to pick up the phone and call her, to tell her about this amazing trip that we've been on, and I can't. The day that she died, it ripped a hole into my heart, and I never thought it would heal."

I noticed the tears that slid down his cheeks but said nothing. I didn't reach up to wipe them away like I wanted to. John was opening up to me for the first time, and I didn't want to do anything that would stop it.

"When the doctors wouldn't tell me if you had made it, that hole grew bigger, Emma. I felt like I couldn't breathe while I waited to find out if both the women who I loved and adored had been taken away from me. I know that you can't stand the thought that you're replacing Charlotte, but I assure you, you're not. Nothing that you do will ever replace her, and I don't mean that in a bad way."

He pulled in a deep breath, along with the courage to keep going.

"You can't replace her because my time with Charlotte is now frozen. The things that you do for Lily and me, they aren't things that Charlotte could do for us because she's gone. You're not stepping on her toes or taking anything from her. I hate that you feel like you are."

Now, it was my turn to let the tears fall as I listened to him talk.

"I love you, Emma. In a way that I can't even wrap my head around right now, and that scares the shit out of me. I've always loved you, and Charlotte knew that. It wasn't a romantic love that she had to be worried about, but a deep love that I had for my closest friends and the little bit of family that I choose to have. I don't know if it's because we've spent almost every day together for the past two months, but something between us has shifted. I feel it, and I know that you do too. You wouldn't be trying to run away every chance you had if you didn't."

I picked up a tissue and quietly blew my nose, surprised that Lily was still sleeping through all of this.

"I know that we've shared a kiss—and I don't regret it, but please don't run from me because you're worried that *I'm* trying to replace Charlotte with you. That would never happen, Emma. And while I can't even begin to wrap my head around the idea of dating or being romantically involved with anyone right now, I don't want you to think that I would ever try to replace her. *If* I'm ever given a second chance at finding love, that person will be just as special as Charlotte was."

I nodded quickly, deciding then and there that the rest of the dream would be an embarrassing detail that only I would keep secret for as long as I lived.

Hearing John talk about our relationship and how he felt about me helped clear some of the murkiness that had started to develop. Maybe he was right that we did love each other, just not in the way that was causing me so much stress. I took comfort in knowing that I meant so much to him but that he wasn't interested in anything romantic.

"Thank you for telling me," I whispered, wiping my face with a clean tissue. "That did help clear out some of the mess that was starting in my head."

"Of course," he said softly, patting my knee. "But, like I said, this only works if we're both open and honest with each other."

I could hear something in his voice like he was waiting for me to confess something. If it was about the rest of the dream, there was no way that I was going to tell him about that. It was embarrassing enough for me to have to think about it. I didn't need to make him uncomfortable, thinking that I was having these kinds of thoughts about him. Before the dream, I had never thought about John in that way. Well, not until after our kiss. But even then, my thoughts never got anywhere past the panic of knowing that I had kissed my best friend's husband.

"I agree. Honesty is important," I replied, not knowing what else to say.

"Okay…" He gave me a pointed look and waited.

"I'm not sure what you're waiting for," I laughed nervously, glancing at Lily as she shifted position.

I could still feel his eyes on me, not letting up as he waited.

"Fine," he sighed.

I felt a tiny bit of relief when I thought that he was giving up on the subject.

"Are you moving out and interviewing for this job because you're in love with me, and you're trying to run from your feelings?"

My jaw dropped open as all the air inside rushed out. *How did he know?*

"I… umm…" I stuttered, unable to find the words. My heart was racing again as panic flooded through me that my secret had been exposed.

I closed my eyes and leaned my head back against the headboard. Maybe if I stayed like this and ignored him, it would all just go away?

I waited patiently, with no such luck. Finally, when I opened my eyes, I found him staring at me, a stern look on his face.

"I'm interviewing for the job because it's my dream job. It's what I've always wanted."

I kept my answer short and simple, avoiding the other half that I knew he was wanting.

"And are you moving out because you're in love with me?"

"I'm moving out because it's the right thing to do." I swallowed hard, feeling the intense heat from his eyes as they bored into me.

"Right thing for who?"

"All of us."

"So, that's it? You just get to decide what we need, without even talking to us first?"

I could hear the anger in his voice and flinched.

"I'm just trying to make things easier. I don't want anyone to get hurt."

"Too late for that," he muttered under his breath as he got up and walked into the bathroom, closing the door behind him.

I let out the breath that I had been holding and let my shoulders fall. I felt like shit for how things had just ended between us, but he asked me to be honest with him. A few minutes later, I heard the shower running. I looked over at the clock. It was already four in the morning, and Lily would be up in a few hours. I hated the idea of John driving the seven some hours to New Jersey today, especially with little sleep.

I laid down and curled into my pillow, hoping to rest for a few hours so I could help with the driving. In his effort to make things better between us, I had only made them worse.

Twenty Eight

Lily was up by six, bright and chipper as if there wasn't a thick fog of tension filling the room. I knew when I heard the shower earlier that John was up for the day. He was sitting at the small table in the corner of the room, looking at the map he had brought on the trip while Lily took her time in the shower.

I was still tired but didn't want to delay us getting to New Jersey by sleeping all morning. My body was sore, but thankfully, it seemed like I was over the worst part of the cold and was starting to feel better. I heard the low grumble as my stomach growled, ready for breakfast.

John looked up and glanced at me, not saying a word before turning his attention back to the map. He wrote something down on the notepad the hotel provided and tossed his pen onto the table when he was done.

"I'm going to go find breakfast. Can you keep an eye on Lily?"

I felt the knot in my stomach from the way he was acting. The added *can you keep an eye on Lily* comment really got under my skin. Since when did he have to ask? That's what I've been doing for the past few months, and I would do it without him even asking.

But he was making it clear where we stood, and I had to remind myself that by separating myself from them now, it would make things easier for everyone when I left.

"Yes." I gritted my teeth as I pushed the words out.

The door closed quietly behind him, leaving me with the

quiet peacefulness of the room and the muted sound of the shower under the bathroom door.

I stood next to the bed, digging inside the duffle bag to find a clean outfit to wear that would also be comfortable. It was already Sunday, and I was planning to leave on Thursday, which meant that I really only needed a handful of clean clothes to last me until I got back home. Then, I could sit around and cry in my cereal over the mistakes that I made while doing loads and loads of laundry.

I picked a pair of shorts and a tank top, anticipating another hot and humid day. A few minutes later, the shower turned off, and I could hear Lily singing along with Taylor Swift. I smiled and repacked the bag, setting my clothes for the day to the side.

I grabbed my cosmetics bag and debated whether to bother with getting ready today. We were going to be driving most of the day, so it wasn't like anyone would see me. But then again, we would be seeing Charlotte's parents tonight, so that seemed like a good enough reason to make an effort.

John got back at the same time Lily had finished in the bathroom, letting the steam from her shower float into the room as she opened the door.

"How long were you in there?" John asked, rushing past the sticky heat to get to the air conditioner.

"Not that long," Lily shrugged.

"Not that long?" He lifted a brow. "You were in the shower when I left, and you're just now coming out. I'd say that it was long."

I laughed, then stopped when he looked at me. It wasn't

a sharp, angry look like I had expected. Instead, it was soft and warm, inviting almost. I rubbed my lips together nervously and looked away.

John set the bag of food and the drink tray down on the table. Lily was still humming along to the song she was singing while running a comb through her hair.

"Well, now that the shower is free, I'm going to go get ready," I said, grabbing my stuff so I could get out of there as fast as possible.

"I brought you breakfast," John replied with a stern tone. "I thought we could all eat together. As a family."

It felt as though there was a snake wrapped around my throat, squeezing it shut as it tightened around me. His eyes locked onto mine, neither of us looking at Lily, as he pinned me with a look. He was challenging me to stay, and I could hear it in his tone as I felt the intensity of the green eyes that were still staring at me.

If I sat down to eat with them, *as a family,* then I would be going back on what I said I wanted. I would be doing the opposite of what I should be doing—putting distance between us—separating myself from them because I'm *not* part of their family.

I chewed the inside of my cheek, trying to figure out how to get around this without drawing Lily's attention. I didn't want her to worry that something was wrong or to stress about the tension between her dad and me.

"You guys are being weird again," she muttered, tucking her comb back into her bag before joining John at the table.

He raised his eyebrows and stared. I could feel my palms

sweating and hated that he was having this effect on me.

"The food is getting cold," he warned, not moving an inch.

Lily worked on unpacking the bag of food, setting stuff out on the table while we continued in this awkward stare-down.

"Fine," I muttered, dropping my stuff to the bed. "I'll come and have breakfast with my *friends*."

I raised an eyebrow and gave him a smug smile.

"We're not family?" Lily asked, looking up at me with a hurt look on her beautiful face. She reminded me so much of her mom with her baby blue eyes and the way her face looked so thin with the thick blond hair framing it.

"That's not what I meant," I replied cautiously. "Of course you're family. You're my god-daughter." I offered her a smile, but it was tight and unconvincing.

"What about daddy? He's not your family?"

"Well… umm…" I was stammering, trying to find the right words to say.

"Eat your breakfast before it gets cold." John pointed to her food with his fork and ended the conversation for me.

I kept my head down as I picked pieces off the bagel and popped them into my mouth. I wasn't ready for these conversations with her and didn't know if I would ever be. I thought I was doing the right thing by walking away and giving them space, but now I worried that Lily would feel abandoned by me. Which she had every right to feel that way, given that was exactly what I was doing.

"So, I decided what I want to do for my birthday this year," Lily said around a mouthful of the breakfast sandwich she was eating.

"Yeah? What's that?" John asked, taking a sip of coffee. He had set the other cup in front of me without bothering to acknowledge it. It was like he was trying to prove to me that regardless of what I wanted, he was still going to try to take care of me.

"I want to have a party on the beach! But I want to do it in New Jersey, with nana and pop. That way, we can celebrate as a family."

She looked over at me, staring me down the same way her father does.

"Can you come back for my party?" she asked with so much hope in her voice that I couldn't hear anything else.

I glanced at John, who was staring coldly at the table, his fist clenched around the fork in his hand.

"I'm not sure, but I will try. When are you having it?"

"I was thinking fourth of July? It's on a Saturday this year so we could spend the *whole* day at the beach, and then watch fireworks that night. I know that my birthday isn't until the eleventh, but I really want to watch the sky light up and pretend that it's mommy sending me birthday wishes. Plus, you only get to turn eleven once. Why not make it a big celebration?!"

Her enthusiasm overrode the heartache that I felt when she mentioned Charlotte. I hated that she had to spend her first birthday without her mother, but I was happy that she found something that she wanted to do. It would be a hard day for her regardless, but at least she was finding her way. Something that I still needed to do.

"You only get to turn every age *once,*" John teased, taking a bite of his eggs. "But I think that will be a fun celebration. I'll talk to them when we get there, and we'll plan it out. We'll have to get back on the road to head home shortly after that, so think about where you want to celebrate your birthday, and I'll plan our trip around it."

"Okay!" she was even more excited than before. She went back to eating her breakfast as I struggled to keep my bagel down.

I reached for the coffee at the same time John gently slid it over to me as if reading my mind. I hated that he knew me so well and could read my emotions better than anyone. It was a gift and a curse at the same time. I smiled and grabbed the cup, fighting the urge inside of me to fling it against the wall.

Instead, I pushed away from the table and stood up.

"Thank you for breakfast," I said, my voice shaky as I struggled to talk past the lump in my throat. "I'm going to get ready real quick, so we can get on the road."

I took the coffee and grabbed my stuff from the bed before I disappeared into the bathroom. I stood under the hot water, hoping it would wash away the rush of emotions that were overwhelming me right now. I knew that I had to find a way to make it back for Lily's birthday. I would hate myself if I didn't. But that was barely a month away, and who knew what would happen with the interview and finding an apartment.

I couldn't stress over any of that right now. I had to keep pretending that everything was alright before Lily caught on. The last thing that I wanted was to ruin her trip. I got ready as quickly as possible and tossed my dirty clothes and cosmetics bag into my duffle bag, ready to get moving again.

We were on the road, heading to DC, when Lily looked out the window and yelled for John to stop. We both panicked as he looked around to see what's wrong.

"Can we go?!" she asked excitedly, pointing to the side of the road up ahead where a sign for a U-Pick-It farm was located.

"You want to go pick fruit?" John asked, clearly confused.

"It's on the bucket list!"

I calmed down, thankful that nothing was wrong.

"If you are what you eat, make sure to pick—"

"Something sweet," John finished for her with a chuckle.

"Well, it's fitting," I offered, noticing the sign below it that read 'pick fresh strawberries here.'

Fifteen minutes later, we were walking through the field, holding our buckets as we plucked strawberries from the vines and added them in.

It was already hot and humid as we continued the last few rows before our buckets were too full.

"What are you going to do with all of these strawberries?" I asked Lily, looking down at the three buckets that were almost overflowing.

"I have no idea," she giggled. "We can make strawberry shortcake at nana's house. Or maybe dip them in chocolate?"

"Those both sound delicious," I said with a cheesy grin.

"Well, let's get going before we all melt out here," John groaned, not a fan of the humidity.

We paid for our harvest and climbed back into the motorhome. John got us back on the road while I had Lily watch Sammy so I could wash the strawberries in the sink. I was thankful that we had a few colanders after our trip to Walmart. I knew they would come in handy for the pasta that I made but didn't know that we would need even more for all these strawberries.

Lily hung out with Sammy for the first half of the drive, and I found myself googling whether fish could get motion sickness after Lily forgot to brace his tank when John went through curves a little too quickly, and he got sloshed around.

By five o'clock, we had made it to New Jersey. I looked out the window, watching the houses pass by as we made our way to Charlotte's parent's house. I remembered these streets, and the memories of my childhood came flooding back to me. For a moment, I closed my eyes and tried to feel the happiness that I had felt long ago before everything that I loved in life was taken away from me.

Twenty Nine

"It's so good to see you! Welcome home!" Alice cried excitedly, holding me tight as she hugged me. I felt a surge of emotions course through me as I thought about how much this really did feel like home. A strange pull at my heart made me miss being here and spending time with Alice and Charles. Charlotte's parents had always been so kind to me and took me in as one of their own after my parents died, and then again when my aunt passed away.

I was reluctant to let go of her as she pulled away. I missed having someone to hug like family. It was the kind of hug that fully enveloped you and made you feel whole again, no matter how broken you were.

"It's my turn!" Charles said, scooting around John and Lily to get to me. It was a fun dance of moving around to greet each other. Finally, he pulled me into his arms for a hug and kissed the top of my head. "How are you? I feel like we haven't seen you since…."

His voice trailed off when he remembered that the last time we had seen each other was at Charlotte's funeral.

"Well, it's good to see you," he added, clearing his throat. "How was the drive?"

"It was long but fun," I laughed, looking over at Lily. "We've had a great time going on different adventures while working on the bucket list."

"I've been so excited to hear all about it," Alice said, wrapping her arm around Lily's shoulders as she led her toward the house. "Why don't we go have some lemonade and cool off, and you can tell us all about it."

I smiled as I watched Lily walk in between them while John and I grabbed the items we needed out of the motorhome before joining them.

I was putting together an overnight bag when John startled me.

"How are you doing being back here?" he asked, leaning against the wall as I sat on the bed and finished packing.

"It's weird," I sighed, dropping my hands to my lap. "It feels like home."

"In a good way?" he questioned, noticing my tone when I said it.

"Yeah? I guess. It's hard to explain, but I'm not as sad as I thought I would be. It's like I remember all the fun times that I had here growing up, and even though it makes me miss my family and Charlotte, it's not as painful as I had imagined. Maybe it's because I miss them regardless of where I am? I don't know."

I started to ramble nervously, forcing myself to stop before I said something stupid.

"I get it," he said, breaking the awkward silence that had started to fall over us.

I looked down at the stuff that I had packed, feeling confident that I had what I needed. Alice and Charles had graciously invited us to stay in their house, so we didn't have to sleep in the motorhome while we were here. Their home was plenty big enough with four bedrooms and three and a half bathrooms, plus it was on the beach, which meant that we weren't likely going to spend much time inside anyway.

"I think I have everything that I need," I replied, grabbing the strap of the duffle bag and pulling it over my shoulder.

I hadn't realized that he had been staring at me until he flinched when I spoke.

"Yeah, um, me too." He turned around and grabbed the bags from the kitchen table before picking up Sammy's tank.

"We probably need to clean his tank soon," I said, looking at the water that was starting to look a little murky.

"Yeah, I'll go to the store and get more food too. He's almost out."

"Honestly, I'm surprised that he's still alive," I confessed, giggling.

"Me too. I've been dreading having to deal with it when he passes."

"I'm sure. I wouldn't want to have that conversation either."

We walked inside the house, greeted by the sound of Lily telling them about the night she saw a shooting star and made a wish.

"Wow, that must have been amazing," Alice replied with a tone that only a grandmother has.

"It was! But now I have to wait and see if my wish comes true. I don't know how long it's supposed to take, but I'm hoping that it's soon."

John and I paused in the living room, stopping when we heard her. It sounded like such a personal confession that we didn't want to intrude. Not that it was any better that we were technically eavesdropping from the other room.

"I'm sure your wish will come true when the time is right," Charles assured her.

"But what if it doesn't? What if it's too late, and then it never happens?"

John and I exchanged a curious glance, unsure of where this was going. Whatever it was, she seemed upset about it.

"It sounds like this is something that you really want," Alice said softly.

"It is," Lily rushed to confirm. "Like more than *anything* in the whole wide world."

I felt my stomach drop and knew that it had to be something to do with Charlotte. It was the only thing that I could think of that she could want so desperately.

"That is a big wish," Charles added.

I loved that they were being so nice to her and didn't push her to tell them what it was.

"I doubt it will come true," she mumbled unhappily.

I looked to John for guidance on whether we should go in yet or not. He nodded and took the lead, clearing his throat before he pushed open the double swinging door to the kitchen.

"Hey, kiddo," he said, setting Sammy on the kitchen counter across from where they were sitting. "We're going to have to get some food soon and clean his tank. Do you want to go to the store with me later?"

"Sure," she said sadly, her mood not lightening yet.

"Is everything okay?" he asked, looking over his shoulder at her as he got Sammy situated so his tank wouldn't get bumped.

"Yeah. I'm fine."

"Well, I don't know about you guys, but I'm starving," Charles said, pushing away from the table and standing up. "Why don't I go get the grill started?"

"I'll work on the potato salad," Alice added in. "Emma, do you want to help me?"

"Sure, I would love to."

"Can I go upstairs to my room for a little bit?" Lily asked, looking around the room.

"Of course, dear. I'll show you which one is yours."

Alice helped Lily get her stuff, and they headed upstairs while Charles and John grabbed a couple of trays of meat from the fridge and headed out to the grill. I was left by myself in the kitchen with no one to talk to but Sammy.

I pulled the duffle bag off my shoulder and set it down on the chair. Sammy was swimming along the top of his tank, searching for food, so I walked over and opened the almost empty container, and shook a few flakes in.

"You're lucky that you don't have to worry about anything other than eating, swimming around, and looking cute," I mumbled to him. I leaned down to watch him, resting my elbows on the counter. "I wish that my life was that easy. Instead, it's filled with all these tough decisions that I have to make that I don't want to. Being an adult sucks."

"What decisions do you have to make?" Alice asked,

walking in behind me and scaring me.

I jumped up, and my hand flew to my chest.

"I didn't hear you come in," I said as my heart beat wildly against my chest.

"Sorry. It didn't take long to show her to her room. She wanted to be alone, so I didn't stick around longer than needed."

I nodded and pulled my lips into a thin line.

Alice opened the fridge and started pulling bowls out, setting them on the island beside us. She worked quietly, starting an assembly line of ingredients for the potato salad. I stood beside her, waiting for her to tell me where she wanted me to start. It had been a long time since I stood in her kitchen and helped her cook.

"I've already boiled the potatoes and cut them up," she said, pointing to the biggest bowl on the counter with her elbow while she opened the jar of mayonnaise. "Go ahead and grab the eggs from the sink. I just finished boiling them right before you guys got here. They should be cool enough to peel now."

I did as she asked and worked quietly at the sink. I glanced over my shoulder to see her mixing the mayonnaise into the bowl with the potatoes before adding the chopped pickles and a splash of the juice from the jar. I tried desperately to learn how to cook from her when I was growing up, but it was difficult given that she used the eyeball method and never any actual measurements. I tried my best, but countless meals were inedible due to my *eyeballs* being a poor judge of quantity.

"So, does this big decision that you have to make have

anything to do with the wish that Lily made?" she asked casually while mixing the ingredients together.

I blew out a heavy breath, feeling the weight on my shoulders. She had always been like a mother to me, and I wanted to confide in her and ask her for her opinion, but it didn't feel right. Not when my big dilemma had to do with her daughter's husband.

"I don't know," I said, avoiding the question. "She hasn't told me what she wished for."

"Well, she seems rather stressed about it. And if I'm being honest, you seem pretty overwhelmed right now too." She stopped what she was doing and turned around, waiting for me to do the same. I set the last egg down and wiped my hands on the towel hanging over the edge of the sink.

"I'm not going to pry Emma, but I hope that you know that you can still talk to me. About anything. Just because Charlotte is gone doesn't mean that our relationship has changed. You're still like a daughter to me, and I care greatly about your happiness."

"I'm happy," I lied, looking down to avoid the knowing look that she was giving me.

"No, you're not. I saw it on your face the moment you stepped out of that motorhome."

I lifted my head, my eyes meeting hers and finding the comfort that I've been longing for, for so long now.

"I've really missed you," I said shakily, my voice faltering.

She took the few steps that separated us and wrapped me in a hug.

"I've missed you too. It's so wonderful to have you back home again, even if it's just for a few days."

I pulled my head back and looked at her, shocked that she knew that I was leaving before John and Lily.

"John told me yesterday when he called to update us on when you guys would be here. After you had been so sick, he was keeping us in the loop on how you were feeling and if you guys would need more time before you got back on the road again."

"I didn't know that he was going to tell you that I wasn't staying the entire time."

"He didn't mean any harm by it. I asked if you guys should be pushing it, trying to get here so quickly, and he told me that you wanted to make sure you got to spend some time with us before you had to head home for your interview."

My stomach dropped, and I felt a wave of nausea hit me again. It happened every time I thought about going back to San Francisco. It was the end of everything that I had known and come to love over the past few months, and I wasn't ready to face it—even though I needed to.

"He sounded as miserable as you look right now."

"Did he tell you why?"

At this point, I had no idea how much John had told her and didn't want to be blindsided if she knew what was really going on and why I was leaving.

"He didn't. He just said that things were complicated. Now, with John, I usually take that to mean that he's having trouble with something at work. But since you guys have been on the road for almost two weeks, I'm guessing that this is more personal."

I felt my hands tremble slightly at my sides, wondering if I was going to regret what I was about to do. The worst that could happen was that she would hate me for what I had done, which I had constantly been beating myself up over anyway.

"John and I kissed," I blurted out. "Just once, and it was an accident. But then Lily found out about it, and things have been weird between us ever since."

I looked up to find the shock on her face before it was quickly replaced with understanding.

"I see," she said quietly. "I can see now why you're both acting the way you are."

I waited patiently for the verbal lashing that I was expecting, only it never came. Instead, she turned back around and went back to making the potato salad. I didn't know what to do, so I stood there, staring dumbly at her back.

"Finish up with those eggs, then bring them on over. The boys will be done grilling soon."

I turned around and finished the last egg. I cleaned up the shells and tossed them in the trash before joining her at the island and setting them down.

"Go ahead and grab that knife, then start cutting them." She nodded to the extra paring knife that was sitting between us.

I grabbed the knife and started cutting, surprised by how satisfying it felt to cut into each egg.

"So, is the problem that you guys kissed, and Lily found out? Or is that you guys kissed, and something changed with how you feel about each other?"

"I don't know. Both, I guess?"

"What does John think about it?"

"He apologized right after it happened and admitted that it was a mistake."

"And what did you do?"

"I tried to forget that it happened. I wanted to move on, but he kept wanting to talk to me about it later. Then, things got weird, and he wouldn't stop trying to take care of me."

"So, why is that a problem?"

I pushed the bowl of eggs over to her and set the knife on the counter. She dumped them into the big bowl and started mixing with the wooden spoon while she waited for me. I planted my palms on the island and tried to find the best way to talk to her about this.

"Because I can't have him taking care of me. I was supposed to be taking care of him and Lily—not the other way around. But things keep changing, and I find that I'm getting too close, and I don't want to overstep. Lily started her period last week, and I was the one who helped her through it. That's something that her mom should have done for her, not me."

"But her mom's not here. So, if you didn't help her, then she would have had to figure it out on her own."

I tilted my head back and looked at the ceiling in frustration. She was right, and I knew it. But no matter how hard I tried to justify that I had been overstepping in my role, it didn't seem to matter.

"Do you remember when you started your period? You didn't have your mom either, but your aunt helped you. No one looked at her and thought she was overstepping. So why would it be different for you with Lily?" She tilted her head and looked at me as she stopped stirring.

"Okay, I get what you're saying. But still, it feels like I'm constantly overstepping. Lily was having a hard time at school with these girls that were bullying her, so I talked to John about it. I'm constantly there, helping with her homework, teaching her things that Charlotte had started— it's like I'm replacing her, and I don't want to do that."

"Has she said that she thinks you're trying to replace her mom?"

"No."

"Has John?"

"No."

She set the spoon against the edge of the bowl before wiping her hands on the front of her shorts.

"You seem to be the only one who's concerned with this. I think that maybe there's some guilt that you haven't allowed yourself to deal with, and it's forcing its way out now."

I pressed my lips together tightly, hoping that the pressure would force the tears away from my eyes.

"It should have been me that day," I whispered, looking away. "I should have been the one that was taken. Not

Charlotte. She had a family that she left behind, and they need her."

"Just like *we* need you. All of us. John, Lily, Charles—myself. There's not a single person in this house who wishes that it would have been you instead, Emma. We miss Charlotte more than anything, but we would miss you just as much if you were gone."

Her words wrapped around my heart, squeezing it so tight that I felt like I couldn't breathe. I sucked in a deep breath and held it, trying to pull myself together as I heard the guys outside, getting ready to come inside.

"Oh, and another thing," Alice added quickly, checking over her shoulder to make sure we were still alone. "Don't be so afraid of love that you can't even see it when it's staring you in the face."

She smiled and winked before she walked away. I looked out the window and found John watching me.

Thirty

I felt like I weighed twenty pounds more after dinner than I did when we first got to Stone Harbor. One thing that I missed about Charlotte's parents was their cooking. But then again, I didn't miss how uncomfortable my stomach would be hours later from eating too much.

By eight-thirty, we had cleaned up dinner and were getting ready to call it a night. Lily had already gone to bed and was quite content in her bedroom at the end of the hall, right across from Charles and Alice's room. John and I had the two rooms at the other end, which shared the jack and jill bathroom.

I was tired but felt gross and sticky from the humidity after sitting on the patio for dinner. I didn't bother to unpack my duffle bag, knowing that I wouldn't be staying long enough to justify unpacking and repacking the bag. I pulled out a pair of light cotton shorts and a tank top to sleep in and went to the bathroom to take a quick shower.

I opened the door and gasped, dropping my clothes to the floor as I shielded my eyes.

"Oh my God! I'm so sorry! I didn't know you were in here," I apologize, continuing to look away from John. He was wearing nothing but a towel wrapped around his waist and his body still damp from the shower.

"It's fine," he laughed. "I guess I should have given you a heads up before I jumped in. Sorry about that."

I was still looking down at the floor, avoiding him while he twisted a q-tip around in his ear. He was oddly relaxed, not at all phased by the fact that he was standing naked in front of me, in just a towel.

"I'll come back when you're done," I said quickly, turning to walk away.

"I'm not naked," he replied coolly. "Just in case that's what you're freaking out about. I have underwear on underneath."

I felt the heat pinch my cheeks.

"Okay."

I left it at that, too uncomfortable to trust myself not to say something stupid. Besides, it wasn't any of my business what he was or *was not* wearing under that towel.

Once he was done, I waited for him to go to his room and locked both doors before I got in the shower. It had already been a long day full of surprises, and I didn't need anymore.

I tilted my head back and closed my eyes as the hot water ran down my face. It felt good to just stop for a moment and not have to worry about where to go or what to do. The trip had been great, don't get me wrong, but almost two weeks on the road was starting to wear on me, and I was thankful for a bathroom that felt like home.

I thought about what Alice had said while I shampooed my hair. I still couldn't believe that I had told her about our kiss, but I was even more in shock when she talked about us being in love. There was something about the way that she said it that made it feel alright and not icky. Maybe because she was able to see it from the outside and could tell that there weren't any romantic feelings involved for either of us? Or was I simply *hoping* that she didn't assume that there were any?

My mind had been foggy all evening, and while I still didn't have the answers that I needed, I knew one thing that was for sure. John wasn't interested in me in *that way.* That was crystal clear when he talked about Lily's teacher Ms. Summers at dinner and emphasized how he wasn't ready to start dating again any time soon and wasn't sure that he ever would be.

I got ready for bed and tried to force my mind to shut down long enough to make up for the lack of sleep that I got last night.

The next morning, I woke up to the smell of freshly brewed coffee and bacon—two of my favorite things. I smiled when I bounced downstairs, seeing Alice and Charles cooking in the kitchen. The table was already set with plates full of pastries and a fruit platter that Lily was picking at when she thought no one was looking.

"It smells *delicious* in here," I said when I walked in, stopping to give Lily a quick kiss on her head. "Good morning, sweet Lily. How did you sleep?"

"Good," she replied cheerfully, popping a grape into her mouth. I was happy that her mood seemed better than it was yesterday.

"Daddy said that we could go down to the beach today," she added, looking up at me with a smile.

"That sounds like a fun time."

"Nana said that it should be cooler today than it was yesterday, and if the weather is good, we can take a boat ride on the ocean so I can finish another item on the bucket list. You know, the one where we sail across three different types of water?"

"I remember." I smiled at the memory of us spending the day floating along the Rio Grande River in Taos, trying to keep our balance, so the little boat didn't tip over.

"How many items do you have left?" Alice asked, pulling a quiche out of the oven and setting it on the trivet on the counter.

"Just two more," Lily commented, pulling the worn piece of paper out of her pocket and unfolding it on top of the table. "If you build it, they will come. But when the water comes, you better run."

Charles laughed, earning a cheek-splitting grin from Lily.

"Well, that sounds like an easy one," Alice replied, adding another plate to the table. The smell of sausage and bacon floated up in front of me as I sat down, and I fought the urge to sneak a piece like Lily had been doing with the fruit.

"I think she wanted to build a sandcastle," Lily said with a small ounce of uncertainty.

Charles scooped some scrambled eggs onto a plate and moved the skillet to the back burner. He set the plate down in front of Lily and placed his hands on her shoulders, looking down at her with a mischievous grin.

"Not just *a* sandcastle. A GIANT sandcastle! Your mom always wanted to build a huge one, but it was never as big as she had envisioned it. She wanted a three-story castle, with a moat around it and flags sticking out of the top of it."

His eyes traveled over to me as he offered a soft smile, remembering how many times she and I had sat on that beach and tried. Each attempt a disaster as the water always reached us before we could finish and wiped-out half of our castle with one quick wave.

"Well, then I guess we have our work cut out for us today,"
I said, trying to find the excitement that I needed for Lily.

"But we don't have flags." Lily frowned.

John walked in and grinned, holding something behind his
back. He bent down beside her as Charles walked over to
sit down beside me.

"Do you mean flags like… these?!" He pulled out a gallon
Ziplock bag that was packed full of different plastic flags.

"Where did you get those?" she asked, taking the bag from him.

"I've been collecting them." He shrugged and stood up, a
look of satisfaction on his face that she had the reaction he
was hoping she would have.

I reached for the pitcher of orange juice and filled a
glass, debating whether I should fill one for John as well.
Deciding against it, I picked it up and took a drink.

"Is this one from that restaurant in Las Vegas? The one
where Emma choked on a pickle?"

The acidity from the juice burned my nose on the way out
as I choked—again, reaching for a napkin to dry my face.

"She did what?" Alice asked in disbelief as she joined us at
the table, handing me a handful of napkins.

"Thank you," I managed to get out before turning away to
blow my nose, hoping to expel the rest of the juice.

"She choked on a bite of her pickle," John explained
calmly, looking to make sure I was okay. "We were at
dinner, and they had this karaoke contest that I signed us up
for but didn't tell her until they called our names—which

happened to be at the exact moment that she took a bite."

"Oh my, I bet that was embarrassing, dear," Alice said sympathetically.

"It was," I replied, finally able to breathe, even though I could still feel the burn in both nostrils. "You kept the flags from my sandwich?" I asked, tilting my head at John.

"They were special."

We stayed staring at each other for a few minutes, completely oblivious to everyone around us. I hadn't seen him take them, but the fact that he thought that they were special was pulling at something in my heart that I couldn't put my finger on.

"What was special about them?" Charles asked, scooping a serving of quiche onto his plate. He was oblivious to what was going on, which meant that Alice hadn't filled him in on anything after we all went to bed last night.

"Well, I thought they were special because they came in the *biggest* sandwich that I had ever seen. Emma and I both ordered the club, and it was stacked so high that it was impossible to eat. Except, our sweet Emma here, tried."

I could hear the laughter in John's voice as he told the story, remembering how much he and Lily had laughed about that night as well. I scrunched my face and pretended to give him my best scowl.

"Why didn't you just take it apart and eat it like a regular sandwich?" Charles asked, looking at me as he passed the plate of bacon.

I took it, thankful to finally dive in.

"Honestly, I didn't even think about it until I saw John do it. It came as one giant piece, so I figured it should be eaten that way."

The laughter floated around the table as I grabbed a few pieces of bacon and passed it to John.

Soon, we had our plates full, and the conversation died off while we ate. I already knew that I would regret such a heavy breakfast when we were going to spend the day at the beach. The nice thing was that the beach was literally their backyard, and we didn't have to walk far to get to the water.

By ten o'clock, we were sitting in the sand, under an umbrella, with all the supplies that we needed to make a massive sandcastle. We made sure that we were far enough away from the water to have a couple of hours to work on it. John and Lily worked on clearing the area and smoothing it out while I dug a hole a few feet away. We needed mud to make the sand stick, so once I had a big enough hole, I went to the water and collected buckets full to take back to my hole, creating our own little mud shop.

Alice sorted through the different buckets and tools that she had brought with her while Charles set up the blanket and some chairs behind us. He had packed an ice chest full of snacks and bottles of water, even though we were close enough to go back and grab what we needed. I loved his kind heart for making it more convenient for everyone.

He had even called his friend to see if we could take a boat ride out on the ocean today, but he had a meeting in New York that he had to get to, so we scheduled for tomorrow instead. That meant that we had all day and all night to build the perfect sandcastle for Lily.

"Alright, I think we're ready to get started," John said, getting up to check his work. He was wearing a white t-shirt and swim trunks, yet I couldn't stop panicking over the fact that I had seen him in his towel last night. I hadn't been able to figure out why it had been bothering me so much until I had another dream like the one I had the other night, where Charlotte came to yell at me for trying to steal her family.

"What should we build first?" Lily asked, looking up at her dad. Her long, blonde hair was braided behind her back, and she was wearing a cute visor that Alice had loaned her to keep the sun out of her eyes so she could work.

"I say we start with the first level. We can get some sand and make a giant rectangle. That will be the main entrance into our castle."

"Okay," she giggled.

"I have some mud ready for you guys over here," I said, pointing to the hole that was already starting to dry up. Well, so much for that idea.

"Perfect," John said, walking over and bending down in front of me to fill the giant bucket he brought with him.

He reached back and set it to the side before filling another one for Lily.

"Where's your bucket?" he asked. I felt like he was staring at me, but behind the dark lenses of his sunglasses, I couldn't see anything.

"I don't have a bucket."

"Why not?"

"Why would I?"

"Because we're building a sandcastle, and it's going to be a lot more work if you're planning to carry globs of mud in your hands, back and forth."

He paused for a moment and lowered his head, tipping his sunglasses down his nose so I could see his eyes.

"Is this going to be another sandwich adventure?" he teased playfully, his cheeks dimpling from his grin.

"No." I rolled my eyes and then wondered if he could even see me through my sunglasses. "I was on mud duty. I did my job, and now I get to sit and watch the workers do theirs," I joked, pursing my lips.

"I don't think so," he grumbled, setting the bucket down next to the other one. He reached over in one quick swoop and picked me up out of the chair, tossing me over his shoulder. I squealed, praying that my bikini wasn't getting moved around to cause a wardrobe malfunction once he put me down.

"We're *all* building a sandcastle," he said, setting me beside Lily, next to the smooth sand. He walked back and grabbed the buckets and brought them over, sitting Lily's beside her and the other one between us as he plopped down next to me.

I could feel Alice and Charles' eyes on us as they watched but didn't say anything. I knew that his knees wouldn't allow him to get down here to join us, and she had insisted that she wanted to watch and help with the decorating once it was done. That left us—just the three of us—to build this thing together.

John reached into the bucket and pulled out a handful of mud, dropping some on my leg before he slapped it down on the sand. The cold, wetness sent a chill through me as a small gust of wind passed by us.

"Hey, buddy, keep to your own side," I joked, wiping the mud off my leg.

"There are no sides when it comes to teamwork."

He reached in and grabbed another handful, this time *purposely* letting a chunk fall onto my thigh.

"You can't be afraid to get dirty out here," he said proudly. "We've got a luxurious sandcastle to build. We're not trying to look cute for the frat boys down the beach."

He nodded to where a group of guys were playing football—shirtless. I hadn't even noticed them, and from the looks of it, they hadn't seen us either, probably because there was a large group of girls in teeny tiny bikinis on the other side of them.

I huffed out a snort, laughing at how ridiculous he was being. Then it occurred to me—was he *jealous*?

"Well, if you don't want the cute frat boys to look your way, then maybe stop looking theirs." I kept my voice even, not wanting to draw Lily's attention to another awkward conversation between her father and me.

"I wasn't talking about me, and you know it." He kept his voice quiet enough for only me to hear.

I glanced over at Lily, who was busy dumping her mud onto the smooth sand, frowning when it didn't stay in the shape she had started with.

"Is there something that you want to say to me?" I snapped under my breath, turning to look at him.

"No. Nothing that would make a difference." He leaned forward and started working his mud into a pile on the sand.

"What's that supposed to mean?"

"It means that you've already made up your mind, and I know that nothing that I say or do is going to change it."

I pulled back as if his words had physically hurt me.

"I'm trying to do what's best for everyone, John. For once, I'm not worried about myself or how I feel about everything. I'm only thinking about you guys and what you need."

He stopped and leaned back on his heels, turning toward me.

"You have no idea what we need."

It was a cold, harsh statement. One that I couldn't argue with, even if I wanted to. How could I sit there and say that I knew what they needed when I barely even knew what *I* needed.

"Well then, maybe it's for the best that I go."

He pulled his lips together in a thin line and thought for a moment before deciding not to say anything.

I tried my best to keep it together and have fun with Lily as we worked, but my mind was scattered, and my emotions were barely holding on by a string.

Finally, around one o'clock, we stopped for lunch and took a much-needed break. We had the first two levels done and secure after several mishaps and crumbled walls. John took Lily down to play in the water for a little bit before we started working on the sandcastle again.

I laid on the beach towel with my sunglasses on and let the sun warm me up. Alice was sitting beside me on another towel, reading a book while Charles scanned the sand for hidden treasures with his metal detector.

"I wanted to talk to you about last night," Alice said, setting her book down next to her. I turned to look at her, pulling my glasses down, so she had my full attention. I braced myself for what she was about to say and knew that she had every right to be upset with me for falling in love with her son-in-law.

"Okay," I said softly when she didn't say anything more.

"We started talking about love, and I could see that it made you uncomfortable. I'm sorry about that. Sometimes, I don't think before I talk, and it makes for a messy situation later."

I rolled onto my side, adjusting my swimsuit to make sure it stayed in place.

"There are different kinds of love, Emma. But what I was talking about with you and John, that's been there for as long as I can remember. It's the kind of love that starts as a friendship and then turns into being best friends before anything else. It's where they know you so well that they can read your mood without you having to say anything. It's them surprising you with your favorite food when they know you've had a bad day or when you have something to celebrate. It's all of the little things that we don't stop to think about, but we feel them when they're missing, and there's suddenly a void inside of us."

Memories of the past few weeks rushed through my mind with all the things that John had been doing for me. From taking care of me when I was sick to getting me my favorite foods to eat without me having to ask. Making sure that I had my own room and some privacy when we would stay at a hotel. Spoiling me rotten on my birthday. Almost every single day, he had done something special for me, and I didn't always see it. I had gotten so used to him taking care of me and doing nice things for me that I hadn't noticed just how much he was doing.

"I know that you're afraid of falling in love, Emma. And I understand why. But I think that you're running because suddenly it feels too real, and it scares you. I'm not suggesting that you guys rush off and start a romantic relationship, but I don't think that you're being very fair to either of you by pushing him away."

I rolled onto my back and pushed the sunglasses up to hide my eyes as the tears slid down the sides of my face.

Thirty One

I pulled at the hem of the black satin tank top, studying myself in the mirror as I wore the outfit that Charlotte had bought me for this very interview. It felt weird to finally put it on three months later, but I prayed that it still had some of her good luck vibes hidden somewhere in it because I needed all that I could get today.

I had been back in San Francisco for almost two weeks, and of course, it was just my luck that they would schedule my interview for Friday afternoon, the weekend of Lily's birthday party on the beach in New Jersey. Since I hadn't been working, I couldn't afford to fly back for it, especially during a holiday weekend.

Lily had cried on the phone when I told her that I wasn't going to be able to come after all, and I felt like shit for it. It wasn't a complete lie, but it was also heavily swayed by my firm determination to walk away from them before she got any more attached than she already had.

I glanced at the clock, confirming that I only had twenty minutes to finish getting ready and get out the door before I was late for the interview. The last thing that I wanted to do was make a bad impression by being late, so I quickly swiped my lips with a light peach-colored lip gloss and tossed it into my purse before leaving.

My anxiety was so bad that my entire body felt like it was covered in sweat. It wasn't hot out, especially compared to the weather we had endured on our trip, so it had to be my nerves. I pulled into the parking lot and found a spot up front, in the shade. I took one last look in the mirror before I got out and walked into the interview that could change my life.

When I got to the lobby, I felt sickened by the number of people filling the chairs in the waiting room, all there to interview. I knew that it wasn't for another position because I had been researching everything I could about the company to prepare for today and hadn't seen any other openings. That meant that I had to be at my absolute best today and work hard to impress them.

They were running late and finally called me back twenty minutes after the scheduled time. I walked into the large boardroom, my stomach tightening as I looked around at the different faces staring at me and sizing me up based on physical appearance alone. I knew that group interviews were common, but I hadn't expected to meet with *ten* people at one time. A handful of them were easily recognizable from my recent searches and served on the board of directors or were in upper management. Then my eyes landed on the man of the hour, Mr. Henry Crawford, the man whose job I was here to steal.

"Ms. Monroe, please have a seat," a woman who looked like she was in her late thirties said, extending her hand to the only empty chair at the table.

I tried to smile but wasn't sure if it was coming across as pleasant or if it looked more like a snarl. My body was so rigid that my facial muscles couldn't relax enough to focus on the task.

Laid out in front of each person on the large mahogany table was a copy of my resume, a notepad, and a pen. It felt so serious and tense in the room as they studied me. I squirmed under the heavy gazes as I waited for someone to start.

Finally, the woman who had asked me to sit down began asking some general questions, which felt easy enough to answer. They weren't too personal, but I had no idea what to expect next.

Once she was done, the interview moved to Mr. Crawford, who sat at the head of the table, holding a pen between his hands with just the tips of his pointer fingers.

"Why do you want to work at BayView Advertising?" he asked, looking away from the pen to make eye contact.

I swallowed hard. I hated these types of questions and hoped that there wouldn't be many more. The worst thing to try to answer was *where do you see yourself in five years?*

"I've worked in creative marketing for most of my career. It's what I know and love. I think that my knowledge and expertise are what this position needs. My passion and drive are what will make me succeed."

He smirked at my response, and I wondered if he was already ruling me out. I shifted uncomfortably in my seat, hoping the next question would be better and not so personal.

A few of the board members jumped in and asked me questions related directly to my experience and focused on the skills I was eager to discuss. I was finally starting to feel better about the interview. This was what I had planned for, what I had spent the last two weeks preparing myself for. If I could focus on what I've already done, I could impress them with what I could do for their company if given the Creative Marketing Director position.

Just when I thought we were finished, Mr. Crawford lowered his glasses and peered at me over them.

"Ms. Monroe, where do you see yourself in the next five years?" he asked, drawing everyone's attention to him.

I imagined myself on the beach in New Jersey with John and Lily, laughing and building sandcastles. As quickly as the thought rushed into my mind, I forced it back out, reminding myself that those days were over. I cleared my throat as subtly as possible and answered.

"I see myself excelling as the creative marketing director for BayView Advertising."

He smiled, but it didn't meet his eyes. Instead, it was sad, as if he was disappointed that I hadn't said something he was expecting instead. He looked down and studied my resume for a moment before looking up at me.

"Where do you see your *personal* life in five years?" he asked with a heavy emphasis on personal.

"I'm not sure that I understand what you're asking. My job is very important to me, and I'm willing to dedicate the time needed to do this job. I don't have any personal commitments that would interfere if that's what the concern is."

Did he assume that I wasn't serious about this job because there was a small gap of time between when I had been laid off at my last job? There would have been a history of me applying for the creative marketing manager position in April, which would confirm that I had been actively looking right after I was let go.

"Being the creative marketing director for BayView means that a lot of your time will be spent here. There are times when you'll work long hours—late evenings, possibly weekends, and the occasional holiday. This job can be as demanding as you let it be, and I think it's important to think about where you see yourself five years down the line, so you have an idea of whether this job is the right fit for you. I would hate for someone so young and ambitious to be tied down to a job that keeps her from living the life she envisions for herself. Maybe something to consider before you make any quick decisions."

My jaw dropped slightly as I felt taken aback by his words. It was like he had somehow been inside my head and knew what I was thinking about when he first asked me. Was I that transparent?

I didn't say anything. I just waited for the interview to be over and left. Once I was outside, I took a deep breath and replayed what had just happened in my head as I got into my car. I was almost back at John's house when my phone rang. I parked in the driveway and climbed out, answering Alice's call on my way inside the house.

"Hey," I said, wondering if she was calling to try to convince me to come to New Jersey for Lily's birthday. It was so last minute, but I wouldn't be surprised. I kicked off my heels and sat down on the couch. "What's up?"

"I was calling to see how the interview went," she said excitedly. There was a lot of background noise behind her, and I wondered where she was since everything around them is usually calm and quiet.

"It seems like it went well. I won't know anything for a week or two until after they've completed all of their interviews."

"Wow, that seems like a lot of people."

"I agree. I'm not sure how many people have applied for the position, but at least twenty people were waiting before me, and probably fifteen more who were still in the lobby when I left."

"Well, if it's meant to be, you'll get it."

I loved that she felt so calm about it when I felt on pins and needles, wondering if I would have better odds at winning the lottery.

"What are your plans for dinner?" she asked, cutting the silence that had fallen between us.

I glanced down at my watch. It was already after five, and I hadn't even thought about it. I wasn't in the mood to cook, which meant that I would order pizza and call it a night.

"I'm not sure, probably just make a salad or something," I fibbed, feeling guilty for my pizza obsession.

"Well, I'm sure the salad will go great with the pizza you're about to order," she teased, laughing loudly in my ear. I pulled the phone away and cringed from the noise.

"How did you know?" I joked, laughing along with her.

"Because I know you so well. But I think you should do something better than pizza tonight. You should go celebrate your interview and treat yourself to something nice."

I groaned and closed my eyes as I leaned against the couch. I was too much of an introvert to go to a restaurant on my own—there was no way that I was going to do that. So what if I preferred the company of the fictional characters on tv to real people? It wasn't like I had any friends that I could call and invite out to dinner.

"Pizza is nice," I countered. "I can stay home, in my pajamas, eat my pizza, and drink a glass of wine without having to deal with anyone."

"Or you could go get changed and meet us outside in twenty minutes, and we can all go grab dinner together."

I felt my heart skip a beat. What did she just say?

"What are you talking about? You guys are in New Jersey, getting ready for Lily's birthday party on the beach tomorrow."

"Well, about that. Lily decided that she didn't really care *which* beach she had her party on, so we all hopped on a plane and flew back to San Francisco so you could be there for her party. We were getting our luggage when I called you."

My stomach knotted in a mixture of happiness and stress. Why didn't John tell me that they were coming when we talked the other day? A little bit of a heads up would have been nice given that I hadn't cleaned up in a few days and was still working on Lily's birthday present that was scattered across the coffee table.

"Twenty minutes?" I asked, paralyzed by the shock.

"I can ask the Uber driver to go slower if you need a few more minutes. John will run in and drop off our luggage, and then we can head out to dinner. Think about where you want to go, and we'll see you soon!"

The line went dead, and I was left scrambling to figure out what to do. I jumped up and started collecting the stuff from the coffee table, making sure not to damage anything as I loaded it on top of the clean clothes that were already folded but still sitting in the laundry basket by the stairs. Once I had everything packed up, I swung the basket up on my hip and rushed upstairs to get ready.

Twenty-five minutes later, I heard the front door open, and John called out to let me know he was there.

"I'll be down in just a second," I called back, giving my hair a quick fluff with my fingers before grabbing my purse from the bed and heading downstairs. I hadn't changed out of the outfit that I had worn to the interview, there just wasn't enough time, and I had no idea where we were going.

I walked barefoot into the living room, looking for the shoes that I had kicked off when I first got home. I sat down on the couch and was slipping them on when John came in from the garage with more suitcases lined up by the stairs. Seeing them there made it feel more real that this was really happening. They had all flown back to San Francisco so that I could celebrate Lily's birthday with her. There was no doubt about it, I was already in too deep, and it was going to hurt like hell to walk away from her.

"Hey," he said casually, shoving his hands into his shorts. He looked tanner than the last time I had seen him, his green eyes more vibrant against the darker color of his skin. "You almost ready?"

"Yeah, I'm good," I lied. Good implied that I was doing okay and that I didn't feel like a hot mess, ready to explode at any moment from the dozens of thoughts that were rushing through my mind. "Did you want to take two cars?"

"Everyone's already situated in the Sequoia. The middle row is pretty roomy."

I felt silly for even asking, knowing that his SUV was plenty big enough for the five of us. There was just something about being in such close proximity to him that made me feel like we needed to take separate vehicles so I could clear my head and think.

I got up from the couch and walked over to where he was waiting for me, holding the garage door open. It felt weird, and I didn't know what I should do. Did I hug him and tell him that I was glad to see him? Or did I ignore any physical contact and pretend that things were normal between us when they weren't.

As I got closer, he rested his hand on my lower back and guided me out, pulling the inside door closed behind us. The garage door was open, and the Sequoia was parked in the driveway, next to my car.

"It's nice to be home for a few days," he said quietly as we walked together to the car. I could barely see inside, but when the light hit just right, I noticed that they were all piled into the back, leaving the front passenger seat open for me.

"It's nice having you back," I replied with a soft smile, meaning every word.

Something flickered across his face, forcing him to frown before he shook it off and climbed inside.

The drive to the restaurant was filled with Lily filling me in on what had happened since I'd left. It had only been two weeks, but she had enough details to fill in for two months. They had a few picnics on the beach, she went boating with Charles and got to do some deep-sea fishing, and in the evenings, she and Alice were building a puzzle of New York City that was super hard.

I laughed and stayed turned in my seat, watching her face light up every time she talked about something that had excited her. I asked about Sammy and was happy to hear that he was doing well and staying with their neighbor while everyone was in San Francisco. My heart felt happy, and for once, I started to second guess whether I was right about walking away from them.

The past two weeks had been depressing, and I hadn't found joy in much of anything. But now that they were here, I felt alive and found my cheeks hurting from smiling so much. Maybe Mr. Crawford was right; I did need to stop and think about where I saw myself in five years and what I wanted out of life.

Thirty Two

"So then, Mrs. Williams—she's the nice lady who's watching Sammy for us while we're gone—she went running down the beach, trying to catch the seagull that stole her hat!" Lily burst into laughter as she told the story, her face completely illuminated by her happiness.

We were finishing our dinner at Azalia's, an upscale restaurant with the most divine lobster tail that I'd ever tasted. The room was decent sized with plenty of tables scattered throughout, each one dressed with a crisp white linen tablecloth and a vase of fresh flowers in the center. Our table was against the wall of full-length windows that looked over the ocean, the vibrant colors of the sunset reflected off the water.

Everyone had been quiet for the most part, with Lily doing all the talking, but I could still feel a slight tension in the air between us. While it didn't feel any different than what I had been feeling with John before I left New Jersey, it struck me as odd that I was starting to feel it from Alice and Charles as well. Had they started to realize that maybe John and Lily had been happy without me and that it wasn't a bad idea for me to leave after all?

Finally, after John had insisted on paying for the meal, we headed home. I imagined that they were all tired and jet-lagged from their flight today, and honestly, I needed some time to wrap my head around the conflicting messages that my heart was trying to send to my head. I said goodnight to everyone and made sure that Alice and Charles had what they needed in the other guest room before I went to Lily's room and wished her sweet dreams.

She was already falling asleep, clutching the teddy bear that she got for Christmas when she was five and hadn't parted with it since. I sat on the edge of the bed, watching as her eyelids fluttered before she gave in and drifted to sleep. My fingers itched to reach over and brush the strand of hair off her face, but I had to remind myself that I couldn't do those things anymore. It was bad enough that I had come into her room to begin with, but some habits were harder to break than others, which was why it was important for me to find a place to live before they came back for good.

I spent a few minutes beside her, soaking up the feeling of being so close to her that it made my heart ache. I couldn't imagine a world without her in it, and I hated that soon, I would have to. I wiped the tears from my eyes and gently stood up, making sure I didn't wake her. When I turned to the door, I saw John standing there with his arms crossed over his chest and a stern look on his face.

My stomach soured when I imagined what he was about to say to me. I deserved to be scolded for what I had done. It wasn't going to make it any easier for me to leave Lily behind. I padded across the room and followed him down the hall per the nod he gave me.

Once we were in his room, he closed the door and turned to look at me. I couldn't read him right now, and that scared me. Was he mad at me? Disappointed? He definitely didn't look pleased.

"We need to talk, Emma," he said, his tone colder than normal.

I knew it. I clasped my hands together and squished my toes up in my heels, trying to expel as much of the nervous energy as I could without him noticing.

"Do you want to sit?" he asked, nodding to the chair by the window, next to the window seat.

I shook my head, too desperate for him to get this over with and put me out of my misery.

"Okay," he said heavily with a sigh. "I don't really know how to say this…."

Oh God, he was trying to let me down easy as he fired me from their lives.

"John, you don't have to say it—I was planning to be out of the house before you guys came back. I didn't expect the surprise visit. I can find somewhere to stay this weekend, so you don't have to worry about it," I blurted out, ready to head for the door.

He pulled his head back in surprise before narrowing his eyes at me in disbelief.

"*That's* what you thought I was going to say? That I want you to *leave?*"

I waited impatiently, a pinch of heat flaming against my cheeks.

"God, Emma. When is it going to stop?"

He put his hands on his hips and scowled at me.

"I don't know what you're talking about," I admitted sheepishly.

"I can see that," he muttered, running a hand down his face.

"I didn't ask you to come in here so I could tell you to leave, Emma. I would *never* ask you to leave, but for whatever reason, you keep trying to run away, and it's really pissing me off."

"I've told you why John. You don't want to listen," I said softly, trying not to upset him further.

"I don't think that *I'm* the one who has the problem listening."

"What do you want me to do? Act like things between us haven't changed? I can't do that, John. It's not fair to you, to me, or Lily. She deserves better than that, and that's what I'm trying to give her."

"I get that things have changed!" His voice boomed through the room, and I hoped that it wasn't loud enough for anyone else to hear. "My life has been in a constant state of change for three months since Charlotte died, and I'm still waiting for it to turn right side up again!"

"That's why I'm trying to walk away—so you guys can find your new normal and get back to the life you're supposed to live."

"Do you *really* think that there is a normal for us *without* you in it? You've been in my life for fifteen years, Emma. You've been in Lily's life since the day she was born. That makes you family—whether you want to believe it or not. I don't know how you can just turn your back and walk away from that so easily."

I could hear the anger in his voice as my emotions bubbled over the surface. I fisted my hands at my side and tried to control my temper.

"You think that this is *easy* for me?! You have *no idea* how freaking hard it is to walk away, knowing that I will never see you guys again. The only thing that I have known in life is about to be ripped away from me, and I'm doing my best to keep my head above water right now!"

My body shook with anger as I stared at him, wondering how he could think that this was easy for me.

"You're the one who keeps walking away, Emma. Not us. Maybe you should reconsider that the next time you think that this is the hardest thing that you *have* to do. Lily has been through a lot over the past few months, and she's about to go through another big change. I thought if anyone could be there to help her, it would be you. I guess I was wrong."

I felt his words stab straight into my heart, holding my breath in place as the hurt paralyzed me.

"What are you talking about? What big change is happening to Lily?"

He unclasped his watch and slid it down his hand as he walked over to his nightstand and set it down. He kicked off his shoes, purposely making me wait for his answer.

"John," I said curtly, forcing his attention my way.

"Lily and I have decided to move to New Jersey. She loves it there, and it turns out that Charles has a friend looking for someone to take over his company. It's a good fit for me, and it will allow me to have more free time to spend with Lily."

I felt like the wind had been knocked out of me as his words swirled around me like a tornado. That must be why Alice and Charles were acting so tense at dinner. They already knew that he was going to tell me tonight.

"The reason that I asked to talk to you was because I was going to ask you to come with us. Lily and I want to be close to family, and we've come to love New Jersey." He paused for a moment, standing on the other side of the bed, watching me. "I guess I just thought that maybe you would consider it, given how happy you were while you were there."

I wanted to talk to him about it, but the words were lodged so deep in my throat that I couldn't get them out.

"When are you moving?" I asked, forcing my voice past the lump that had formed in my throat.

"We're packing up some stuff while we're here and then flying back on Sunday with Alice and Charles. I'll have the packages overnighted, so they'll be there when we get back. I start the new job on Monday. Lily and I talked about finishing the other half of our trip, but we've decided to postpone it for now given the change in plans. Instead, we're going to focus on finding a house and getting settled in before she starts her new school in August."

"I'll make sure to have my stuff out as soon as possible," I said quietly, still processing this bombshell he dropped on me.

"You don't have to leave until the house sells, Emma. If anything, it will help me to have someone living here while I'm in New Jersey, so I don't have to worry about anyone breaking in."

I felt the burning sting as I realized that he had already accepted that I wasn't going with them. He didn't even put up a fight about it or try to convince me otherwise, which was fine—I knew where I belonged, and it was better this way.

"Okay, I'm happy to help however I can." I turned away before the tear could slide down my cheek and rushed out of his room, closing the door behind me.

As I stepped into the hallway, I spotted Alice at the other end, heading to the bathroom. One look at me, and she clutched her hand to her chest as the sadness washed over her. I didn't bother to look back before I darted into my room and closed the door. I quickly stripped off the outfit that Charlotte had bought me and wondered if maybe it wasn't lucky after all.

Thirty Three

"Okay, open my gift!" I said excitedly, handing Lily a box wrapped in pink shimmery wrapping paper. There was a white ribbon tied around it that she was trying to get off with no luck. I reached into the drawer behind me and pulled out a pair of scissors, handing them to her. She cut the ribbon and started tearing through the paper as her face pulled tight with an ear-to-ear grin.

I leaned forward on the couch, resting my elbows on my knees while folding my hands together in front of my face. I tapped my feet anxiously, hoping that she would love her gift. Finally, she had the box free from the paper and opened it. Her eyes went wide as she looked inside, then looked up at me. I smiled back, nodding for her to take it out.

Her fingers dug in and pulled out a thick photo album that had a picture of her and John on the front. Beneath it was the words *Lily's Epic Adventure*. She took her time flipping through the pages of the scrapbook that I had made for her with the pictures I had taken on our trip.

She laughed at the silly ones, and I watched her eyes get glossy with a few of the more serious ones, like her and John sitting side by side at the beach after we finished the sandcastle. It was such a huge accomplishment, and she was overwhelmed with emotion when we were done. John had taken her down on the beach to talk, and I snuck in a picture of the two of them with his arm wrapped protectively around her.

There were plenty of pictures of the sandcastle itself, plus the few that Alice had sent to me of the three of us working on it as we went. I wanted her to always have this memory and know how thrilled her mom would have been to see her biggest dream come to life.

Once she got to the end, she stopped and looked down at the piece of paper that was by itself in a protective sleeve. I felt the tug at my heart, knowing that she was as emotional about it as I was. It was the original bucket list that Charlotte had written. The copy that Lily was afraid to take with her because she didn't want anything to happen to it.

I had also taken the time to write each of the riddles down on a new piece of paper, along with what the adventure was and where we did it.

"What is it?" Alice asked softly, leaning forward to see what had Lily in tears.

"It's mom's bucket list. Aunt Emma saved the original one and made me a new one that has the answer to each clue."

"Why don't you read them out loud to us," John asked, leaning closer to see over her shoulder.

"Okay," she said shakily.

As she worked her way down the list, she got too worked up and started sobbing, unable to continue. I looked away, feeling terrible for giving her a gift that had upset her so much. John was holding her as she cried, assuring her that it would be alright with each word he whispered.

After a few minutes, she calmed down enough to get up and come running over to me, wrapping her arms around me.

"Thank you for the gift," she sobbed, her tears wetting my face. "But you forgot one."

She pulled back and wiped her face as she looked at me. I

pulled my brows together in confusion, wondering how that could have happened. I was focused when I worked on it, but surely it was possible that I accidentally missed one.

"Which one did I miss?" I asked, reaching out to touch her hand before she jerked it away and ran upstairs.

My heart was beating in my ears as the blood rushed through me, bringing me to my feet quickly before I squatted down in front of the table and looked at the pages that were arranged so they would be side by side.

On the left side was Charlotte's list, and on the right was mine. I counted the number of items on both and confirmed that they matched. I quickly scanned the one that I had written, making sure that I hadn't accidentally listed the same one twice.

Eat with the ants, but you can't wear pants

You might get a tummy ache from the funnel cake, but if you sink a ball in, you just might win

If you are what you eat, then make sure you pick something sweet

Go high in the sky, but not faster than the birds can fly

You might need more than a breeze to travel across all three of these

Just when you've crossed the line, take a step back and go back in time

Be entertained while under the stars; it's even better if you're in the car

Keep your eye on the night sky, and you just might see one pass by

Sit and be still; maybe they'll come. When they light up, it's even more fun

If you build it, they will come, but when the water comes, you better run

Everything matched between the two of them, so I couldn't figure out what had Lily so upset. I reached inside the clear sleeve and pulled out the copy that Charlotte had written and found one more on the back that I hadn't noticed before. I sucked in a deep breath and closed my eyes, holding it against my chest when I read it.

"What does it say?" John asked behind me.

"When you think you've found happiness, check to see if it's true love's first kiss."

I pressed my lips together when I was done, hearing John sigh behind me before he sunk back against the chair.

"I don't get it," Charles said, confused. "Is she trying to find true love?"

John and I stayed silent, neither of us knowing what to say. It had hit me like a ton of bricks after I remembered her talking to me about her friend's mom, who was suddenly happier than she had ever been because she had fallen in love again. Lily was so adamant that was what she wanted for John, for him to be happy again.

"It's not about her, dear," Alice said softly, knowing what was being said by our silence.

"I'll go talk to her," John said, pushing out of his seat.

I didn't want to overstep, but I also didn't trust that he would know the right thing to say to her right now.

"Do you mind if I try instead? I think this might be better girl to girl, if you know what I mean?"

He nodded and sat back down as Charles watched, still confused.

"Why don't we go make some tea?" Alice offered, helping him off the couch. I knew that she was going to go fill him in on what was happening while she gave John some space to not have to be in the middle of that conversation with his father-in-law.

I took the stairs two at a time, then waited outside of Lily's room, afraid to go in and break her heart even more. I knocked softly, hoping that it was enough for her to hear.

"Go away," she muttered.

I closed my eyes and rested my forehead against the door, frustrated at myself for creating this mess. I only had a few seconds for self-pity before I had to move on and get this over with before I made it worse.

"I'm coming in, Lily," I announced, turning the knob slowly and pushing the door open.

She was lying on her bed, curled into a ball with the blanket she was working on with Charlotte wrapped around her. It felt like the walls were caving in around me, smothering me with the grief that I felt for her.

I didn't bother trying to sit on the bed with her. I wanted to give her whatever space she needed and knew that she might not want me in here, period. I sat down on the plush rug in the middle of the room and waited a few minutes.

"I'm really sorry that I upset you," I said softly. "I didn't mean to, and I feel terrible about it."

She laid there quietly, pulling in ragged breaths as she clutched the blanket tighter.

"I didn't remember that there was another clue when I wrote them down for you. It wasn't on purpose that I left that one off. It just happened to be the luck of the draw that it was the only one on the other side and the one that we didn't talk about on the trip while we were marking the others off."

She stayed quiet, but her breathing started to level out as she calmed down some.

"When your mom wrote that one, she was head over heels in love with this guy at school—or so she thought. She believed in fairytales and wanted to believe that you can tell if it's true love by the first kiss," I explained. "But Lily, this was when she was your age and didn't even know what love was yet. I'm sure that this one was already crossed off her list after she met your daddy."

"That's not true," she countered, shifting to sit up. She kept the blanket held tight against her. "You guys have always told me how mommy didn't want anything to do with daddy when they first met and that it took her a while before she gave him a chance. They didn't fall in love with their first kiss."

"That's not really how it works, though," I tried again, already knowing that this wasn't what she wanted to hear based on the scowl on her face. "Just because someone doesn't fall in love after the first kiss doesn't mean that it's not true love."

"Yes, it does!" she yelled angrily. I pulled back, shocked by the outburst. "Mommy and daddy didn't have that after their first kiss, but you and daddy did! That's why you guys have been acting so strange since it happened. Because it's *true love*! You can't fight it, even though you guys are trying. Daddy found happiness, and you guys shared true love's first kiss!"

I opened my mouth to speak but stopped when I felt John's eyes on me. I turned around to find him standing in the doorway, eyes narrowed and piercing through me.

"Emma, can you give us a minute, please?" His tone was clipped. "Alone."

I stood up on shaky legs and walked out of the bedroom, jumping when the door closed loudly behind me. I sat at the top of the stairs, waiting impatiently.

"How's she doing?" I asked when I heard John come out of Lily's room a few minutes later.

"She's fine," he replied, sitting down next to me. "She's going to rest for a little bit before we head to the beach."

I covered my face with my hands and rested my elbows on my knees as I leaned forward.

"I made a huge mess out of this," I grumbled. "I'm so sorry. I didn't mean to ruin her birthday. You guys flew all the way here, and I had to go and—"

"You didn't ruin anything. It was a beautiful, very thoughtful gift, Emma. It means a lot to her, just like it does to me too."

I sat there hiding my face for a few minutes before I turned to look at him.

"I didn't remember that last one," I admitted, the guilt still eating away at me.

"I know. Me neither."

"I didn't expect her to think..." My voice trailed off with the words that I didn't dare speak.

"I wish she hadn't heard us talking about it," he admitted, looking straight ahead of him and away from me.

I lowered my eyes in shame, knowing that he had regretted it from the moment that it happened.

"I'm sorry that it happened. It really hurt Lily, and I never wanted that to happen."

"Do you know what I'm the most upset about?" he asked, turning toward me.

I stilled as I waited.

"I'm upset because I thought that we would be able to just move past it. Given everything that we've been through together, I figured we could get through this too because you're not like other women. I knew that I didn't have to worry about whether or not you were worried that I had crossed the line or if you would question whether I had loved my wife. You've always been real with me, Emma, and then all of a sudden— bam! Something changed, and now I feel like I don't know you anymore. You're running from me every chance you get because I made one mistake that changed something between us."

I swallowed back the tears that were threatening to spill over.

"I got scared."

"Me too," he admitted. "But Emma, how are we ever going to move past this if you don't talk to me?"

"What was I supposed to say? That I *had* accidentally fallen in love with you? Because I am John— I'm madly in love with you and Lily, and the thought of leaving you guys rips my heart open. I don't know what *this love* is, but it's different, and that scared me." I gestured to the space between us.

"I would be more worried if things *didn't* change between us. We've spent a lot of time together since she died, grieving our loss as a family and putting the pieces back together to start a new life. So, it's easy to see that our love for each other would change too."

His voice was soft and reassuring as he reached over and gently squeezed my shoulder.

"The thing that I hate the most about all of this is that the moment things got hard, and you got scared, you ran and put a wall up that no one can get through. You are so afraid of letting yourself love— or be loved— that you push people away until there's no one left. We're sitting here, trying to love you with everything that we have, and you're basically saying that it's not enough."

The tears started to slide down my face as I kept my eyes on the front door below us.

"I know that you have your own life to live and that you need to decide what's best for you, but I really wish that you'd come to New Jersey with us. I think it's a great opportunity for all of us."

He patted my knee and got up, walking to his room as he left me speechless.

Thirty Four

"Aunt Emma, I'm sorry about what I said earlier," Lily said as she plopped down on the sand next to me. I scooted over, making room for her on the blanket under the shade of the umbrella.

"You don't need to say sorry," I assured her, wrapping my arm around her shoulders. "I'm the one who should apologize. I didn't mean to upset you."

"You didn't. I've just been trying to figure out how to make daddy happy again, and I guess I just started to overthink everything. He reminded me that you guys were just friends and that it might have made you uncomfortable for me to say that you guys were supposed to fall in love."

I smiled softly at her, letting her talk.

"I guess I just didn't think it would be a bad thing if you were in love because I like how things are when the three of us are together. I know that you're not my mom, but you still take care of me like she did, and you're really nice to my dad and me. If I had to pick a new family, that's the one that I wanted. But I understand that it's not how things work, so I'm sorry if I made you uncomfortable. I know that it's my fault that you don't want to move to New Jersey with us."

Her bottom lip trembled as she fought to keep away the tears.

"Oh, sweetie!" I pulled her in closer to me and held her as she cried.

"*You* are not the reason that I don't want to move to New

Jersey. Honestly, I haven't decided what I want to do yet, and a lot is still in the air because I don't know if I'll get that job."

"And you really want it," she said sadly, sniffling.

"I do. But that doesn't make you or your dad any less special or important to me. Sometimes, we have things in life that we have to do for ourselves to prove to ourselves that we *could* do them. This is one of those things that I have to do. I have to know that I gave it my everything, and if it doesn't work out, then I won't be upset that I didn't try."

"That makes sense," she agreed, turning her head up to look at me. "So, if you don't get the job, then will you move to New Jersey with us?"

"We'll just have to wait and see," I replied loosely, not wanting to commit to anything.

I looked down the beach at John, who was on his cell phone, pacing back and forth barefoot in the sand. He looked serious, his face etched in frustration with whoever was on the phone. Alice and Charles were walking along the water, holding hands and looking like the perfect couple in love.

We had been at the beach for a few hours already, and Lily had built a sandcastle that she was satisfied with before giving up and deciding to play in the water. The plan was to hang out in Santa Cruz until the fireworks were over, then drive the hour-plus drive back home. Since we didn't have the luxury of being right by Alice and Charles's house, Lily wanted to do the cake and gifts at home, so we didn't have to pack much up or lug it down to the beach.

Lily had gone down to join her grandparents on the beach

as John walked back to where our stuff was set up and sat down on the ice chest behind me. He looked angry. His eyes were such a dark shade of grey that they almost reminded me of the charcoal color of mine. Whatever had happened, it wasn't good.

"Everything okay?" I asked, keeping my focus on the waves crashing ahead of me to give him space in case he didn't want to talk about it.

He worked his jaw back and forth, slightly shaking his head.

"That was my lawyer. The cop who killed Charlotte was released, and his case was deemed a mistrial."

"What?!" I gasped, whipping my head around to look at him.

"Yup. Apparently, when you're high enough up the chain, you get special favors."

"What are you going to do?"

"He thinks that we should sue the city. Go after them and make sure that word gets out that their chief was involved in DWI *while* on duty in an unmarked car. There isn't much that we can do other than that. Hopefully, it will be enough to get him fired, though."

"Wow," I stuttered, trying to wrap my head around it. "I can't believe that they just let him off. He killed someone…"

John turned to look at me, the heat from his gaze burning into me.

"He *almost* killed *two* people, and he's damn lucky that he didn't."

I hated the feeling that crawled up inside of my throat and tried to claw its way out every time someone reminded me that I had survived the accident that should have killed us both. It was the same feeling that had been eating away at me since I was a little girl and the lone survivor of the fatal crash that ended a happy family.

"I'm really sorry," I said quietly, feeling the weight of the grief between us.

"Me too," he answered, giving me a half-smile.

"It's things like this that make me eager to get the hell out of here and start over in New Jersey."

The words hurt every time I heard them, and nothing dulled the pain that they inflicted when I thought about the countdown that had already started for when they would leave and begin their new life.

"Well, you deserve happiness, and I'm sure you'll find it in New Jersey."

I turned my attention back to the waves, forcing a smile as Alice, Charles, and Lily came walking back to us.

Before long, the sun had set, and we were snuggled up on the blanket, eating funnel cake that John had bought on the boardwalk while watching the fireworks. Lily's eyes lit up with the kind of joy that you only see with the innocence of a child who can still see the beauty in things without searching out its flaws.

I felt a tug at my heart as she closed her eyes and took a deep breath. She was making her birthday wish, the one that she had been holding onto for this special night. I looked up and watched the sky flash with beautiful shades of pink and green as the colors burst and then fizzled in the sky. For a brief moment, I allowed myself to pretend that it was Charlotte putting on this beautiful show for Lily.

Thirty Five

"I'm going to miss you so much," Lily cried, hugging me tighter against her. Her backpack was filled to the brim with stuff she was taking back with her to New Jersey and almost tipped her over with the weight of it.

I held her as tight as I could and forced back the tears.

"I'm going to miss you more," I whispered in her ear. "Promise me that you'll call when you get there and give me an update on Sammy?"

"I promise," she said through another burst of tears. She stepped away into the comforting arms of Charles as Alice wrapped me in a hug to say goodbye.

"Have a safe flight," I choked out, feeling her hands rub my back in the motherly way that had always calmed me.

"We will, dear. We're going to miss you greatly. Promise that you'll call as soon as you hear anything about the job?"

I nodded, too emotional to get any words out. As if sensing the pain that I was in, she nodded back and wiped her thumb gently across my cheek, brushing the tear away.

Charles opened the door and helped Lily out, pulling their luggage behind them. While Alice and Charles had only brought a small duffle bag with a few changes of clothes for the short trip, they had packed up some of John and Lily's stuff in the extra suitcases to take with them.

Everyone walked outside where the cab was waiting for them. John hung back, his face rigid with emotion.

"Are you sure you can't come with us?" he asked, a hint of desperation in his voice.

I shook my head, not trusting my voice right now.

"Okay," he sighed, sucking in a deep breath as he reached over and pulled me into a hug. "You take care of yourself and call me if you need anything."

"I will."

He stepped back, not in a rush to leave. It felt like he was stalling, trying to find a reason to stay.

"Well, then. I guess they're waiting for me."

I felt the tension between us as it got thicker, the air heavy to breathe in.

"Be careful out there," I forced out, my voice cracking. "Please let me know how Lily is doing once she gets settled in."

"I will."

He let out the air that he had been holding and grabbed his suitcase, rolling it behind him as he walked out and shut the door behind him.

I rushed over, ready to fling it open and beg him to stay. But, instead, I turned around and slid down it, holding my head in my hands as I cried uncontrollably.

The house felt empty once they were gone, and the happiness that used to be here was instantly missing as well. I stayed sitting there on the floor, crying for the only family that I had left as they moved on, starting their new life without me.

Thirty Six
October

I missed the warmth of summer as I pulled my jacket tighter against me, shielding me from the bitter wind as it whipped past me. It wasn't supposed to storm today, but the dark grey clouds hanging above me said differently than the local weatherman, who was overly confident at four o'clock this morning while I was getting ready.

I rushed through the parking lot, eager to get into my office where I could warm up for a few minutes before I would be stuck in back-to-back meetings for the rest of the day. I was supposed to Facetime with Lily tonight so she could show me the Halloween costume that she had been working on with Alice, but I already knew that I was going to miss another one.

Mr. Crawford wasn't lying when he had mentioned the long hours and possible weekends when I interviewed for this job. I couldn't remember the last time that I had a day off or when I had gone to bed in my empty apartment without dreaming about a work-related crisis. The worst nightmare that I had was the one a few nights ago when I showed for today's meeting, completely naked and with no time to find something to wear. As silly as it sounded, I had checked my outfit a handful of times before I left this morning to make sure I hadn't missed any crucial articles of clothing.

I walked through the door, thanking the front doorman for holding it open, and made my way inside. It was still early, which allowed me to walk through the building without the loud chatter of voices interrupting my thoughts. I sat down at my desk and pulled out the cold bagel that I had stuffed into my purse at the last minute, knowing this would likely be my only meal until I got home late tonight.

It was ironic that six months ago, I was unemployed and lecturing John about working too much and not taking care of himself. Now, here I was, working at my so-called dream job, busting my ass and working more hours than I knew even existed in a day.

John had flown in a few weeks after he had started his new job and worked on packing up the rest of their stuff to send back to New Jersey. While he was busy doing that, I made myself scarce as I worked on unpacking at my new apartment. John hated that I had already moved out by the time that he came back, but I reminded myself—and him—that it was better for everyone.

I don't know how many times he came back to town after that since I wasn't at his house to see him. I kept busy at work, and between his new job, the lawsuit against the police department, and getting the house ready to sell, he was probably even busier than me. Every now and then, I would get a text message from Lily, checking to see how I was doing and to give me an update on how things were going in New Jersey.

Unfortunately, Sammy had passed away while they were here for her birthday in July, but John had agreed that it would be fun for her to get another fish, which also meant a bigger tank when she decided she wanted two this time.

Luck seemed to be in their favor because while John was looking for a house out there, Charles and Alice's neighbor—Mrs. Williams decided to move to Florida. John joked that she gave him a good deal on the house because she felt bad about killing Lily's fish while she was gone.

By the end of August, there was a For Sale sign up in front of their house. I vowed never to drive by it again after that.

"Emma," Randall's voice interrupted my thoughts as I shoved the last piece of bagel into my mouth and looked up. "Did you want me to go ahead and set up for the meeting in the boardroom?"

"Yes, please," I said around my bite, trying to multitask without being rude. I covered my mouth as I spoke, sparing him the unpleasant view. "I'll be down in just a few minutes."

I took a sip of my cold coffee to wash my food down and glanced at my computer. Forty-seven new emails in an hour that I would have to deal with in the few minutes I had between meetings today. Every second of my day had become valuable and was allotted to things that I used to take for granted—like using the restroom.

When I thought back to the day when Mr. Crawford asked me where I saw myself in five years, I should have given it a little more thought before I rushed to accept this job.

Thirty Seven

December

"Merry Christmas!" I squealed into the phone, smiling at Lily, who was decked out in Christmas pajamas that matched the rest of them as they all tried to fit into the screen.

"Merry Christmas!" they called back, smiling and looking genuinely happy.

I recognized the living room from the handful of times that Lily had given me the grand tour of their new house while we Facetimed. It was similar to Charles and Alice's house, just flipped in the opposite order. The tree was beautifully decorated with white lights and a mismatch of decorations that Lily had found when they unpacked a few months ago. There was an angel on top that had long blond hair that cascaded over a white dress and matched the glittery halo on top.

They didn't have to tell me how much it looked like Charlotte. I had noticed the moment I saw it.

"So, what are you guys doing? Did you already open presents?" I asked, leaning forward as if it would help me get closer to them.

Lily pulled the phone in to focus on her while the others scattered about, waiting for their turn to talk to me like usual.

"We haven't opened them yet. We're waiting for Celia to get here."

I furrowed my brow. Who was Celia? I hadn't heard Lily talk about her before. Maybe she was a friend from school? But that didn't make sense why they would be waiting for her friend to come over before they opened presents.

The confused look on my face must have given it away because then she added, "she's my dad's new girlfriend."

I tried to keep the look off my face as an odd—but overwhelming feeling of jealousy washed over me.

"Oh," I said as casually as I could. "I didn't know that he was seeing anyone."

"He hasn't really, not that long anyway. Just a few months."

I felt like my jaw was hanging open. I had talked to him a handful of times over the past few months, so why hadn't he mentioned it?

"Well, I'm happy for him," I lied, suddenly wishing that I could hang up and not have to go through the rounds of talking to everyone now that my mood had been soured.

"I have to go help nana in the kitchen, but let me find my dad, and I'll put him on real quick."

"Actually," I said, a little too loud. "I'm getting a headache, so I'm going to go lie down. I'll try to call back later if I'm feeling better. Tell everyone I said Merry Christmas, and I love them."

"Okay, feel better," she replied, completely oblivious to my lie.

I hung up and tossed my phone on the bed next to me. I hadn't bothered to get up or get ready yet. Why bother? I was spending the day by myself with a turkey tv dinner that would be ready in seven minutes as soon as I wanted it.

I closed my eyes, feeling the bitterness bite at my thoughts, tainting everything quicker than I could stop it. Why was I that surprised that John was already seeing someone? It was going on ten months since Charlotte died, and he was a good man who didn't deserve to be lonely. If I were really a good friend, like I had claimed to be, I would be happy for him.

I rolled over and looked at the small tree that sat on the floor beside the TV. There were a handful of presents from John and Lily and some from Alice and Charles that I had planned to open while on the phone with them. While I wasn't in the mood for anything Christmasy right now, I would make sure that I opened them and sent a quick thank you message to each of them for their wonderful, thoughtful gifts.

As much as I tried to make it feel like Christmas, it just didn't. I tried to convince myself that it was because I was too busy at work to bother with decorating. Hell, I hadn't even bothered to buy furniture other than the necessities. It was a small studio apartment to get me started before I could get back on my feet, but now that I was making good money—*exceptionally* good money, I didn't have the time to spend it.

I could consider quitting my job and finding something that was less demanding, but for what? I didn't have anyone to spend my free time with, and a huge part of my heart felt like it was missing and couldn't be easily replaced.

I curled up into a ball and cried myself back to sleep.

Thirty Eight

April - One Year Later

"I already told you, Miles, I'm not going to be in the office this afternoon. It can wait until Monday," I snapped into the phone, my irritation starting to bubble over. I stood at my desk, watching the new email notifications pop up, feeling a wee bit of satisfaction that the out-of-office alerts were already turned on and every single one was being forwarded to my assistant.

"No, I can't stay late today. If you guys can't handle things while I'm out of the office for half of a day, then maybe I need to find a team who can."

I heard his sharp intake of breath, knowing that I meant business.

"Find someone who can handle it and make sure that things are dealt with by the time I get back."

I hung up the phone, feeling slightly thrilled that someone else would have to deal with things for the rest of the day. It was a whopping six hours without me—if they couldn't handle that, then we had bigger problems.

I packed up my stuff and hung my leather briefcase on my shoulder as I left and locked my office door behind me. I felt the stares of the staff as I walked by with my sunglasses pushed up my face and nothing distracting me as I left for the day. I was usually the first one in and the last one out, but today was different.

My stomach had been a mess all morning as I thought about what was going to happen. Today marked one year since Charlotte died, and John, Lily, Alice, and Charles were flying in to have a memorial for her. Lily was having an exceptionally hard time, and John had some paperwork to deal with for his lawyer now that the lawsuit was over. The court had ruled in his favor, and we all got what we really wanted—the police chief fired, and his name ruined.

We were planning to meet at the park across the street from where it happened, which was only a fifteen-minute drive from my office. I climbed into the car and rolled the windows down, needing as much fresh air as I could get. My fingers were shaky as I started the engine and carefully pulled out of the parking lot.

Ever since the accident, I'd been nervous driving, even though I was the passenger that day. Whenever a car approached when I made a turn, I would have a panic attack and freak out that it was happening again. I forced myself to push through it and tried to keep it from overwhelming me, but my therapist said that it was a normal response and not to rush anything.

I had started seeing her shortly after New Year's when I'd gone over forty hours without sleeping and couldn't find the desire to eat. I knew that I needed help; I just hadn't realized how deep it went. I had confided in her about the grief I was holding onto from Charlotte's death and found that it went even deeper with my parent's death. She confirmed what I had known all along but was never willing to accept—that I close people off when they start getting too close because I've associated love with loss. If I love someone, then surely that means that I'll lose them.

I pulled into the parking lot and found a spot under the tree where we were supposed to meet. Looking around, I could see that they weren't there yet. I had a new text message that I was busy responding to when I heard someone knock on my window, startling me.

John stood on the other side, smiling as I practically hyperventilated, trying to catch my breath. I pressed the button to roll down the window as he stepped back.

"I didn't see you guys. I thought you weren't here yet," I explained, setting my phone in my lap.

"Rental car," he said, nodding to the black truck that was parked two spots over. "They're still inside. Lily was having a hard time getting out."

"Are you sure that it's a good idea to do this?"

He nodded, and I could see the way his Adam's Apple bulged that he was getting choked up too.

"Okay," I said, rolling up the window before I turned off the car. I reached over and grabbed the folder sitting on the passenger seat and prayed that I was ready for this.

I wasn't sure what hurt more—the immediate grief that I felt the day that I lost her or the suffering that I was feeling one year later, standing by the intersection where it had happened.

I followed John over to the shaded grass area that stretched between our vehicles and waited for Lily to get out of the truck. Charles was already out, standing at the front of it while Alice helped Lily.

Once she saw me, she burst into tears and came running to me. I opened my arms and grabbed her, holding her as tight as I could as the folder fell to the grass beside me. We didn't say a word as we cried, feeling the connection between us that hadn't died after all.

I was worried that being away from her for so long would have changed the bond that I felt with her, but right now, at this moment, I knew that nothing ever could.

"Are you alright?" I asked, gently pulling away while holding her face in my hands as I studied her.

Her blue eyes were red and swollen, her face splotchy from crying. I had seen her plenty of times during our Facetime calls, but I hadn't noticed until now just how much her face was changing, and she was looking more and more like a woman instead of a child.

She looked just like Charlotte.

"I'm okay," she whispered, her hands reaching up to squeeze my wrists. "You?"

"Me too."

I sucked in a ragged breath and looked past her at the others who were patiently waiting for us.

"You ready to do this?" I questioned, trying to get a feel for how she felt about it.

She nodded, her chest still as she held the breath that she had just taken.

I bent down and picked up the folder, brushing it off. We walked over to where they were waiting for us and gave quick hugs.

"Does anyone want to start?" John asked, looking between us.

I knew that each of us had prepared something special that we wanted to say to Charlotte, but I didn't know who should go first. I noticed the pain on Alice's face for the first time since the funeral and my heart twisted inside my chest.

Lily was crying hard, trying to wipe her tears away before more could fall.

John and I looked at each other as if silently questioning which one of us should go first.

I cleared my throat and moved to the side, standing in front of them as if on a stage.

"I wrote a letter to Charlotte that I would like to read out loud." My voice was stronger than I thought it would be, giving me the courage to get through this. I inhaled deeply, the way I had been learning in yoga, and started.

"When I was a little girl, I thought I had a perfect life. I didn't have many friends, but I had the best parents that anyone could ever ask for, and I was lucky enough to have them as my best friends. When they died, you were there for me. You stepped in and became my new best friend without any questions asked. You didn't know me that well, but you decided right then and there that I was worthy of your friendship.

"Throughout the years, you continued to amaze me with your generosity and how selfless you were. If someone needed something, you were the first to volunteer to help out. When you found out that I didn't have a date to the senior prom, you dumped yours and went stag with me, so I didn't have to go alone. Over the years, you've been there for me every single step of the way, and I never imagined that I would lose you.

"My heart broke the day that you died, and it hasn't been the same since. I've tried to walk in your path and be the kind, loving, and caring person that you were, but I've found that it's hard to do that when you're missing a huge part of who you are. You had such a profound impact on me that I don't know what to do without you. It's been a year, and I feel as lost as I was the day that it happened. It feels like standing in the darkness and screaming for someone to come find you, but they can't.

"I know that I can never repay you for everything that you did for me over the years, but I can promise you that I will always treasure the memories that we made together. I will strive to be the best person I can be, and I'll always find a way to help those who need it. But most of all, I will love and take care of those who you love the most—your family. I promise you that you never have to worry about them because I will be there for them like you were always there for me."

I felt the tears rush down my face as a loud sob escaped my throat.

"I know that I've let you and everyone else down these past few months, and I'm sorry. I walked away when they needed me the most because I didn't know how to be strong for them. I thought they were better off without me, and maybe they are, but I know that I'm not who I want to be without them. I need them in my life as much as I needed you."

I lowered the paper and covered my face as I cried. I felt John's hands as they pulled me into him and held me as I cried. Charles went next with a beautiful memory of their first camping trip and how Charlotte had made sure that they didn't put their tent over the line of ants that were trying to get back to their home. Even at a young age, she had a tender heart and was concerned about others.

Everyone was crying, which made it hard to stop crying as

we talked about how much we missed her. John's message was short and sweet, and I knew that there were plenty of things that he would say to her later when he was alone.

Lily was the last one, and I wasn't sure that she wanted to go through with it. John's hand rested lightly on her shoulder, letting her know that he was there if she needed him. She cleared her throat and looked up at me.

"When my mom died, I didn't really understand what it meant. I knew that she wouldn't physically be there anymore, but I didn't know how to deal with the emotional part of it. There were so many times when something would happen, and I wanted to go to her for help, but she wasn't there. And then I would feel sad all over again, but then Emma would find me, and she always knew the right things to say to make me feel better.

"Mom, I know that you're in heaven and that you probably can't hear us, but I want you to know that I'm okay. I miss you so much that it still hurts, and I cry a lot. But I know that you can't come back, so I try to be strong like daddy and Aunt Emma were when you died. You always said that if I were feeling sad or scared, to look for the person who was smiling if you weren't around—they would be the one to help me."

She stopped for a moment and choked back her sobs as she looked at me.

"For a while, that was always Aunt Emma. Whenever I needed her, she was always smiling and would make me feel better. I knew that I could go to her and she would make it okay. Like when I wanted to finish our blanket or when I turned into a lady on vacation. She didn't freak out.

She just smiled and made me feel like it was alright." She gave John an obvious wink, teasing him about how much he hated when she talked about her *period.*

I felt my heart swell in my chest. I knew how much these little things had meant to me, but I never knew that they had made such an impact on her.

"Things are different now, and I'm trying really hard to be strong and to find the person who is smiling, but it never feels the same. I think this just means that I'm growing up and that I have to be stronger and less scared. So, I just wanted to tell you that I'm trying, mom, and I won't let you down."

The sound of crying filled the air around us as a gentle breeze passed through us, gently blowing Lily's hair out of her face.

"I love you too, mom," she whispered, her eyes closed as she cried.

I was thankful that I had taken the rest of the day off, knowing that I wouldn't be in any shape to go back to work. And I was right. This was emotionally draining as we spent an hour sitting in the grass, sharing stories about her and how much we loved her.

It was getting late and a little too cold to be sitting in the grass, so we packed up and agreed to meet up tomorrow for lunch before they flew back to New Jersey on Sunday. Alice and Charles had already climbed into the truck with Lily while John walked the short distance with me to my car.

"Do you have dinner plans tonight?" he asked as we stood by the driver's side door. I glanced down at my cell phone that was still sitting in the middle console and debated what to say.

"I have a date," I said nervously. I wasn't sure why I felt nervous about it, but the look that flashed across his face made the anxiety even stronger.

"A date? I didn't know you were seeing anyone," he replied tightly.

"It's not serious, but I've been seeing him for a few weeks."

"A few weeks, and you didn't bother mentioning it during any of the numerous times we've talked?"

"Just like you didn't tell me about Celia at Christmas?" I folded my arms over my chest and glared at him. Suddenly, I was feeling the anger build up inside of me from his smug reaction.

"There was nothing to tell. We went on a few dates."

"You invited her to your house to open presents with your family on Christmas morning." I raised my brows.

"It's a small town in New Jersey, Emma. It's the nice thing to do," he countered, widening his stance next to me.

"Well, either way. You were seeing someone, and now I've gotta go, or I'm going to be late for *my* date."

"Cancel it. Please."

"What?"

"I asked you to cancel it."

"John, you're acting crazy. I'm not going to cancel my date."

In all honesty, I was planning to cancel it the moment I got in the car. Not because he told me to, but because I knew I wouldn't be great company tonight given everything that was rushing through my head.

"Please. Just cancel the date, Emma. For me?"

I was so lost and confused. What was happening?

"Why?"

"Because I asked you to. I want to take you to dinner tonight so we can talk."

The way he said it sent an immediate flashback through my head about the other times that he told me that we needed to talk. The first one was after our kiss in Taos that he immediately regretted. The second time was when he broke the news that they were packing up and moving to New Jersey.

"John, I don't think there's anything that we need to talk about," I whined, already feeling too exhausted for this. "Can't we just talk tomorrow? We can meet up before lunch if you want to talk in private. Just not tonight."

"Is he that important to you?"

"What?" It took me a moment to figure out what he was asking. "It's been a long, exhausting day. I've been up since three-thirty and have been going non-stop since. I just don't have it in me to sit down and talk about whatever it is that is bothering you."

I felt regret the moment the words touched my lips. Here I had just promised Charlotte an hour ago that I would always take care of her family, yet I wouldn't give John my time or attention right now to talk about whatever was weighing on his mind.

"I'm sorry," I quickly apologized. "I didn't mean that the way it sounded. I'm just tired and getting cranky."

I knew that they were likely watching us from the truck and didn't want to keep them waiting.

"You should get going. I'm sure Lily wants to get back to the hotel so she can rest."

"I didn't finish reading what I had written in my letter to Charlotte earlier."

"Okay," I said nervously as he stepped closer to me, pinning me against the car without touching me. "I can walk back to the grass with you if you want to keep talking to her," I offered.

His body was close enough that I could feel the heat radiating off of it, shielding me from the cold.

"Right here is fine." His voice was low. He took another small step toward me, invading more of what little space I had around me.

"When I made my vows to Charlotte, I promised to never love another woman, for as long as we both shall live. We never got around to talking about what we would want for the other if something were to happen to one of us, probably because we didn't think that something *would* happen. But the funny thing about Charlotte is that she was always prepared for everything.

"When I started unpacking at the new house, I came across a letter that she had written that was in a sealed envelope and paperclipped to our marriage license. Imagine my surprise when I found that it wasn't just her wishes for what she would want to happen to Lily if anything ever happened to her, but for me too."

My breaths felt shallow as I hung on to every word, wondering what she wrote. Was it an older letter? Would anything have changed from then to what she would have wanted now?

"The letter was from last year, shortly before the accident, believe it or not," he laughed as if reading my thoughts. "And organized with very clear bullet points."

I found myself laughing, knowing that was in Charlotte's true nature.

"Long story short, she wanted for me to find someone that I would fall in love with and who would be the perfect mom for Lily. Someone who would put their own needs aside to take care of her daughter's. Someone who loves to laugh and is always up for an adventure. Someone that will keep me on my toes and get me back in line if I start drifting in the wrong direction."

He paused and pushed a heavy breath out, chewing nervously on his lip.

"Someone who will be my best friend above anything else and who I can't imagine my life without her."

I felt the pain stab in my chest when I realized that he must have found someone else. It sure sounded like it by the conviction in his voice as he proudly recited what she wanted for him.

"Well, I'm sure you'll find the perfect woman," I said shakily, turning to reach for the door handle.

His hand reached down and stopped me, holding my hand in place to keep from opening it.

"I already have."

I felt the air rush out of me and worried that my legs would give at any moment. This was too much. First, the fresh feelings of grief after talking about Charlotte, and now this.

"I'm happy for you," I lied, avoiding his eyes as they tried to lock onto mine.

He gently pinched the end of my chin and guided my face back to him.

"It's you, Emma. It's always been you."

Okay, now I was *really* confused. What the hell was he talking about?

"John, what are you—"

He placed a finger over my lips and shushed me.

"You don't get to fight me on it, not today. Not ever."

I waited until he moved his finger before I tried to speak again.

"You were the first to admit that the kiss was a mistake. You've said it yourself that you're not ready to date. How is any of that different now?"

He stepped back and took a steadying breath.

"I don't know, Emma. It just is. I can't explain it, but I sure as hell know that no matter how hard I try, I can't get you out of my head. I think about you every waking minute of the day and wonder whether you're happy here or if you're just as miserable without us."

Butterflies flutter in my stomach at the thought that he's been as unhappy as I've been without them.

"Of course I've missed you guys, John. I've said so plenty of times."

"Do you still love me?"

I paused, too afraid to answer the question. Even with as much therapy as I had already been through, nothing could help with the automatic instinct I felt whenever I talked about love.

"I'm not capable of love, John."

I turned and looked away, refusing to meet his eyes that were desperately searching mine for an answer.

"Bullshit."

I stepped away from the car toward him, pulling my shoulders back. I needed to say what I had to say and get the hell out of there before I did something that I would regret.

"You deserve someone who will give you their whole heart, John, and that someone isn't me. My heart hasn't been whole for a long time. It's cracked in so many places that I fear it will shatter if I try to love again, and that's a pain that I know I can't handle."

Satisfied that I was able to be open and honest with him, I turned to get into my car. His hand reached out and grabbed me, spinning me back to him as he wrapped his arms around my waist and held onto me.

"Emma, it's okay to be broken as long as you have someone strong enough to hold you together."

He leaned forward and planted his lips over mine, kissing me softly as his words melted my heart.

Epilogue
Eight Months Later

I had forgotten how cold it was in New Jersey during the winter as I curled up in the oversized cuddler chair by the window that looked out to the ocean. It was hard to believe that I was currently unemployed and living next door to my best friend's parents.

Shortly after John had declared his love for me, I found myself quitting my demanding job at BayView Advertising and packing up the studio apartment to move in with him and Lily. It was one of the wildest things that I had ever done—aside from our epic road trip, and I didn't regret a single second of it.

Lily was the happiest that I had seen her in a long time and was thriving at school. She had made four new friends, and the five of them were inseparable. When she wasn't sleeping over at their houses, they were all piled upstairs in her bedroom, eating junk food and gossiping about the cute boys in their class.

John hated that Lily was starting to see boys as something other than gross creatures with cooties. I had to remind him that it was only going to get worse and pulled him back when he wanted to go to the store to buy plenty of protection for her. It turns out that there *isn't* enough ammunition in the world for an over-protective father, and I had to reign him in.

I curled my feet underneath me, enjoying the warm fuzzy socks that Lily had bought me for Christmas last year. While John was at work in Manhattan and Lily spent her days at school, I had secretly been writing a novel about the journey of a beautiful woman named Charlotte.

It was filled with memories of her and stories of how she touched other's lives without even knowing it. It gave me a sense of pride to be able to bring her story to life, knowing that her legacy would live on and that the world would get to see what a wonderful person she really was.

"Honey, I'm home," he called out playfully from the front door as he walked in. The frigid cold air blew in behind him, sending a chill right through me.

I closed the journal that I was writing in and slid it into my regular hiding place before I got up to greet him.

"Hey, you're home early," I said, reaching up to place a kiss on his lips.

"I decided to take a few days off for Christmas," he said, wrapping his arms around my waist.

"So, you're done being the Grinch?" I teased, earning a quick slap on my butt. He had been overly stressed about a project at work and had been grumpier than usual.

"That depends," he murmured against my lips. "Is Lily home?"

"She's staying the night at Alice's tonight. They're working on some top-secret Christmas gifts and have been at it since ten this morning."

"Well, in that case, I'm the Grinch," he chuckled. "But it's not my heart that's about to grow."

I laughed at the poor attempt at a joke and swatted at his chest.

"You've gotta get better at the jokes," I teased, feeling his hand wrap around my wrist to pull me back to him.

"Does the little *Who* girl think the big, bad, Grinch is funny?" His voice was low and gravely as he pulled me tighter against him. I could feel his length thickening between us.

"Maybe I need to be punished," I flirted, pulling my lower lip in between my teeth. I had him just where I wanted him. Without warning, I turned and ran down the hallway, thankful for the carpet, so I didn't slip and fall, as I rushed into the bedroom and jumped on the bed.

He followed behind me with a hungry look in his eyes. Then, slowly, he stood at the foot of the bed, undoing the knot in his tie as he slowly pulled the silky fabric through to undo it.

I watched him take his sweet time undressing, the ache already starting between my thighs.

"If you don't hurry up and get over here, *I'm* going to turn into the Grinch," I warned, desperate to touch him.

He tugged his shirt off and tossed it to the floor behind him as he crawled across the bed, hovering over me.

"You're so beautiful, Emma," he whispered, gently pushing a strand of hair away from my face. "I'll never get tired of making love to this beautiful woman who stole my heart."

I closed my eyes and relaxed into his kiss as his tongue teased my mouth and his hands skillfully explored my body.

And just like that, my heart felt whole again.

****

Thank you so much for reading One Last Wish! I hope you loved this story as much as I enjoyed writing it!

If you're looking for something new to read and want something fun and spicy, check out my flirty romantic comedy novella, Finding Love In Apartment 2C.

https://books2read.com/u/bze9aZ

If you're looking for another sweet love story that has some steam in it, check out my Stone Creek novella series.

https://books2read.com/u/3LRk9N

If you're looking for something more thrilling, be sure to check out my romantic suspense series, Haven Brook.

https://books2read.com/u/m2RJNR

Other Books By Samantha Baca

The Haven Brook Series:

'Til Death Do Us Part (Haven Brook Book 1)
https://books2read.com/u/m2RJNR

The Cradle Will Fall (Haven Brook Book 2)
https://books2read.com/u/b6O0QE

The Ties That Bind (Haven Brook Book 3)
https://books2read.com/u/mqgoz8

A Very Haven Christmas (Haven Brook Book 4- Novella)
https://books2read.com/u/mvqGjj

Three Strikes, You're Gone (Haven Brook Book 5)
https://books2read.com/u/mvqL2z
****

The Dark Shadows Series

Five Steps Ahead (Dark Shadows Book 1)
https://books2read.com/u/38Q0gO

Ten Seconds Too Late (Dark Shadows Book 2)
Coming 2022

Against The Clock (Dark Shadows Book 3)
Coming 2022

Out Of Time (Dark Shadows Book 4)
Coming 2023
****

<u>The Stone Creek Series (Novellas)</u>
Chocolate Covered Mistletoe (Stone Creek Book 1)
https://books2read.com/u/3LRk9N

Candy Coated Promises (Stone Creek Book 2)
https://books2read.com/u/mldP5Y

Pumpkin Spiced Possibilities (Stone Creek Book 3)
https://books2read.com/u/bojdwV
****

<u>Stand-Alone Books</u>
One Last Wish
https://books2read.com/u/mqg7D9

Finding Love In Apartment 2C (Novella)
https://books2read.com/u/bze9aZ

Acknowledgments

Thank you so much to all of the readers, bloggers, and bookstagrammers that were so quick to pick up this book—I appreciate it! I hope you enjoyed this story and found yourself itching to take a road trip across the country. I know I did!

I would like to thank my amazing alpha readers- Azucena and Chelsea—thank you both for everything you did to make this book as amazing as it is! I love working with you ladies and value your input so much. I'm excited to see what new books come our way in the future.

To my beta readers—Katy, Camille, and Stephanie—I am so appreciative of the time that you took to read this for me as well as all of the wonderful feedback that you provided. You were an incredible asset in making this book incredible!

To my family and friends—thank you for all of your support along the way. I will never grow tired of seeing my books in your newsfeed on social media or hearing about how you recommended my books to a stranger in line at the store. You are all amazing, and I'm so lucky to have you!

My dear, sweet husband—I love you and your big heart so much. You're my biggest cheerleader and the person who grounds me when I need it. I simply adore you and appreciate how much you do for me. I couldn't imagine a world where we didn't work together on some project or another, and I'm thankful that we work so well together in this area as well.

My girls, if you ever learn anything from me, please let it be that your drive and determination will take you as far as you want to go in life. The only thing that can hold you back is yourself, so believe in yourself as much as I believe in you. You have the power to reach for the stars, so aim high, my darlings. I love you and can't wait to see what amazing things you're going to do in life.

About the Author

Samantha lives in the southwest with her husband and two small children after abandoning her childhood dream of living in a cabin in Colorado when she found that she couldn't afford to live there and was deathly allergic to the woods. When she's not writing she's usually spouting off sarcastic remarks while drinking wine out of a coffee mug to look like a functional adult while chasing down her toddlers. She enjoys spending time with her family, watching reruns of Friends, and the 24/7 flow of coffee that can be found in her veins. Be sure to follow her on social media for updates on what she's working on.

You can find her here:

Facebook: https://www.facebook.com/AuthorSamanthaBaca

Instagram: https://instagram.com/author_samantha_baca

Goodreads: http://www.goodreads.com/authorsamanthabaca

Facebook Reader Group:

https://www.facebook.com/groups/2945710968775398/

Webpage: https://authorsamanthabaca.wordpress.com

Newsletter: http://eepurl.com/g0NcSj